Praise for Sue Ann Jaffarian's
Odelia Grey Mystery Series

"Odelia Grey is delightfully large and in charge."
—*Publishers Weekly*

"Jaffarian plays the formula with finesse, keeping love problems firmly in the background while giving her heroine room to use her ample wit and grit."
—*Kirkus Reviews*

"[Odelia Grey] is an intriguing character, a true counter against stereotype, who demonstrates that life can be good, even in a world where thin is always in."
—*Booklist*

"An intriguing, well-plotted mystery that will entertain and inspire."
—*The Strand Magazine*

"…a real treat for chick-lit and mystery fans who like feisty women."
— *Library Journal*, starred review

Praise for Sue Ann Jaffarian's
Ghost of Granny Apples Mystery Series

"*Ghost à la Mode* is a charming tale,
as appealing as apple pie; I predict a long life
(and afterlife) for Sue Ann's latest series."
—Harley Jane Kozak,
Agatha, Anthony, and Macavity award-
winning author of *Dating Dead Men*

"A delectable first in a new paranormal
cozy series from Sue Ann Jaffarian."
—*Publishers Weekly*

"A fun new series. Ghostly puzzles are one of the trendy
new themes in cozy mysteries, and this is a good one."
—*Booklist*

"Emma handles her 'gift' of seeing the dead
with aplomb and class. I'll look forward to seeing
where the sequel will take Emma and Granny."
—*Deadly Pleasures*

About the Author

In addition to the Fang-in-Cheek Mystery series, Sue Ann Jaffarian is the author of two other best-selling mystery series: the Ghost of Granny Apples Mystery series and the Odelia Grey Mystery series. She is also nationally sought after as a motivational and humorous speaker. Sue Ann lives and works in Los Angeles, California.

Visit Sue Ann on the Internet at

www.sueannjaffarian.com

and

www.sueannjaffarian.blogspot.com

SUE ANN JAFFARIAN
MURDER
IN VEIN

A FANG-IN-CHEEK MYSTERY

MIDNIGHT INK
WOODBURY, MINNESOTA

FIRST EDITION
First Printing, 2010

Book design by Rebecca Zins
Cover design by Ellen Dahl
Cover images ©Image Source/PunchStock

Midnight Ink, an imprint of Llewellyn Worldwide Ltd.

This is a work of fiction. Names, characters, places, and incidents are either the product of the author's imagination or are used fictitiously, and any resemblance to actual persons, living or dead, business establishments, events, or locales is entirely coincidental.

Library of Congress Cataloging-in-Publication Data
Jaffarian, Sue Ann, 1952-
  Murder in vein : a fang-in-cheek mystery / Sue Ann Jaffarian.—1st ed.
    p. cm.
  ISBN 978-0-7387-2311-2
  1. Women—Crimes against—Fiction. 2. Vampires—Fiction. 3. Married people—Fiction. 4. Older couples—Fiction. 5. Los Angeles (Calif.)—Fiction. I. Title.
  PS3610.A359M87 2010
  813'.6—dc22

                                                                    2010014233

Midnight Ink
A Division of Llewellyn Worldwide Ltd.
2143 Wooddale Drive
Woodbury, MN 55125-2989

www.midnightinkbooks.com

Printed in the United States of America

For Darrell and Diana James.
Thanks for everything!

Acknowledgments

While writing is a fairly solitary endeavor, the publishing of a book is not. I am truly blessed to be surrounded by so many capable and talented folks.

For *Murder in Vein*, in particular, I would like to express my very special gratitude to Terri Bischoff, my acquisitions editor at Midnight Ink, who supported me from start to finish in the birth of this manuscript and this new series.

And, as always, thanks to Whitney Lee, my agent; Diana James, my manager; and all the good folks at Llewellyn Worldwide/ Midnight Ink.

.ONE

Madison had been in Los Angeles just over two years when she found herself facedown on the ground in a wooded area. Her clothes were in tatters. Duct tape held her hands. A filthy rag muffled her screams. Fear coursed through her battered body, scraping and tearing with jagged edges as she fought to maintain control of her slippery mind. It was the only weapon she had left.

When she turned her head slowly to the side, pine needles and gravel ground into the cuts and bruises on her face, the pain bringing clarity to her mind for a fleeting moment. Bobby Piper had smacked Madison around pretty good while dragging her from the car. After roughing her up and ripping at her clothes, he'd stopped, then moved away, seeming to have second thoughts. He certainly hadn't had any second thoughts an hour ago when he had grabbed her in the parking lot outside the diner where she worked.

The moonlight penetrating the canopy of overhead branches allowed her to see Bobby as he sat with his back against a nearby tree. He was guzzling from a can of generic beer torn from the six-pack resting at his side. He glanced at the cheap watch strapped to his wrist. He seemed to be waiting for something or someone.

There had been several news reports over the past year about missing women. Three had been found dead and mutilated. The others were never found. And even though the police claimed to have the killer in custody, Madison's panic and terror gathered anew as she worried about being the guest of honor at something evil and terrifying. She wiggled, but the tape around her hands and feet stayed put. Bobby noticed and glanced her way, causing her to freeze.

Getting down on his knees, Bobby scooted over and knelt next to Madison. "Steady now," he warned. He bent close and tongued her ear as he spoke. When she squirmed in disgust, he laughed. "Don't go making things worse for yourself."

Worse? Madison thought. *Worse than this?* Her fear splintered, invading every cell of her body.

Bobby glanced again at his watch, then looked off in the direction of Madison's car, which he'd driven with her stuffed in the trunk. "Damn it. Where is he?" he said to the empty night.

These were the last words he ever uttered.

Something came out of the dark. Something large and silent. It struck Bobby hard and fast, sending him into the tree where he'd been leaning just a moment before. Beer, malty and luke-warm, rained on Madison's face. From the corner of her eye, she caught sight of her attacker splayed against the thick trunk of the tree, busted and askew, a rag doll in a disturbing pose. He moaned.

Whatever it was that had attacked Bobby now hovered over his broken body, totally ignoring her. It tore at Bobby's shirt, the fabric rasping loud and foreign against the natural sounds of the night. It looked to Madison like a man, dark and looming in appearance. When it raised its head and looked up at the moon, she saw that it *was* a man—an older man, his face strong but weathered, his jaw line slack with age. Then he looked back down at Bobby. Bobby screamed. It was a short scream, winding quickly down into a whimper, until Madison could hear it no more.

The man raised his head again toward the moon. Even with the rag in her mouth, Madison's breath caught in her throat. He heard it and turned toward her, leaning down until she could smell his metallic breath. He grimaced, displaying fangs dark and thick with fresh blood—Bobby's blood.

Madison passed out.

When she regained consciousness, Madison found Bobby Piper trussed like a Thanksgiving turkey. He was just as white as raw poultry and just as dead.

My name is Madison Rose, she reminded herself in silence while she studied Bobby's body. She hoped that remembering the small details of her life would keep her focused and not allow her mind to drift back into unconsciousness. What she'd seen— the man with the fangs—couldn't have been real. Bobby's killer was just another psychopath like himself. She tried desperately to convince herself that her mind was playing tricks on her.

Madison heard footsteps. The sound brought her focus back to the problem at hand. It sounded like there was more than one set. They moved with stealth over the dead leaves until they were nearby. She didn't close her eyes, but neither did she turn her head to look.

"What should we do with her?" she heard a woman ask in a soft, cultured voice.

"She saw me," a man answered. "We'll have to kill her." His voice was low, rounded out in unexpected civility, and almost apologetic.

Madison. Rose. She repeated it to herself like a mantra. It was her first and last name. She had no middle name like regular people—just a last name for her first name and a first name for her last. People always screwed it up. No matter how clearly she explained it, there was always some jackass who insisted on filing her under the Ms instead of the Rs. On more than one occasion, she'd thought about changing her name to Rose Madison just to make things easier for everyone. But she'd never been known for making things easy on the folks around her—or on herself. After being raised in a string of foster homes, Madison Rose wasn't used to things being easy on any level.

Remembering the details of her twenty-three years of life didn't change the fact that she was still on the ground, still bound and gagged—a sitting duck for whatever hell would come next. Looking again at Bobby's body, she had only one regret: that she hadn't killed him herself.

It also crossed her mind that moving to LA had been a bad call.

TWO

Madison's eyes opened slowly until they caught on a vertical strip of diffused light. It signaled to Madison in the darkness. The last thing she remembered was waiting to die.

Is this death? she asked herself. *Is this the light everyone talks about?* She squinted and concentrated on it, thinking the light of passing should be big and bright, not dim and slim as a reed. She felt disappointed, let down even in death.

She wiggled her fingers, then realized her hands were unfettered and her mouth no longer gagged. She lay on her back, on what felt like a very large, soft bed. Again, she wondered if she'd died and gone to heaven. After a few minutes, she decided if heaven was all about lounging in a big bed, cocooned in expensive linens edged in lace and smelling faintly of lavender, then it was okay by her.

Closing her eyes, she opened her mouth in a wide yawn. A sharp pain stabbed the middle of her lower lip. She touched her tongue to the spot, tasting blood and feeling a small split. Her cheek throbbed. Lifting a hand to her face, she felt a gauze bandage on her right cheek. Gently, she moved her fingers over her face in a Braille examination and detected a small bandage across the bridge of her nose. She felt like she'd been hit by a train. If she was dead, she wouldn't be bleeding—or in pain. She also had to pee and reminded herself that she couldn't recall ever hearing of the dead needing to use the bathroom.

Cautiously, she eased a foot out from under the covers and over the edge of the bed. The room was cool, almost cold. Someone had removed her clothes and dressed her in a long, sleeveless nightgown. Stroking a hand down the front of her chest, she felt pintucking and ribbon trim. Her feet found a soft, cushy area rug, then traveled onto a bare but glossy wood floor. She moved slowly in the near blackness, aiming for the shaft of light.

She'd only taken a few steps when she heard a knock, then a door opened a few feet to the left of the shaft of light. More light entered the room, silhouetting a shape in the doorway.

"I see you're up," a cheerful female voice said.

Before Madison could answer, a small lamp on the far side of the room came on, filling the space with a soft light. She turned her face away, giving her eyes time to become accustomed to the brightness, then turned her head back to see who was speaking. At the door was an older woman. Not elderly but definitely old enough to qualify for the senior menu at the diner.

"How are you feeling, Madison?" the woman asked.

Madison studied her, digging through her cottony brain for recognition. She was pretty sure she didn't know the woman, but she didn't seem totally unfamiliar either.

Madison started to speak but stopped to clear her throat first. "How do you know my name?"

The woman smiled and stepped deeper into the room. "It was on your driver's license," the woman explained. "I hope you don't mind, but we had to go through your purse for your ID." The woman pointed toward a dresser. "Your bag is over there."

Turning her head, Madison saw her beat-up shoulder bag on top of the dresser.

The woman moved toward her, her trim body gliding gracefully across the wood floor on pink velvet slippers. When she reached Madison, she held out a hand with long, tapered fingers to feel the girl's forehead. Instinctively, Madison backed away.

"Don't worry," the woman assured her. "I'm a retired nurse. I need to make sure you're not running a fever."

She moved closer. She was almost Madison's height, about five foot six. This time, Madison didn't half bolt when the woman laid a cool hand on her face. After a few seconds, the woman smiled, satisfied with her patient's status.

"Are you the one who fixed me up?" Madison asked.

The woman nodded and moved toward the bed, where she fussed with the covers, pulling them back and smoothing the sheets underneath. "Yes," she answered. She folded one edge of the sheets and blanket back in a tidy triangle, as fancy as in a luxury hotel, readying the bed for Madison's return. Then she started fluffing the pillows. "You were quite a mess, Madison. But I'm happy to say your nose was not broken." With one final fluff to a pillow, she was done. "I don't even think you'll have any scars. But you'll be feeling the bruises on your body for several days."

With her bladder complaining, Madison had to decide which was more urgent: going to the bathroom or finding out who in the hell this woman was. As if reading her mind, the woman said, "Why don't you freshen up?" She pointed to a door next to the one she'd entered. "The bath is right that way." She started back toward the other door, then stopped. "Take your time," she told Madison with a warm smile. "I'll go find something for you to eat. You must be starving."

Before leaving, the woman asked, "Are you allergic to anything—or a vegetarian? Anything like that?"

"No," Madison croaked out. "I'll eat anything."

The woman gave off a low, almost private chuckle. "In this house, that could be dangerous."

Upon entering the bathroom, Madison discovered the sliver of light was cast from a small night-light positioned just inside the door. The light was in the shape of a purple flower.

Lavender linens, beribboned nightgowns, flower-shaped night-lights, and room service. She had gone from near death on decaying foliage to a fairy tale. Or had she? Madison Rose knew better than to make assumptions based on first impressions. She'd learned early in life that even good things had a way of biting you on the ass when you took a closer look.

The bathroom was spotless. There were no chips in the tile, no water stains on the floor, no birthmarks of mildew in the corners. The room was decorated similar to the bedroom, abundant with lace and floral prints, just on the edge of being Victorian. After using the toilet, she stood in front of the vanity, where fresh soaps in the shapes of roses sat in a delicate white dish next to a matching drinking glass. Carefully picking up a fancy soap, she wet it as if she were washing a piece of antique china. Next to the soap dish was a new toothbrush, still in its package, and a fresh tube of toothpaste. She wondered if they'd been put there for her use. Again, she was unsure. Somewhere, a part of her still wondered if she might be dead.

As she washed, Madison avoided looking into the mirror over the sink, but she knew she couldn't evade it forever. After drying her hands on a towel, she jerked her head up fast, letting her appearance hit her like a baseball bat, which was appropriate, since her face looked like it had done some time with one.

She had a black eye, and her nose was scraped. The gauze bandage she'd felt earlier covered her right cheek from the edge of her eye almost to her mouth. Her long, dark brown hair was loose, with the odd, tiny leaf clinging to a few strands. She pushed strands of hair out of the way and saw another scrape across her forehead. Her wrists were also bruised, the outline of the duct tape still visible.

She opened the toothbrush and started brushing the fetid film from her mouth, careful of her split lip. The toothpaste was a national brand, cool and minty. She wanted to scrub her whole body with it.

As she brushed, Madison opened the door wider, letting the light from the bathroom splash across the bedroom. The woman hadn't returned. The bedroom was beautiful and inviting, the sort of room she'd only seen before in magazines. She rinsed and spit, then studied her bruised reflection in the mirror again, trying to piece together the lost time.

The last thing Madison remembered was a man and a woman standing over her, deciding her fate. She closed her eyes and concentrated. The man had been inclined to kill her; the woman had not. Then something was placed over her face. She'd had dreams while she slept. Dreams of being carried through the woods. Dreams of fangs and blood and Bobby's final cries. The man had killed Bobby... hadn't he?

Looking at the shower with longing, Madison decided against it. Until she had some answers, she didn't want to be naked and standing under running water. She'd seen the movie *Psycho*. Instead, she took up the fancy soap again and wet a facecloth. Gently, she washed her face, traveling carefully around the bandages, then over and around her neck. It made her feel better and helped clear the cobwebs.

The woman.

Madison stopped washing and stared out the door, into the bedroom. The woman hadn't returned yet. Then it hit Madison. It was the woman's *voice* that was familiar, not her face. The older woman was the woman in the woods. She was sure of it.

If the woman, the retired nurse, was the same woman in the woods, then who was the man? She shut the door, locking it. The man had wanted to kill her. To finish what Bobby had started. He—the man—had fangs. The sight of the blood-covered fangs exploded from her deep memory like a ball through a plate glass window. The man had bitten Bobby, torn into him like a barbecued rib on the Fourth of July.

She looked around for a window. Nightgown or not, Madison was ready to squeeze through a bathroom window and hit the ground running. But the bathroom was windowless. The only way out was through the bedroom. She started to unlock the door but stopped, still unsure of what she had seen.

"There's no such thing as vampires," she scolded herself in a barely audible whisper. She paced the small room, repeating the phrase several times. The man had killed Bobby, true, but he'd also saved her life. The biting, the fangs, must have been a product of her overactive and stressed imagination.

She lowered the toilet lid and dropped down onto it, still trying to convince herself. She must have heard wrong that he'd wanted to kill her, too. She was alive, wasn't she? And why would they bring her here if they meant to kill her? Then again, why hadn't they taken her to a hospital? Or to a police station? Her last question hit home. If she'd nearly been murdered, where were the police? Her mind reeled with contradictions.

A knock on the bathroom door sent Madison into near cardiac arrest. "Madison, are you all right?" It was the older woman. "Madison," the woman called, knocking again. "Do you need help, dear?"

"I'll ... I'll be right out." Madison rose and went to study herself in the mirror again. She couldn't stay in the bathroom forever. Her cell phone was in her bag on the dresser, but what good would it do? She had no idea where she was.

Slowly opening the bathroom door, Madison peeked out. The bedroom was empty. As soon as she stepped into it, her nostrils filled with the aroma of something hot and inviting. She followed the fragrant trail to a small desk, on which sat a tray holding a large bowl of soup, buttered toast, and a tiny pot of hot tea with its own matching teacup. The soup looked homemade. Her mouth watered. Sitting down in the desk chair, Madison picked up the soup spoon and stirred it through a broth thick with chicken, potatoes, and chunks of an unidentifiable orange vegetable. With the spoon, she plucked a chunk of potato from the bowl and tenuously put it in her mouth. It was delicious. She'd downed several more big spoonfuls when the woman returned.

"Good?" she asked Madison.

With her mouth full, Madison could only nod.

"That's Pauline's special chicken soup. People love it. It has pumpkin chunks as well as yams and regular potatoes."

Pumpkin and yam. Those were the orange vegetables Madison couldn't identify in the bowl.

In the woman's arms were some folded clothes. "It's a Jamaican recipe. Pauline is our housekeeper. Her family is originally from Kingston."

"It's awesome," Madison said between gulps.

"Here are some fresh clothes for when you're ready to get dressed." The woman placed them on the dresser. "You're about my height but slimmer. Still, these should do for now. And no rush getting dressed. You've been through quite a lot. Feel free to climb back into bed if you like."

Noticing for the first time a white linen napkin next to the soup bowl, Madison picked it up and wiped her mouth. "Thanks," she said bluntly. She wondered if she should offer more words of gratitude, but instead she blurted, "Who are you, and where in the hell am I?"

The woman sat on the edge of the bed nearest the desk. "My name is Dorothy Dedham, but everyone calls me Dodie. My husband is Douglas. You are in our home."

Madison ran her eyes over Dodie's lined face. She appeared to be in her late sixties, attractive, with porcelain skin and light auburn hair, which she wore pulled back in a clip. Her eyes were blue and crinkled when she smiled. She was dressed in sharply pressed khaki slacks and a blue V-neck sweater pulled over a white tee shirt. The sleeves of the sweater were pushed up to her elbows. The pink slippers were still on her feet.

The memory of being carried crept forward from the back of Madison's mind. She blinked and stared at the older woman.

"Did you carry me through the woods?" she asked, hesitating. "I know it seems crazy ..." She shook her head at the thought. "I'm not very heavy, but you're ... old."

Dodie laughed. "Old doesn't mean decrepit, dear. And I had help. Doug helped me carry you to your car, then he drove it here to the house."

It sounded feasible but didn't jive with the picture in Madison's head. Her memory was of being carried through the woods, cradled like a child in the arms of the woman seated in front of her.

Madison looked around the room until her eyes settled on a clock near the bed. She hadn't noticed it before. It was ten minutes after five. Standing, she went to the window and pulled back the heavy drapes. From the second-story window, she could clearly see that nightfall was coming to the October evening and that the house was surrounded by thick stands of trees.

"How long have I been asleep?" she asked, still looking out the window.

"About fourteen hours."

Madison turned sharply on Dodie. "Fourteen hours?" Now it was clear why her head had been so heavy and thick when she woke. "You drugged me?" The tone was accusatory.

"When we carried you to the car, you passed out. Once we got you here and started dressing your injuries, it was obvious you were in a lot of pain, so I gave you a sedative to help you rest." Dodie's words were matter-of-fact, not defensive.

Before Madison could say anything more, Dodie rose and approached Madison, her face calm and comforting. "I called Detective Notchey to let him know you're awake. He wants to drop by tonight to ask you some questions. Do you feel up to it, or would you rather sleep some more?"

Madison hesitated before answering. She wasn't fond of the police, but this was an unusual situation. "No, I'll see him."

"Good." Dodie smiled at her. "Why don't you finish your dinner and get dressed?" She headed for the door. "Feel free to take a shower. Just be careful of the bandages if you wash your hair. There's a hair dryer and clean brush in one of the vanity drawers."

In spite of Madison's concerns, the pieces were falling into place with reasonable explanations. She sat back down to finish her soup. Digging an orange chunk from the bowl, she carefully tasted it. Was it a yam or a piece of pumpkin? Yam, she decided.

Maybe some things were exactly as they seemed.

———————

Freshly showered and dressed in the warm leggings, tunic sweater, and socks provided by Dodie, Madison picked up her dinner tray and headed downstairs. Like the upstairs, the main floor was a harmonious blend of gleaming hardwood floors and antique furnishings mixed with expensive fabrics and area rugs. Once on the first floor, she heard voices coming from the back of the house. In front of her was the front door. For a fleeting instant, Madison thought about running out the front door, but her purse was upstairs, and who knew if her car keys were with it. Instead, she straightened her shoulders and headed toward the voices.

In the spacious, modern kitchen, Dodie was at the counter by the sink fussing with a blender. The older man from the woods sat at the table teasing her. There was a distinguished and knowledgeable air about him. Madison hung back, staying out of sight, not wanting to disturb their intimate banter.

Dodie placed a glass in front of the man. It held a thick liquid the color of red velvet cake. He tasted it, swishing it around in his mouth as if tasting a fine wine. "New recipe?" he asked.

Dodie turned to him and wiped her hands on the cotton apron that protected her sweater and slacks. "Why? Don't you like it?"

He took another sip. "It's fine. A little on the gamey side, but in a good way."

She took a drink from her own glass. "I mixed equal parts domestic and wild. I thought it would be nice after last night's smoky, boozy aftertaste."

"Ah, yes," the man said, lifting the glass again to his mouth. "Last night's dinner wasn't very pleasant, but it was fresh."

Dodie shook her head. "When are people going to realize that they really are what they eat?"

Turning toward the doorway, Dodie waved to Madison. "Come on in, Madison, and meet Doug."

Embarrassed at being discovered eavesdropping, Madison sheepishly stepped into view. "I thought I'd bring my tray down."

Doug downed the rest of his smoothie in two big gulps before turning to greet Madison. When he did, she saw the reddish-brown liquid from the glass clinging to his lips and teeth.

Instantly, Madison was back in the woods—back on the ground, tied and immobile. She saw fangs. She saw blood. She heard Bobby Piper's screams. She staggered. The tray in her hands crashed to the floor.

Doug Dedham wiped his mouth with his napkin and addressed his wife. "If she's going to stick around, we need to have a talk with her. Pronto."

THREE

"They're freaking *vampires!*" Madison shrieked at Detective Notchey. They were in a comfortable wood-paneled den on the first floor of the Dedham home. In the fireplace, a small, cheerful fire danced. The door was closed. Detective Michael Notchey sat in a high-backed leather chair, one denim-clad leg crossed over the other as he calmly reviewed his notes. In front of the fire, Madison paced like a panther. Her arms were wrapped tightly around herself—not for warmth but to hold herself together, as she feared she was falling apart.

"The Dedhams can seem rather odd," Notchey commented dryly without looking up. "But they're nice enough people." He'd just questioned Madison about the events that had led up to her being kidnapped and her time in the woods, but it had been tough pulling the information out of her when all she wanted to focus on was the vampire issue.

"Odd, my ass." Worked into a frenzy, she spun to face him. "Did you not hear a word I've said? They're not *people*. They're *vampires!*"

This time, the detective looked up at her, his face weary with impatience. "How could I *not* hear, with the lungs on you? And just so you know, the Dedhams can hear you, too, even if you weren't shrieking like a banshee. They have very acute hearing."

That's not all they have, Madison thought to herself as she glared at the detective.

After she had dropped the tray, Dodie Dedham had rushed to Madison's side. "Dear, are you all right?"

Madison had slumped to the floor and was sagging against the doorjamb. Her hands were over her face, trying to squeeze out the invading memories from the night before.

"Madison, what's wrong?" Dodie had asked again. She knelt beside the girl, speaking in a soft, soothing tone.

"Last night," Madison began, lowering her hands just enough to stare in terror at Doug. "Last night I saw you kill Bobby. You wanted to kill me."

"Nonsense," cooed Dodie next to her. "You're still alive, aren't you? We took you in and cared for you, didn't we?"

"I heard him," Madison persisted. "He wanted to kill me. He killed Bobby."

Doug Dedham leaned back in his chair, totally unperturbed by Madison's accusations. "Would you rather I didn't? Should I have left that scum to kill you instead?" He let loose a low chuckle reminiscent of dark, dank corners. "Certainly would have saved us all a lot of trouble."

"Stop it, Doug. You're scaring the girl." Dodie started picking up the tray and its former occupants. The teacup had broken, but everything else was sound. When she got to her feet, Madison rose with her but never took her eyes away from Doug.

Rising from his chair, Doug took his glass to the sink and rinsed it out. "Better scared than dead—at least for her. Me, I prefer dead over scared."

"Don't mind him," Dodie told Madison as she took the tray to the kitchen counter. "He has a very dark sense of humor." She turned to her husband. "You behave," she ordered, poking him in the chest with an index finger.

"I am behaving, darling." He smiled at his wife while rubbing his hands up and down her arms in a tender motion. "But she really needs to know, especially if you plan on keeping her."

"Keeping me?" Madison straightened up, her fear downgraded a notch by her indignation. "What am I, some sort of pet?"

The Dedhams turned and looked at her in unison—Doug with amusement, Dodie with frustration. Without waiting for an answer, Madison made a break for the front door.

Upon yanking the door open, Madison screamed in blinding white terror. On the other side, Doug Dedham filled the doorway, tall and elegant with his silver, slicked-back hair and strong jaw. But it was impossible. It had to be. There was no way he could have gone out the back door and made it around the front before she reached the main door. *No freaking way,* she told herself. *Not at his age.*

Madison glanced behind her to see Dodie standing a few feet away in the doorway that connected to the kitchen.

"Madison, please," Dodie pleaded, as if Madison were a young, naughty child misbehaving in church. "Sit down and listen. We're not going to hurt you."

"No!" Madison backed up and weighed her options. To her right was the staircase, and next to it Dodie, moving slowly toward her. To her left, Doug watched her with a hungry eye.

"I saw you," she said to Doug, pointing a finger in his direction. "I saw you bite Bobby." She shot a look at Dodie, keeping track of her movements.

Doug stepped into the house. He was smiling. Madison backed up, a cornered rabbit amid a hunting party.

"You ... you had fangs," Madison continued, feeling at this point she had nothing to lose.

"Fangs?" Doug inquired.

"No, Doug," his wife warned. "She's been through enough."

Doug grinned. Ignoring his wife's caution, he looked right at Madison. "You mean like these?" As if triggered by a spring, fangs shot forward, framing each upper corner of Doug Dedham's mouth as his eyes widened with a red, burning light from within.

Madison felt her mind fading as her body tried to fold in upon itself like a tumbling house of cards. She fought to hang on to consciousness. She tried to scream. Her mouth opened in horror, but nothing came out. Finally, she dropped to the floor out of emotional exhaustion and waited a second time to die.

Her complete breakdown was interrupted by another voice, a different voice. "What's going on here?" the new arrival had demanded. It was Detective Notchey.

Back in the den, Madison had looked at Detective Notchey in disbelief but continued, her voice toned down. "So the vampire thing—this isn't news to you?"

"No, it's not. I met the Dedhams a while back." He paused. "On another case."

Madison's eyes widened with new fright. "You're not a vampire, too, are you?"

Notchey stared at her a moment, then laughed. "No, I'm not. I'm a beater, just like you."

"A ... a beater?"

The detective beckoned to her. "Come here, Madison." When she hesitated, he repeated his request. "Come here." He said it as gently as he knew how.

Madison shuffled over to the detective. He held out a hand to her. With caution, she placed her hand in his. He drew it forward and placed her fingertips on his neck, just under his jaw.

"What do you feel?" he asked.

"Besides stubble?"

"Besides stubble, what do you feel?" He kept his eyes riveted to Madison's face.

Madison pressed her fingers gently into the warm flesh of Notchey's neck. "I feel your pulse."

"And a pulse is?"

"A heartbeat." She pulled her hand away. "Heartbeat ... beater. I get it."

Notchey nodded. "You and I have heartbeats, like all living creatures. The Dedhams do not. Vampires refer to us as beaters."

Before Madison could say anything further, Notchey went back to his foremost concern: asking her questions. "Let me get this straight," he said. "You knew Bobby Piper *before* he snatched you, right? Are you sure you're telling me everything?" He looked at her with a cocked eye, as if she'd left out a vital piece of information on purpose.

Madison wanted to hit him, not once, but twice. Once for disregarding her own concerns, and the second time for his barely veiled accusation. She knew damn well where he was going with his prodding questions, and she was ready for him like a fighter prepped for the fight of a lifetime.

Detective Mike Notchey of the LAPD was irritating and rude, but then so were most of the cops she'd met in her life. Just a bit taller than her and with a slight, wiry build, he reminded her of the bantam rooster that had ruled the back yard at her second foster home. The small, ill-tempered chicken had terrorized her and the other children with its aggressive demeanor and arrogant ways until the day it turned up headless. They'd all been severely punished, even though all evidence pointed to Jodie Hormel, the oldest girl staying at the home, as the culprit.

"I'm telling you the truth," Madison insisted. "Bobby came into the diner every now and then. Sometimes he tried to talk to me while I worked. That's how I knew his name—he told me. That night, I didn't see him until he grabbed me."

"Do you remember anyone ever being with him?"

"No. There might have been from time to time, but I don't remember."

"And the diner, that would be Auntie Em's Diner on Washington in Culver City?"

Madison ran a hand through her freshly washed hair and winced as she grazed the scrape on her forehead. "Yes," she huffed. "I've told you that several times now." She'd been questioned enough by police to know that they asked the same questions over and over in different patterns in the hope of tripping up a suspect or unearthing new information from the victim.

Notchey was dressed in jeans and a Dodgers sweatshirt. His medium brown hair was cut short. He looked tired. Shadows cupped his dark eyes, and his five o'clock shadow had gone into extra innings. He wasn't young and he wasn't old, landing somewhere between Madison and the Dedhams in age. But then, that was a pretty wide spread.

"According to your record, you were picked up twice in Boise for soliciting." The detective eyed her over the top of his notebook.

Madison's jaw set in defiance. "I was never formally charged."

"Why is that?"

"Because I never solicited. I've never, ever been a whore." She spit the words out like rotten food and for the moment forgot about the vampires in the kitchen.

"According to your sheet," Notchey said, consulting his notebook, "you'd go into bars and promise the johns a good time. Once they were nice and drunk, you'd rob them in the parking lot."

"That was back in Boise. I've been straight since I've been here."

"Here? You mean since you've moved to LA?" He scoffed. "So you came to la-la land to start a new life, just like every other skank, crook, and perv?"

"Yes," she answered, as if clubbing him with the word. "I came here to start a new life. I've got a job, a place to live, and I pay my bills. I even take a class at West LA College. I haven't had a single brush with the law since I left Idaho. Ask my boss—he'll tell you. His name's Kyle Patterson. He owns the place."

"I already have. He says you're hardworking and always on time. Also said you're not much of a people person."

"Didn't know that was against the law." She narrowed her eyes at him. "If it was, you and I'd probably be wearing his and hers matching orange jumpsuits."

The edge of Notchey's mouth twitched as a smile fought for its life, then was beaten into submission. "We don't think Piper was working alone. And from what you observed—his waiting—

that's a fairly safe assumption. You're sure you never saw anyone else?"

She shook her head. "No one." Fixing her eyes on Notchey, she gathered her resolve and moved closer. "Just … just Doug Dedham splattering him against a tree, then gnawing on him like a ren faire turkey leg."

Mike Notchey closed his notebook and met her steady stare. "The Dedhams saved your life and took care of you. Be a little grateful, why don't you? They could've left you there. It would have been better for them if they had."

Madison raised her chin in defiance. "He wanted to kill me. She talked him out of it," she repeated yet again.

"Doug Dedham would never have killed you." This time the detective did smile. "No matter how tempting. He just likes to screw with people when he can, which isn't often. For him, it's Halloween every day."

"And what about Dodie?"

"Dodie is just as undead as Doug. She just exercises more common sense and manners. Dodie is kind, warm, and caring, but don't for a minute think she's some fragile old lady. Believe me, when need be, she can be just as scary as Doug."

Madison gave that some thought, sure now that Dodie Dedham had carried her through the woods. If they had super hearing and could move at lightning speed, what was to stop them from having super strength?

Notchey closed his notebook and got to his feet. "I'll stop by tomorrow to see how you're getting along and if there's anything more you may have remembered."

"Hold on," she told him. "Let me grab my purse. I'd feel better leaving with you."

Stopping short of the door, Notchey turned to her. "Didn't the Dedhams tell you? You're staying here for the time being."

Madison's mouth hung open a full fifteen seconds before she found her voice. "The hell I am!"

In two strides, Notchey was in front of Madison, holding her tightly by the arms. "It's the safest place for you, and we need you to stay low for a while—out of the way in case they come back to finish you off."

"Did you not pay attention to me just now? Vampires. They are *vam-pires!*"

Notchey put his face close to hers. She could smell onions. "And did you not understand what nearly happened to you?" He shook her, then let go. "Doug and Dodie are not going to hurt you. There's a killer or killers on the loose, and they're helping hunt them down."

"The vamps are helping the cops?" Madison was confused. "But I thought the guy who killed those women was in jail."

"The Dedhams are helping *me.*" Notchey paused before continuing, running a hand through his spiky hair. "The brass think they've got the guy. I don't; neither do the Dedhams. Someone is going around snatching women, mutilating them. It's going on a lot more than what you're hearing in the news. I think Bobby was just a middleman—the guy who brought the women to the killer. I think the guy in jail was also a murder pimp and not the killer. But he's not talking, except to claim he did it. If I'm right, this guy's more afraid of the killer than he is of going to prison for life."

"So the cops want me to stay here until they solve the case? No matter how long it takes?" Madison shook her head and started for the door. "Uh-uh. No way. I'm outta here."

Notchey grabbed her upper arm to stop her. She winced as his hand covered a fresh bruise from the night before. "Except for me, the cops don't know anything about you, Madison. What happened to you last night never officially happened."

That stopped her short. "But Bobby's body—"

"There is no body. We want the mastermind of these killings to simply think you and Bobby disappeared, hopefully together. We want him off balance, pissed off at his underling."

Madison plopped down on the leather sofa across from the fireplace, her mind burning like the logs in the grate. "So I've been kidnapped a second time?"

"Think of it as a personal witness protection program."

She turned toward Notchey. "But I didn't see anything!"

"Maybe not, but why did Bobby pick you? Or did he? Maybe the killer is someone who handpicked you himself and ordered Bobby to serve you up. If the killer is still on the loose, do you want to take the chance he'll finish what he started?"

It was quiet between them while Madison churned everything around in her head.

"I'm going to lose my job."

"You're a waitress, Madison. You'll find another job." After a slight pause, Notchey toned it down. "I didn't tell your boss I was a cop. I told him I was a friend of the family and that you had a family emergency and will call him in a few days. He told me that stuff about you when I told him I didn't know you well and asked what you were like."

Notchey sighed and walked over to where Madison sat still as stone. "Trust me, the Dedhams will treat you well. They have a housekeeper who comes in during the day, so you'll have some … some non-vampire company. Being vampires, the Dedhams mostly sleep during the day anyway."

"In coffins, right?" Madison shuddered.

After giving her an eye roll, Notchey answered, "No, not in coffins. They sleep in real beds, just like you and me. Modern vampires seldom sleep in coffins."

Madison wasn't convinced.

"Hang out," Notchey continued. "Watch TV. Read a book. Sleep 24/7 for all I care. But I want to catch this bastard, and so far you're the only one who's been snatched who's still alive."

She looked up at Notchey with suspicion. "What's it to you? Why are you going rogue over this?"

Mike Notchey turned to look at the fire, then rotated his head back to Madison. He started to say something, then changed his mind and headed for the door. "See you tomorrow night," he shot over his shoulder at her.

When Notchey opened the door, the Dedhams were waiting on the other side. Dodie was holding a large bag, which she handed to him. "Pauline made her chicken soup today, and I wanted to make sure you got some. There's also a few oatmeal cookies in there."

Notchey took the bag and kissed Dodie lightly on the cheek. He shook hands with Doug. With one last grunt at Madison, he left.

Doug and Dodie entered the den. They stood in front of Madison, their arms wrapped lovingly around each other's waists. They looked like an ad for AARP membership or an upscale retirement community.

"Don't worry, Madison," Doug said, his voice now tender. "We won't bite … at least not unless you want us to."

Using her sharp elbow, his wife dug him hard in the ribs.

.FOUR

After Detective Notchey left, awkwardness as thick and heavy as motor oil settled between Madison and the Dedhams. They were trying to be solicitous and charming, yet Madison eyed the vampire couple warily, still wondering if she was to be their next meal.

"Can I get you something, Madison?" Dodie asked with a smile. "Maybe just a little nibble?" When she saw Madison flinch, Dodie edited her comment. "Well, perhaps later. Maybe we should get better acquainted instead."

Doug glanced at his watch. "*The Amazing Race* will be starting soon." He picked up a remote from the table in front of the sofa and aimed it at the large flat-screen TV mounted above the fireplace. The TV popped to life. "We love that show. Never miss it." He looked at Madison. "You ever watch it?"

Madison slowly shook her head from side to side, continuing to stare at the retired couple with a cocktail of fear and curiosity. Inside her chest, her heart thumped fast with anxiety. *Beaters.* That's what she was to them—a beater.

"It's great," Doug continued with enthusiasm. "It's like a worldwide scavenger hunt with multiple teams of two competing against each other." Satisfied with his channel choice, he put the remote back on the table and eyed Madison's position on the sofa. "Scoot over a bit," he told her, "and we can all watch it together."

Instead of scooting over, Madison got up and started for the stairs. She might not be able to leave the house, but that didn't mean she had to stay in the same room with them.

"Please don't go, Madison," Dodie said in a soft, pleading tone.

Madison hesitated, her mind weighing her options and not finding many. After a glance at the doorway, she returned to the sofa but at the last minute chose to sit in the big leather chair next to it that Notchey had occupied earlier. After exchanging glances, Doug and Dodie sat side by side on the sofa, with Dodie sitting nearest Madison.

On the TV, Lesley Stahl was interviewing an environmentalist about global warming for *60 Minutes*. "Dodie's right, Madison," Doug said after muting the sound. "We do need to get to know each other, especially if you're going to be staying with us for a bit."

"It's not my choice," Madison said sullenly, keeping her eyes on the TV. "Believe me." She slouched in the chair like a petulant child.

"I'm sure it's not," Doug continued with soft amusement in his voice. "Until tonight, did you even believe vampires existed?"

Madison shot him a glance, then aimed another at Dodie. The Dedhams looked like grandparents straight out of a Disney family movie. Grandparents trying to have a heart-to-heart chat with an errant granddaughter. She shook her head and turned back to stare at the TV. After a few moments of silence, she turned back toward them and straightened in her chair.

"No. And I'm not a hundred percent sure they exist now." She narrowed her eyes at the couple. "What's the catch? If you two are powerful vampires, why do you need me, a lowly *beater*?"

Dodie looked embarrassed. Doug laughed.

"I'm guessing," Doug said, still chuckling, "that Mike told you about that term."

Madison nodded. "Yes. And he said you're helping the cops find some killer that's on the loose."

"No," Doug corrected. "We're helping Mike. In general, we don't like the police much and tend to stay away from them. We find them a bit too nosy."

For the first time, Madison offered the Dedhams a small smile. "That much we have in common."

Encouraged by Madison's slight thaw, Doug got up from the sofa and sat on the edge of the coffee table, directly in front of Madison. "You can go at any time, Madison. We're not going to hold you prisoner here. But we—and that includes Detective Notchey—feel you'd be safer here for the time being."

"So he told me." Madison looked at the TV, where *60 Minutes* had gone to commercial. She turned back to the Dedhams. "Like I told Notchey, I don't know anything. Bobby Piper came into the diner once in a while, usually alone, although Notchey told me that Bobby might not have been working alone."

The Dedhams exchanged meaningful looks, which put Madison on alert. "What?" she asked, looking from one vampire to the other as her heart pounded faster. "There's something you're not telling me." She sat up straight in the chair. "And why are you two involved anyway? Why would you care if a few *beaters* die?"

Frowning, Doug snapped, "Why don't you quit *beating* that term to death."

Dodie put her hand on her husband's knee, letting him know that she would field the questions. "These murders, Madison, could adversely affect our way of life. By 'our,' I mean the entire vampire community."

Madison scooted hard back into her chair, putting distance between herself and the Dedhams, even if only a few inches. "There's a whole freaking *community* of you?" She quickly looked around as if more vampires would come oozing out of the wall paneling any second.

"Madison, dear," Dodie told her in a motherly tone, "please calm down. And, yes, there are other vampires in the world and quite a few right here in Los Angeles."

"So a vampire is behind these killings?"

"No," Doug answered with blunt confidence. "Definitely not. But we believe someone posing as a vampire may be behind them."

Dodie nodded in agreement. "A lot of people are into vampires these days, Madison. Some even pretend to be us. I'm sure you've seen or heard of that."

Madison had. "Yes, but they're usually harmless goth types, aren't they? Creepy posers?"

"Most of the time, yes," Doug answered. "For obvious reasons, real vampires don't wear their true identity on their sleeves for public viewing. Over the years, most of us have learned to adapt and blend in. Others simply stay away from the living. We just want to live quietly. If these murders continue, it could trigger a serious scare in Los Angeles. A lot of innocent people could get hurt, and I don't mean just the women who get kidnapped."

On the TV, Andy Rooney was doing his end-of-show monologue. Madison stared at the screen while she digested the information she'd just received. "But how can I help if I don't know anything?"

With a soft smile, Dodie rose and left the room, but not before giving her husband a nod of encouragement.

Doug got up and paced in front of the fireplace, stretching his long legs. "For starters, you can keep yourself safe. We don't know if there is a pattern to how the victims are chosen, but if there is, it could help lead us to whoever is doing this. Mike is going to come by again tomorrow. I'm sure he'll have more questions."

Madison thought about her previous conversation with Notchey. "Detective Notchey said the police think they have the guy who's been doing this. But Notchey doesn't think they do."

"They don't, or else why were you grabbed?" Doug's eyes zeroed in on her with intense frankness.

That thought had also occurred to Madison. Unless it was some copycat creep, the real killer was still on the loose.

"Whoever it might be, Madison," Doug continued, "he is still out there. And he's powerful, able to control others and get them to do his bidding. If it was a vampire, the rest of us would know, even if it was a vampire from outside our area. We're a very tight community."

Dodie returned with a small tray. On it was a plate of oatmeal cookies studded with plump raisins, along with a large mug of steaming hot chocolate. She placed the tray on the coffee table in front of Madison and resumed her place on the sofa. "Here's a little snack for you, Madison. I made the cookies yesterday."

Doug came to stand near Dodie. "You will be safe here, Madison. I promise you that." As he spoke, he placed a hand on his wife's shoulder. Dodie looked up at him, and again the couple exchanged looks before Doug's attention returned to Madison.

"We understand that you will miss work," Doug continued. "And Mike told us that you might even lose your job. If you decide to stay, you will be well compensated for your time here."

Madison shook her head as if she hadn't heard correctly. "You want to pay me to stay here until this is over?"

"Yes," Doug said firmly. "It's that important to us."

"And I will *not* be considered a food source?" she pressed, determined to know all the details.

Doug threw his head back and laughed loudly. "Do you want to be?"

"Hell, no!"

"Then you won't be. In this house, no means no." He looked down at his wife and smiled. "Both Dodie and Pauline are excellent cooks. We have a nice large place here. Think of it as a little paid vacation."

"That's it?"

"Not exactly," Doug informed her. "The deal does come with some fine print."

Madison rolled her eyes. "I knew it. Economics 101—there ain't no such thing as a free lunch."

Ignoring her sarcasm, Doug fixed Madison with a burning look. "You can never talk about us or our way of life, or about the other vampires you might meet while here. Not to anyone. Ever. That understood?"

"Sure," Madison said with a cocky grin. "Whatever happens in the coffin, stays in the coffin."

"We're serious, Madison." Doug's tone turned thick and menacing. Dodie cleared her throat; it brought Doug's ire down a few notches.

"I get it," Madison assured them. "Keep my mouth shut." She shrugged. "No problem. I'm good at that. You want me to sign some sort of confidentiality agreement?"

Dodie reached over and patted Madison's knee softly. "That won't be necessary, dear. You see, if you betray our trust, we'll have to kill you. And I'd really hate to see that."

Doug picked up the remote to the TV and turned on the sound. "*The Amazing Race* is starting." He settled on the sofa next to his wife. "You know, Madison, Dodie and I thought about trying out for this show. With our special powers, we'd kick ass. Show them what a couple of old farts can really do." He glanced at Madison, his former hard demeanor wiped clean. "Problem is, most of it takes place during the day. Then there's the food issue." Next to him, Dodie giggled.

Slack jawed and shaking, Madison stared at the two of them. When she spoke, her voice trembled, barely audible over the opening credits of the TV show. "Notchey promised you wouldn't hurt me."

Doug dragged his eyes away from the TV and looked at her with a blend of compassion and gravity. "If you betray us, Madison, and *we* don't kill you, you'd be tried and sentenced to death by the local vampire council. Trust me, you'd rather be killed by our hands than theirs."

Dodie noticed the girl's terror and smiled reassuringly. "Everything's going to be fine, Madison. You'll see. Now drink your cocoa before it gets cold."

FIVE

Dodie Dedham studied the photo in the cracked, blue wooden frame before picking it up and adding it to the bag of clothes in her hand.

"Rather a sad little place," said her husband.

Dodie looked around Madison's tiny Culver City studio apartment. It was a single small room with one window that looked out over a parking lot. There was a kitchenette with a two-burner stove, a microwave, and several shallow cupboards separated from the rest of the room by a counter. To the right of the kitchen area was a dining alcove. Madison had used this instead for her sleeping area by cramming a twin bed, nightstand, and lamp into the space. At the foot of the bed, a squat four-drawer dresser faced out, lending some sense of separation between the bed and the rest of the room. The bed was neatly made. A short hallway between the bed and kitchen led to a tiny bathroom on one side and a full closet with sliding doors on the other. The main part of the room held an old loveseat and assemble-it-yourself end tables with more cheap lamps. Across from the loveseat was a long folding table with a rolling desk chair and a tall bookcase stuffed with books. On the table was a laptop, a printer, and more books. The computer equipment, although not the best quality, was clearly the most valuable item in the room.

"Sad, maybe, Doug," Dodie agreed, "but not hopeless." She pointed toward the dresser that had been painted to match the sofa and the end tables. A colorful cotton dhurrie covered much of the old, worn carpet. The walls were adorned with posters of classic paintings, including those of Manet, Monet, and Georgia O'Keeffe.

"Madison may not have much," Dodie said to Doug, "but she's made a real effort to make this into a home."

"And she's neat as a pin," Doug observed. "Everything is spick and span." He pointed at the makeshift desk. "She also seems intent on bettering herself. Also a good sign."

"Although," Dodie continued, "I'm rather disturbed by the lack of personal items such as photographs and keepsakes. Most young women would have snapshots of friends and family stuck here and there, wouldn't they?"

"You'd think."

"Did Mike say anything to you about Madison's family?"

Doug shook his head. Even though they'd not turned on any lights, the two of them could see quite clearly in the dark, their natural habitat. "Just that she came from Idaho and had been in some trouble before she left. Nothing too serious, mostly petty theft, I believe. He didn't elaborate."

"I checked her cell phone last night," Dodie told him. "It's a disposable. There were no recent incoming calls except one. I called it back, and it was an auto repair place. And Madison had made only a couple of outgoing calls. One to the auto place and the other to the diner where she works." Dodie pointed at the table. "Make sure you get the computer and her schoolbooks. I'm going to pull a few more things from the closet."

Doug went to the table and started packing up the items on Madison's desk. "Let's step on it, Dodie. Samuel said he'd meet us back at our place in about an hour."

When they reached their home, Doug and Dodie found a large black Mercedes sedan parked in front of their door. Standing nearby was Gordon, Samuel's bodyguard and driver. They nodded to the serious man with the thick neck and crew cut and made their way inside, leaving the items from Madison's apartment in their car.

Samuel wasn't waiting in the living room as they expected, but two young women were. Slim, leggy, and gorgeous, the women, one black, the other Asian, lounged on the Dedhams' sofa dressed in expensive evening clothes. They looked bored. Both were beaters. The black woman was new to them, but the Asian woman they'd met before. Her name was Kai.

"Kai, where's Samuel?" Doug asked.

Kai swung her head in the direction of the stairs, her long, glossy black hair swaying like a dark curtain moved by a sudden breeze.

Doug flew up the staircase, Dodie fast on his heels.

Samuel La Croix was seated in a desk chair that he'd pulled close to the bed. He was leaning back, one tuxedo-clad pant leg crossed over the other, casually watching Madison sleep.

"She looks like an angel, doesn't she?" Samuel addressed the Dedhams without taking his eyes, which were shielded by sunglasses even in the dark room, off of the sleeping young woman. "Once those bruises and cuts are gone, she'll clean up nicely."

Dodie stepped forward. Her husband reached out and put a warning hand on her arm, keeping her from approaching further. "She's not for you, Samuel," Dodie told the vampire in the chair. Her voice, though firm, was respectful.

Samuel La Croix turned toward the Dedhams and smiled. His smile was wide, his teeth stark and gleaming against his mahogany skin. He stood, stretched his limbs with the ease of a jungle cat, and approached the bed. With a soft touch, he ran two fingers across Madison's cheek. She didn't stir.

"Given her something, have you?" he asked Dodie. "Making sure she slept while you two went out tonight?"

"She was still in pain from last night," Dodie explained.

Samuel laughed under his breath and picked up Madison's limp left hand, turning the palm toward him. He studied it, running a finger across the lifeline. "She's not one of us," he observed.

Doug stepped forward. "No, Samuel, she's not."

"Interesting." He paused and turned toward the Dedhams. "Haven't most of the victims been marked?"

"Yes," Doug answered. "At least we think most, if not all, had bloodlines. But Madison doesn't. Rather shoots our original theory in the foot."

Samuel placed Madison's hand gently back on the bed and once again studied the sleeping woman. After a moment, he moved toward Doug and Dodie in a long stride of authority.

Placing a hand under Dodie's chin, Samuel raised her face to meet his. Nearby, Doug tensed. Samuel was much taller than Dodie but not nearly as tall as Doug. His head was bald, his jaw strong, his brow thick and serious. A pale scar raised against his dark skin like a thin, curved levee and traveled down from behind one ear, disappearing into the collar of his shirt.

"I've always admired your courage, Dodie, and your concern for your inferiors." Samuel's voice was even, spiced with an accent of far-off places and centuries of travel. He took off his sunglasses, revealing two large milky eyes, which he fixed on Dodie. "But if I want the girl, she will be mine."

Samuel replaced his glasses and took one last look down at Madison. "Now let's leave this sleeping beauty and go back downstairs. We have a lot to discuss before sunrise."

SIX

When Madison opened her eyes, she again saw the sliver of light from across the room. She stretched in the big bed, smelled the familiar wisp of lavender, and glanced at the clock on the nightstand—8:55 in the morning. Thanks to the heavy lined drapes, the bedroom was still cloaked in inky blackness.

When she'd gone to bed, it had been around eleven. She'd taken another pain pill—only a half dosage, though the fuzzy feeling in her head made her wonder if it had been more than half. When Dodie had offered her the medication, Madison had hesitated, but her body still ached from her assault by Bobby Piper. She also decided that just in case the Dedhams were of a blood-sucking mind, she didn't want to be awake if and when they came after her. She wanted to trust them, and they were trying hard to win her over, but even with the vampire thing aside, Madison wasn't used to trusting people, dead or living.

After a trip to the bathroom, Madison opened the drapes. She had no idea where she was, and in the shock of discovering the truth about her hosts, she'd forgotten to ask. The view outside her window showed the house was located in a woodsy area surrounded by uneven ground, as if on a hillside. Just beyond the trees at the end of the driveway, she caught sight of a road. Beyond that, she could make out the roof of another house. As she studied the view, a car went by on the road. The other building and the car soothed her. Wherever she was, it wasn't in the middle of nowhere, as she had suspected.

Madison stretched in the sunlight, going through moves she'd learned in a yoga class. Ignoring the protests of her bruises, she enjoyed the feel of her body. No matter what was ahead, for now she was alive. She'd decided to approach her time with the Dedhams much as she did her childhood in foster care—one day at a time. Although in the case of the Dedhams, it might be one night at a time.

During her final stretches, Madison noticed the desk chair had been moved to the side of the bed, as if someone had been watching her sleep. She'd had a dream about a man, a very dark man, watching over her. When he'd touched her in the dream, she'd been both thrilled and terrified. Madison moved the chair back to the desk. Dodie had probably come in to make sure she was all right, but Madison still found it slightly disturbing.

Something else was different. On the desk was a laptop and a stack of books. Not just any books, but her schoolbooks, along with a few other books she'd had in her apartment. The laptop was hers, too. Her eyes swept the room and came to rest on the dresser. On the top of the dresser were neatly folded clothes that also looked familiar. She crossed the large room and fingered the articles, instantly recognizing several pairs of her jeans and various sweaters and tee shirts. There was also a plastic bag filled with her personal cosmetics and toiletries, including her hairbrush and comb. Then her eye snagged on two other recognizable items.

Half hidden by the pile of clothing was Pookie, a raggedy stuffed kitten, and a photograph in a blue wooden frame. It was a photo of a very young Madison with her mother. Leaning against the frame was a folded piece of stationery monogrammed with a stylized *D* at the top. With a shaking hand, Madison picked up the paper. It was a note from Dodie. The handwriting was clean and precise.

> *We thought you'd be more comfortable with some of*
> *your own things. There are a few more in the closet.*
> *Your lingerie is in the dresser.*

Madison yanked open the top dresser drawer to find an assortment of her panties, bras, and socks. Dashing to the closet, she flung open the doors. Neatly hanging from wooden hangers were the only two pairs of dress pants she owned, a few blouses, and a dress. On the floor of the closet were a couple pairs of her shoes, including her favorite boots.

Returning to the dresser, Madison picked up the photo and studied it as tears ran down her cheeks. She traced the outline of her mother's face. She'd died when Madison was five years old. The stuffed kitten was the last thing she'd given Madison before her death.

Madison put down the photo and picked up the stuffed animal. Clutching it to her chest, she slipped back into bed and buried her head in a pillow, sobbing until she was too exhausted to cry anymore.

It was nearly ten by the time Madison showered and went downstairs dressed in her own clothing. Much to her surprise, the drapes were open and the house was flooded with sunshine. She heard noise coming from the kitchen and headed in that direction.

Bustling around the kitchen was a squat African-American woman with long, braided hair. The mixture of black and gray in her hair gave it the appearance of a tweed veil. She wore gray leggings and a long tunic sweater the color of a ripe banana. An apron was tied around her thick waist. Her feet were stuck into white Keds. The woman's back was to Madison. She was humming a tune that sounded like church music.

Madison cleared her throat before speaking so she would not scare the woman. "Are you Pauline?"

The woman turned around, not surprised at all. She appeared to be in her fifties, with a broad face, high cheekbones, and small, sharp bird eyes. "That's me—Pauline Speakes. And you must be young Miss Madison." The woman eyed Madison up and down without apology. "Thought you were going to sleep the day away, but now that I see that black eye and those cuts, I'm not surprised."

Madison self-consciously touched the bandage on the side of her face. "Dodie gave me a pain pill last night. Those things knock me on my ass."

"Hmmm." Pauline crossed her arms and stared at Madison. "You need to know right off, I don't take to girls with potty mouths."

Madison started to say something coarse in retort, but one look at Pauline cautioned her not to pick the fight. "I'll remember that," she said instead.

"Good, that's getting off on the right foot. Now, what would you like for breakfast?"

Madison shrugged.

"Speak up, girl," Pauline told her. "Dodie had me pick up a few things on my way in today. Things like eggs and bread, some pouches of tuna—stuff like that. She said you drink 2% milk with your Honey Nut Cheerios, that right?"

"How did she know?" Madison asked, then remembered her personal items upstairs. "Of course, they went to my apartment, didn't they?"

"Seems so. Shall it be cereal, then?"

When Madison nodded, Pauline went to a cupboard and retrieved a bowl. From a drawer she pulled out a spoon. "The cereal's in that cupboard," she said, pointing to one near the refrigerator.

Madison went to the cupboard and found a fresh box of her favorite cereal. The pantry was well stocked, though most items appeared newly purchased. After grabbing the box from the cupboard and milk from the refrigerator, she took a seat at the kitchen table, where Pauline had placed the bowl and spoon. In the middle of the table was a large bowl of fresh fruit.

"Where am I?" Madison ventured as she poured cereal into her bowl. Even as she asked the question, it sounded lame to her.

Pauline turned from the sink to face her. "You mean geographically?"

Madison nodded and added milk to the bowl. "With everything that's happened, I forgot to ask. Kind of stupid of me, I know."

"This house is in Topanga Canyon. You know where that is?"

Again, Madison nodded.

Pauline went to the refrigerator, pulled out a container of juice, and poured two glasses. She put one in front of Madison and the other in front of another seat at the table. Pauline settled herself in the chair by the juice.

"Seems like now would be a good time to go over some house rules," she told Madison. "First off, I'm not here to wait on you. Got that?"

Madison jabbed her spoon into her cereal. "I wouldn't expect you to."

"You take care of your room. Pick up after yourself. Make your own bed."

"It's already made." Madison popped the first spoonful of cereal into her mouth and chewed, being careful of her split lip. It was delicious. She'd not eaten much the day before except for soup and a couple of cookies, and she was famished. She shoveled another bite in on the heels of the first.

"Mrs. D said you were neat. Glad to hear it." Pauline took a drink of juice and watched the girl. "Secondly, you have the run of the house except for the Dedhams' master suite. That doesn't mean you can go snooping around or anything like that, but you're not restricted on where you can go—except for their room. The master suite is at the end of the hallway, down from your room. There are two small bedrooms that share a bath across the hall from your room. Mrs. D uses one for a kind of sewing or craft room. She loves to do handwork—knitting, needlepoint, anything with a hook or needle. The other room is empty except for a bed and dresser. Down here, there's the living room, dining room, den, and a small study Mr. D uses. There are lots of books in there. I've heard you like to read, so help yourself, just don't disturb Mr. D's paints. He likes to dabble in oils.

It's the only messy place in the entire house." The last sentence was spoken with frustration mixed with pride.

"Don't worry," Madison told her between bites. "I'm used to living in other people's homes." When Pauline gave her a quizzical look, she added, "I grew up in foster care. Five different places between the ages of eight and eighteen."

Again, Pauline quietly studied Madison, taking her measure. Dodie Dedham had seen something special in the girl. She'd told Pauline so this morning when she arrived, just before Dodie had gone to bed. Dodie had specifically waited up to talk to her about Madison.

Pauline got up from the table and moved to the sink. She pointed out the window. "Out back there's a lap pool, hot tub, and large patio. The pool's heater isn't on, so you might not want to use it this time of year. The Dedhams both love to swim, but the cold don't bother them any."

"Doesn't matter. I don't have a swimsuit."

"I'm sure I can find you one of Mrs. D's if you want to go into the hot tub. Nothing sexy, but it should do."

Madison finished her cereal but stayed at the table, wiping her mouth with the paper napkin Pauline had provided along with the spoon. "So the house and the patio, that's it?"

Pauline moved away from the window. From a set of wooden key pegs by the back door, she removed a set of keys and brought them to the table. She dropped them in front of Madison with a discordant clang. Madison immediately recognized that they were her keys.

"The Dedhams wanted me to tell you that you're no prisoner here. You can go anytime, but they think it best you listen to them and stay, at least for a few days. So do I."

Remembering what Doug had told her the night before about the killings and the person impersonating a vampire, Madison fought the urge to grab her keys and run for the door. So far, the Dedhams had treated her decently—better than most everyone else in her life had treated her to date, except for her mother and her great aunt Eleanor.

"As for food," Pauline said, moving to the refrigerator, "you can cook and eat anything you find, except for stuff that looks like blood."

Madison shivered and Pauline noticed. She chuckled softly as she opened the refrigerator door. "Most of these plastic containers have blood in them. There are similar containers in the freezer, and all are clearly marked with what type of blood."

This time, Madison turned a pale shade of green, and again Pauline noticed her discomfort. "Don't worry, in time you'll get used to it, and none of it's human blood. The Dedhams don't store human blood in the house." She paused before adding, "Doesn't mean they don't enjoy it, but it would be tougher to explain to the authorities if for any reason someone stumbled upon it here. They go out for that—sort of like you and I would go out for a nice slice of prime rib and fried shrimp."

Madison rested her arms on the table and lowered her head onto them. "Oh, god," she moaned as the reality of the situation made itself crystal clear. There really were vampires, and she'd managed to happen upon them.

Pauline ignored Madison's distress. "Mrs. D loves to bake. Seeing how you're a bag of bones, she'll probably try to put some meat on you."

That caught Madison's attention. Remembering the cookies, she asked, without lifting her head from the table, "She loves to bake? Can they eat any of it?"

"Not a lick, but both of them love the smell of fresh baked goods in the house, especially Mrs. D. I think it reminds her of when she was … well … it reminds her of another time." Pauline paused, then added, "Makes her feel more normal, I think. She hasn't been a vampire very long, only about fifteen years. Became one when she married Mr. D."

Curious, Madison raised her head and pushed aside the thought of the Dedhams' liquid meals sharing space in the fridge alongside the cereal milk. She was about to ask Pauline more about the Dedhams, but the housekeeper moved back to the kitchen counter where a Crock-Pot was set up. There she continued with her instructions. "This here is a pot roast for your dinner tonight. There's a nice chunk of beef in there with carrots and potatoes. You should let it cook until at least three o'clock; anytime after that you can eat it. There'll be plenty for leftovers, too. Storage containers for the leftovers are in the cabinet under the microwave."

"You're not staying today?" Madison asked with slight alarm. "I thought you were here all day."

"Usually, I'm here five days a week from about eight in the morning until two or three in the afternoon, but today my great-niece is in a play at school. But don't worry, just relax and get used to the place. The Dedhams get up around five, a little later in the summer months when the days are longer. Mrs. D told me she has a surprise for you, so be ready to go out around six or so. Nothing fancy, just girl stuff."

Madison felt like a ship buffeted by a capricious storm. One minute she'd fallen into a heart-warming movie of the week, the next she was in a cult horror picture.

"We've only had one other living houseguest before, and that was Mike," Pauline told Madison with a skeptical shake of her head. "So this should be interesting, to say the least."

"Do you mean Detective Notchey?"

"Yes. He stayed here once, in the same room you're in now. It was while Mrs. D nursed him back from a shooting injury." Pauline was about to say more about the detective when she suddenly remembered something. "Oh, I forgot," she said, pulling a message out of the pocket of her apron. "Mike called. He wants you to call him as soon as you can. I believe he wants to come by today and ask you more questions."

Madison picked up her keys and rose from the table. She went to Pauline and took the note, which was a phone number scrawled on the back of a grocery receipt.

"He left his cell number," Pauline explained, "in case you misplaced his business card."

Looking out the window, Madison could see the pool, hot tub, and large, lovely patio. The property was edged with thick natural trees and shrubs, like it had been carved out of the dense vegetation with a soup spoon. She'd hiked in Topanga Canyon several times. It was located in the Santa Monica Mountains, not far from the Pacific Ocean and Malibu. Bobby Piper had taken her to a wooded area, and she wondered if it had been here, close to the Dedhams' house.

"I saw Doug kill the man who kidnapped me," she said to Pauline without turning around.

Pauline moved closer to Madison but didn't touch her. "You forget about that now, Madison," she instructed. "Sometimes the Dedhams kill, but they never do it wantonly like some vampires or like those you've seen on TV. If they have to end a life, it's for a good reason and usually with considerable thought and regret." When Madison didn't respond, she continued. "Would you rather they'd left you to die? Because as I understand it, it was either that scum or you."

Madison looked down at the keys in her hand. Pauline noticed and could read her thoughts of flight as if they were stamped in ink on the girl's scraped forehead. She placed a dark, rough hand on Madison's shoulder. "The Dedhams are good people, Madison."

"But they're not people, are they?" Madison turned to look into the eyes of the housekeeper. "Not really."

"At one time they were alive." Pauline moved the hand to touch her own chest. "I know in my heart they were good people then and try to be good people now, even when the dark side of their circumstance leads them in a different direction."

The two women stood face to face in silence for a moment before Pauline spoke again. When she did, her tone was respectful and quiet. "My family has served Douglas Dedham for over two hundred years."

Madison's eyes widened, silently urging Pauline to continue. "It started when Mr. D saved my ancestor, Micah Johnson, from the hands of an evil and sadistic slave trader. Mr. D took him in, trained him as his personal valet, and educated him. In those days, it was dangerous to educate slaves. Mr. D did it himself in secret. From that point on, someone in my family has been employed by Mr. D to see to his needs." She paused for emphasis. "And keep his secret."

Pauline picked up a cloth and started wiping down the spotless counter as she talked. "Before me, it was my Aunt Izzy. After me, either my cousin Sara or my niece Keisha will work here in my place. Both help around here now. Even my husband does things for the Dedhams." She looked up at Madison. "Through the years, my family has been completely loyal to Douglas Dedham, and now to Dodie, and we've been the better for it."

SEVEN

Madison studied the photographs spread across the Dedhams' kitchen table. "Sorry," she said without looking up. "I've got nothing."

Mike Notchey paced the tile floor. Today he was dressed in a dark rumpled suit. As soon as he'd come into the house, he'd removed his jacket and loosened his tie. To Madison, he looked younger than he had the night before. He still sported the haggard look, but today he was clean shaven. Madison downgraded her estimate of his age to mid-thirties.

The detective stopped pacing and leaned against the counter, where just a few hours earlier Pauline had stood giving Madison the skinny on the Dedham house. "You're sure?" he asked.

Madison shrugged. "One of them might have come into the diner at some time. Who knows, *all* of them could have—Auntie Em's is very popular, especially during the lunch rush. It picks up a lot of business from Sony and some of the other studios during the day."

"The day? I thought you worked the night shift?" He narrowed his eyes at her.

"Except for the times I had class," she explained. "I worked whatever hours they threw at me."

A spark of interest ignited in Notchey's eyes. "Did you have any normal hours? You know, hours that might be considered a regular schedule?"

Madison gave it some thought before answering. "Up until Labor Day, I worked mostly the day shift." Madison repositioned herself in her chair and crossed her legs. "You see, the tips were always better during the week at lunch. On the weekends, it's the yuppie Sunday brunch crowd that tipped best. Evenings were slow, with mostly older, less trendy customers who didn't tip well. Saturday nights were the worst, especially later in the evening as people came out of the clubs drunk and in search of food. Kyle likes to spread the schedule evenly so that his waitstaff all have a shot at decent tips. He's good that way, but he always put his best staff down for lunch, to serve the important studio crowd."

"And you were once one of his best? Did you fall from grace?"

"I am his best," Madison said with assurance. "And up until this fall, I always worked the lunch shift four days a week and Sunday brunch. Until then, I was taking night classes at the community college, but there was a class I wanted this semester that was only offered Tuesdays and Thursdays during the day. Tuesdays I already had off. When I asked if I could switch my Thursday with the guy who worked Saturday breakfast, Kyle told me that the woman who worked Friday and Saturday nights was leaving and I could have her Saturday night shift."

"So you worked Monday, Wednesday, and Friday during the day, and Saturday night, and then came back again early on Sunday for brunch? That's a pretty grueling schedule on the weekend."

Madison shook her head. "Because of Saturday evening, he switched me with someone else on Sunday. I lost the brunch hours and worked Sunday late afternoon through dinner. We closed earlier on Sundays."

Notchey hung his head in confusion and frustration. "Okay, let me get this straight. It wasn't until after Labor Day when you started working Saturday evenings?"

"That's right. I lost some good tips, but I got to take the class I wanted." Madison's mouth took a nose dive. "Seems now it was for nothing. Might lose the job and the class—guess it will depend on how much time I spend hanging out here."

"Did you call your boss? Maybe you won't lose your job."

"I called him this morning." Madison's shoulders sagged. "He said he could give me the week, but after that he'd have to find a replacement. He said he'd call Evie to see if she would work a few shifts just until I get back." She looked up at Notchey. "Evie's the waitress who used to work just Friday and Saturday nights."

Mike didn't comment but continued with his line of questioning. "It's early October, so you'd only worked a couple of Saturday nights before you were grabbed by Piper."

Madison crossed her arms and considered the timing. "So what does that mean?"

"It could mean Piper wasn't stalking you for very long, or it could mean nothing." Notchey moved over to the table and placed both of his hands flat on it while he faced Madison. "Think hard, Madison. Do you recall Bobby Piper being in the restaurant any specific day or time? And do you recall seeing him before you switched to Saturday and Sunday evenings?"

Avoiding the scrape on her forehead, Madison combed a hand through her long hair while she dug deep into her recent memory. "Come to think of it, I don't recall seeing him except for those nights. He was kind of scruffy—and not in a hip way. He would have stood out in the film crowd. And we knew our weekday regulars pretty well—who they were and what they ate. Kissing Hollywood asses meant bigger tips."

As soon as she said the words, Madison looked around for Pauline, then relaxed when she remembered that the formidable housekeeper had left two hours earlier.

Notchey pressed, "And you're sure he wasn't part of that crowd?"

"Pretty positive. And he certainly wasn't part of the usual Sunday brunch clientele." She looked down at the photos on the table. There were about a dozen candid photos of people of various ages. Two were of women. All the people in the pictures wore looks of intensity and brooding like they were mad at the world, and they probably were. Several were dressed in the goth style.

"Who are these people?" she asked.

Mike picked up his jacket and pulled out a pack of cigarettes. He clutched it in his hands and started to answer, then motioned for her to follow him out the back door.

Once they were on the patio, Mike pulled a lighter from his pants pocket and lit up. Leaning against a support post, he took a deep drag of the cigarette and looked out at the trees beyond the property line. Madison sat on a chair in the sun, soaking in the warmth from the rays, and waited.

"I don't know how much Pauline Speakes told you about the Dedhams," he began, "or about the local vampire community."

After taking another deep drag, he stubbed out the cigarette on the bottom of his shoe. Making sure it was out, he put it back into the pack and put the pack into his pocket. He glanced up and saw Madison watching him with interest.

"I used to be a two-pack-a-day guy," he explained. "Now I'm down to ten puffs a day. Guess that's progress. Feels like shit, though." He leaned against the post. "Sorry I didn't offer you one, but the Dedhams hate cigarette smoke. So if you do smoke, might as well get used to not having it while you're here. Although Doug does enjoy a good cigar once in a while, but only outside."

"No problem," she told him. "Never been a smoker. Don't drink either."

"No booze, no butts. Probably don't do drugs."

She shook her head. "Seen the damage those things can do to people." Madison recalled some bad memories, then just as quickly shook them off. "And to the people around them. Especially booze and drugs."

Mike eyed her. "Guess your only vice is rolling drunks."

Madison puffed with indignation. "That tune's getting old, Notchey. I told you that was another time, another place." She hugged her arms protectively around herself.

"You cold?" Mike asked. "You want to go back inside?"

She shook her head. "It's a little cool, but I'm okay. I like it out here. Topanga, I mean. Sometimes I come out here to hike. Never thought for a minute I might die here." She let loose a low, tinny laugh. "Certainly never thought vampires lived here—or anywhere else, for that matter. Not for real."

She went quiet, and Mike gave her some space. Shortly, she turned to him. "Pauline didn't say anything about vampires in general. She mostly gave me a list of do's and don'ts about living here. Told me some of the things the Dedhams like to do—about how nice they are. She seems very loyal to them. If they weren't vampires, they'd be too perfect."

"Wouldn't surprise me," Mike said, still watching Madison, "if Pauline was willing to take a bullet for them."

"Would that be a silver bullet?"

A small smile crossed the detective's face. He turned away as if embarrassed by it.

"And how about you?" Madison asked. "Would *you* take a bullet for them? Or have you already?"

Mike Notchey jerked his head in Madison's direction but didn't say anything.

"Pauline told me that Dodie nursed you back to health after you'd been shot."

He nodded and stared into her eyes as he spoke, his emotions raw and just below the surface. "Happened a couple of years ago. But the bullet was meant for me, not them. And it wasn't silver, it was a cop killer."

"I'm sorry." Madison looked away, giving them each another gap of privacy before speaking again. "Pauline didn't tell me anything about any vampire community. But the Dedhams told me last night that if I talked to anyone about them or what I learned about other vampires, I'd be killed."

When Mike didn't respond, she turned to him, brown eyes blazing with both fear and anger. "That true?"

"Yes," he answered, looking straight back at her, leaving no doubt as to the accuracy of his response.

Madison stood up and stalked over to Notchey. She faced him, their bodies just inches apart. "You said I'd be safe here." Her voice was low but accusing. "You said they wouldn't hurt me." Jaw set, mouth tight, she glared at him, the heat from her eyes demanding an explanation. Her black eye looked particularly menacing.

"They won't, but beyond the two of them it's complicated. Just keep your mouth shut and you'll be fine," he told her. "And when you do meet other vampires, stay close to Doug and Dodie. They're well respected."

Madison wasn't buying it. "I don't need to know about any more vampires. I'll just stay here until I can go home."

"That's not possible either," Mike told her. "With what's going on, there's no way for you to avoid meeting more of them."

"But—," Madison began, pointing her left index finger close to his face.

Mike interrupted her by grabbing her hand and roughly turning it over, palm up.

"Ow," Madison let out in surprise. She tried to pull her hand away, but Mike held onto it with an iron grip. He stared at her palm. With his other hand, he traced her lifeline—the line that curved across her palm, separating the thumb from the rest of the hand like a peninsula. He twisted her hand back and forth to get a better look in the sunlight. Finally, he let go.

Madison pulled her freed hand close to her chest and rubbed it. Taking a couple steps back from Mike, she grew quiet. "That's really weird."

"What? Taking your hand?" He shrugged. "Thought I saw something, a cut or bruise. Sorry." He looked down at the ground. "We should go inside." He started for the back door.

"No, what's weird is that I had a dream last night about that. Someone was checking out my left palm, tracing it like you did, but they were much nicer about it."

Mike Notchey stopped in his tracks and turned back to her. "Might have been Dodie," he suggested while keeping an eagle eye on Madison's bruised face. "She might have been making sure you were all right."

She shook her head. "No. It was a man. A black man, I think, or someone very dark." Madison's voice lost its hard edge.

Mike held his breath.

"He stroked my palm and was very gentle," Madison continued. "It was actually quite awesome." Her voice held a tone of wonder, like a small child on Christmas morning. "Yet terrifying at the same time." She shivered, as if shaking off a spell. "Isn't that weird?"

"Just an odd dream," Mike told her. "Not surprising, with what you've been through." He jerked his head toward the door. "Let's take another look at those photos."

There was a deeper urgency in his voice that Madison, still on the edge of her dream, didn't notice. She shook herself again to bring her thoughts to the present and faced Notchey with the will of a stubborn child.

"I'm tired of looking at those old photos," she told him. "I told you everything I know. I want to go home as soon as possible. I may not have a posh life, but it's mine. Those people mean nothing to me."

With the speed of a striking snake, Mike Notchey grabbed Madison's hand again, but this time he didn't look at it or stroke it. He headed for the back door, pulling her behind him like a reluctant canine at the end of a leash. She growled in protest, but he ignored her. Once inside, he dumped her back in her seat at the table.

"Look again, Madison," he ordered. "This is very important. A matter of life or death for some folks, maybe even for another girl."

When Madison didn't answer, Mike picked up a large brown envelope that he'd brought with him. It had held the photos that were now scattered on the table. Without a word, he reached inside and took out more photos. One by one, he slapped three photos of young women on the table in front of her. They were enlarged snapshots showing the women, two brunettes and a redhead, smiling for the camera. All were lovely and around Madison's age.

"Recognize these women?"

Madison casually looked over the photos and shook her head in a slow, bored manner.

Mike reached inside the envelope again and pulled out more photos. He slapped them on the table in the same manner. "Maybe you'll recognize them now."

Madison's eyes widened in horror and her mouth went dry as dust. In front of her were a half-dozen photos of dead women. In half the photos, the women's necks had been slit in a wide, curved gash, like a second mouth laughing into the camera while the face above it stared in horror. The other photos showed their torsos, each with deep, short cuts covering the naked white skin. In spite of the cuts and slashing, there was little blood.

Madison fought to keep her breakfast down. She turned away from the photos, a hand over her mouth. Mike came behind her and grabbed her head, forcing her to look at them. She closed her eyes, but it was too late. The vision of the carnage had already been burned into her brain. Pushing Mike aside with all the strength she could muster, she ran to the sink and retched several times. Finished, she clung to the counter, afraid she would collapse if she let go. Tears ran down her hot face, soaking the bandage on the one side and stinging her cuts. Strands of damp hair clung to her cheeks and forehead. She didn't turn around but looked out the window, focusing on the playful ripples a gentle wind was making across the pool.

"What do you want from me," she finally squeaked out in a nearly inaudible voice.

"Cooperation, Madison. Any one of these three women could have been you. Doug said Bobby Piper was hovering over your neck when he saw you. That's why Doug attacked him. He thought you were going to wind up like this."

For a few minutes, Madison and Mike were silent. The detective waited. Madison tried to digest, then erase, the horrible photos. She ran water in the sink to clean up her vomit. Stripping off the bulky bandage, she splashed some of the water on her face. After taking a deep breath, she turned to face Mike, willing herself not to look down at the photos of the dead women.

"I'll cooperate," she told him in a small, compliant voice. "But take those pictures away."

He studied her injuries a long moment in silence, then gathered up the photos of the women and stuffed them back into the envelope. Madison returned to her seat, weak and broken, and waited for the next level of hell.

"These people, Madison," Mike said, pointing again to the people in the photos spread on the table, "are all involved in local vampire cults. They're not vampires, but they believe in them, worship them, even want to *be* them."

Madison once again examined the photos. She swallowed and said, "I can tell you right now, most of these folks have never been in Auntie Em's—at least not looking like that or when I've been around. We don't get goth types in the diner."

Mike vibrated with frustration. "Why didn't you say that earlier?"

Ignoring him, Madison pulled out the only three photos of people not dressed in the goth style—two men and a woman. "These people don't look like they're into vampires. They look normal."

"See, that's the thing, Madison," Mike explained, his voice straining in its attempt to be civil. "Not all goth types are into vampires. And you don't have to be part of the goth culture to be involved in vampirism. With the near-hysterical interest in vampires now—with all the movies, books, and TV shows—those who worship the undead easily go unnoticed. There are nightclubs, social groups, even religious orders now centered around vampires. Some of it is very well organized."

Mike took a seat at the table, trying on patience as if it were a too-small shirt. "Practicing vampirism, in our day, can involve anything from mind control to absorbing other people's energy to the drinking of human blood. It has nothing to do with real vampires like Doug and Dodie, who are actually immortal. And very few real vampires want anything to do with these wannabes."

Madison was horrified all over again. "People like you and me drink human blood? Isn't that dangerous, with diseases like AIDS and HIV and hepatitis?"

"Extremely dangerous, Madison."

"But what about Doug and Dodie? Aren't they worried about disease?"

"They're immortal," he repeated. "Blood-borne diseases won't harm them." Mike offered a small smile at Madison's concern for the Dedhams. "The people in these photos are all leaders of various vampire cults here in Southern California. We think it's someone from one of these cults who is kidnapping and killing these women." He tapped the envelope, now resting on the table, for emphasis. Madison leaned back as if the photos might reach out and touch her, leaving behind prints of blood.

"Someone," Mike continued, "who probably practices mind control over his or her followers. As I told you last night, we're pretty sure Piper and the creep in custody didn't do this on their own. They weren't smart enough. Someone else is calling the shots, and it might be one of these characters." He indicated the photos spread between them.

A mind-numbing chill went through Madison as she looked down at the photographs again. Suddenly, being in the house of real vampires didn't seem that scary.

EIGHT

Madison watched Dodie sip a beverage from a tall, colorful mug. Something didn't seem right. Madison took a drink from her own mug. It was a heavenly mix of coffee, chocolate, and spices.

"I thought you guys couldn't eat regular food," Madison observed.

Dodie delicately touched a burgandy-colored napkin to her lips. "We can't. This isn't the same thing you're having."

The girly stuff Dodie had planned for the two of them had been a visit to a salon that was open very late. Dodie had her hair cut and colored, along with a manicure and pedicure. She'd treated Madison to the same, minus the color. At first Madison demurred, but she finally caved. She'd been cutting her own hair with kitchen shears and couldn't remember the last time she'd had her nails professionally done. She'd nearly cooed herself into a pampered puddle during the pedicure and almost, but not quite, forgotten about the horrific photos Mike Notchey had shown her. Whenever the visions of those mangled bodies reared their ugly and evil heads in Madison's mind, she worked hard to push them aside. If not, she feared she would go mad. After, Dodie had taken her to a restaurant a few doors down from the salon. The restaurant didn't have a sign, nor was it accessible from the street. They'd entered through a bright red door that faced an alley.

A part of Madison didn't want to know what was in Dodie's mug, but another part of her had to know. "Is it … you know?" she asked.

"Human," Dodie completed. "Yes, it is. While all the blood at the house is animal, human blood is best for us."

When Dodie saw Madison's face turn the color of campfire ash, she quickly added, "Don't worry, no one died so I could drink this. In fact, it's rare that anyone would die from a vampire drinking their blood. It's not like we need to drain a body dry to be satiated." She added a small chuckle, accompanied by a small shake of her head. "The movies have really done us a great disservice over the years." Her face took on a serious flicker. "I'm not saying a vampire has never torn a human asunder in bloodlust, but that was more in days gone by, not the present. Today, most of us live quite peacefully among the living, totally undetected."

Torn asunder. The words vibrated in Madison's head like a tuning fork. The women in the photos had been torn asunder in bloodlust, and Mike Notchey was sure it had not been done by a vampire. Madison watched as the seemingly sweet and warm Dodie Dedham raised the mug to her lips and sipped, looking like a grandmother enjoying a spot of tea after shopping. But the mug held in Dodie's elderly hands did not contain tea. It held human blood—the same blood that coursed through Madison's own veins.

Dodie looked at Madison, her wise eyes reading conflict in the girl's facial expressions and demeanor. Catching Madison's attention, she indicated the restaurant in which they sat. It was a large room with a small bar at the far end and two dozen tablecloth-covered tables with chairs, half of which were occupied. The décor was modern and sleek. It had no windows but was well lit. One wall was painted black and covered with interesting and bright paintings. The other walls were painted a pale silvery gray and also held artwork.

"This place is called Scarlet," Dodie told Madison, "after its owner. It's a vampire restaurant. A living person can only come in here accompanied by a vampire. It's a place where the two can come together socially for a meal, each of their own kind. It has a limited food menu, but I'm told the food is quite good. Are you hungry?"

Madison shook her head and mumbled, "No, thanks." She'd nibbled on the pot roast earlier. It was delicious, but she hadn't had much of an appetite, eating what she did only because she knew she needed to eat something.

"Don't worry," Dodie said, seeing Madison stare into her coffee mug with concern. "The kitchen where the food is made is separate from where the blood items are prepared." She laughed lightly. "Think of it as a kosher kitchen, where the meat dishes and the dairy dishes are never allowed to mingle."

Madison looked around the restaurant, thinking maybe some small talk would get her mind off of the photos. "So," she began, swallowing hard before continuing, "are the waiters here also vampires?"

"Yes, though the chef for the food is not. Since vampires don't eat, how could a vampire chef tell if something tasted good or not? Although most of us do enjoy the aroma of a well-cooked meal."

"Pauline told me that's why you enjoy cooking—for the smell."

"Yes, and I like seeing people enjoy what I make. Did you enjoy the pot roast?"

"I wasn't too hungry, but I had some. It was very good, but I thought Pauline fixed that."

"I put it on before I went to bed. It's one of my specialties, like the chicken soup is one of Pauline's. It was also a favorite of my first husband."

In spite of her continued wariness, Madison found her tension begin to melt and the memory of the photos retreat from the forefront of her thoughts. Dodie's company was as pleasant and soothing as the coffee and chocolate beverage in the mug she held. For the first time since she was a young girl, Madison felt a little spoiled and pampered, even cared about. She also warned herself not to get too used to it. As soon as this thing with the murders was over, she'd be back to her own life in a lonely, dingy apartment, slinging burgers and juggling classes. There would be no indulgences, but there also wouldn't be photos of bodies or blood in the fridge.

"You were married before?" Madison asked with surprise. "To a beater?"

Dodie laughed. "I was a beater then, too." Taking on a faraway look, she traveled through her memories. "I was a widow living in Arizona when I met Doug Dedham. My husband had died six years earlier. Our only son had died years before in the military. I was waiting to die myself. Doug didn't tell me right off about being a vampire. Probably a good thing he didn't, but he gave me back my enjoyment of life. We fell in love. I became a vampire to spend eternity with him. After losing my first husband, there was something very appealing in knowing I couldn't lose my second."

"So you can never die?" Madison was sitting at attention, wondering what it would feel like to know that life could go on forever. Would it be a curse or a blessing? She decided it would depend on the life you had to lead for eternity.

"Vampires can die, Madison. We can be killed by a couple of methods."

"Like being in the sun?"

"Another myth spread by movies and literature." Dodie shook her head in amusement. "We can be out in the sun without exploding or turning to ash, but we prefer not to be, because we're very sensitive to it. It tends to sap our energy and powers, and it makes us feel under the weather. It's almost like it gives us the flu." Dodie paused to think about the subject further. "Perhaps if we were exposed to it continuously over a very long period of time, it could kill us, but I've never heard of that." She looked at Madison and winked. "But I do know you won't find many vampires traveling to places where there's extended daylight, like Greenland."

Dodie took a drink from her mug. "We're also not sensitive to crosses, garlic, holy water, or silver. Those are concepts created by the early Christian church to give people comfort and a sense of protection. And except for what the sun does to us, we don't get sick." Dodie screwed up her face in pretend confusion. "The funny thing is, even though we're technically dead, our hair and nails still grow. Not sure why, but they do. But I'm glad, because I love going to the salon."

Madison ran a hand through her newly shaped hair and loved its silky feel. Dodie had also purchased some makeup, and the stylist had shown Madison how to apply it to cover the black eye and other bruises. When they were done, Madison didn't look half bad. "Was that a vampire salon we went to?"

"It's owned by a vampire. By day it's a regular salon. Several nights a week they stay open to serve us. It's also a popular tanning salon. Many of us get spray tans so we don't look so pale. Others use makeup when they go out in public, but Doug and I prefer the spray tan. It covers everything and lasts longer."

Madison closed her eyes tight and shook herself. "I feel as though I've fallen into a Tim Burton movie. One minute I'm freaking out, the next minute I'm fascinated."

Leaning forward, Dodie patted Madison's hand. "Ask any questions you'd like, dear. Just be discreet about where you do it. Here or at home is fine."

The two women sat quietly. Madison tried not to stare at the other patrons but couldn't help herself. She wondered which were vampires. No one looked particularly dead to her, though it was easy to spot the living. They were the few using knives and forks.

After a minute, Madison turned her attention back to Dodie and wasn't surprised to find the older woman watching her much like she had been watching the vampires.

"That was nice of you to get some of my stuff for me," Madison said. She paused, then added a quick and quiet thanks.

"And thank you, Madison, for not leaving when Pauline gave you your car keys. We really do need you to help us solve these murders before our way of life is threatened. Not to mention averting the panic that would occur if the people of Los Angeles found out about us."

Dodie hesitated, choosing her next words and tone carefully, understanding that Madison was skittish and uncomfortable in personal situations. "Madison, is that your mother in the photo?"

In answer, Madison buried her nose into her mug and nodded.

"Where is she? Do you mind telling me?"

Madison put down her mug and stared at one of the paintings. It was an abstract blend of yellows, reds, and oranges, with the occasional surprise of blue—sharp angles that came together in smooth and pleasing harmony.

"She's dead," Madison told Dodie in a voice devoid of emotion. When Dodie didn't comment, Madison continued. "She died when I was five. I was raised by my father's aunt, Eleanor, until she died a few years later. After that, I made the rounds of foster homes until I turned eighteen." Madison's voice began to break. She swallowed the lump in her throat and corralled her emotions. "You know that ratty old stuffed animal? The one you brought over from my place?"

Dodie nodded. She had sensed the battered toy meant something significant to Madison.

"My mother gave that to me right before she died. It's all I have left of her—that and the photo."

"How did she die, Madison? Was she sick?"

"No, she wasn't." The words came out of the girl spiced with bile. Seeing that Madison looked about to break into tears, Dodie didn't prod. After another few moments, Madison said, "My mother was killed in a robbery."

"I'm so very sorry, Madison."

Madison, considering she'd gone this far, decided she might as well complete the story she hadn't told anyone—ever. "My mother and father and I were coming home from something, not even sure now what, when my father decided to stop at a convenience store. Mom was driving. My father went into the store. Then there was the sound of shots. My father ran out of the store and yelled at my mother to get going. She screamed at my dad. I remember her asking him over and over about what he'd done. He kept screaming for her to drive. A man came out of the store and fired a gun at the car. My mother was killed."

Dodie's lips were pressed tight, holding back tears that in reality she couldn't shed. "And your father?"

Madison shrugged. "He's in jail—or was. He shot one of the store clerks, paralyzing him. Even before then, I don't remember him around much. And when he was around, he was mean to us, especially to my mother."

Madison filled her lungs with air, held it, then expelled it, as if doing that would rid her of the horrible memory. When that didn't work, she shoved the pain back into the shadows to sit next to the photos of the dead women. "Aunt Eleanor left me a little money. Not much, but I couldn't get it until I turned twenty-one. As soon as I did, I left Boise and headed here to start over."

In a sharp motion, Madison pushed away from the table. "Where's the ladies' room? Or don't they have one?"

"It's over there, dear." Dodie pointed to a door just to the left of the bar. "It's for their live customers."

NINE

When Madison headed back to their table, she saw that Dodie wasn't alone. Seated with her was another woman. She appeared to be in her late thirties, with straight brown hair pulled back into a ponytail and bangs worn just past her eyebrows. Her body was compact and athletic.

"So this is the girl," the woman announced rather than asked as Madison reached the table.

"Madison," Dodie said with a smile. "I want you to meet a good friend of ours. This is Stacie Neroni. She's an attorney who does a lot of work for the community."

Stacie held out her hand to Madison, who took it with a slight hesitation. They shook, and Madison noticed that Stacie's hand was ice cold.

"You're a—," Madison started to say as she took her seat.

"Yeah, yeah, yeah," Stacie said, cutting her off with a wave of her hand. "I'm a vampire attorney. I know, go ahead and say it—it's redundant." Her words came at Madison fast and aggressive, like the beat of a hard metal rock song but without the harshness.

"I've heard it all before," Stacie continued with a smirk. "'Blood-sucking should come easy to me. It's a natural career step. I want to bite your wallet.' In the forty-two years since I was turned, I've heard it all."

"Turned?" Madison ventured.

"Turned," Dodie answered her, "means when Stacie became a vampire. It's the term we use to denote the event of going from living to undead."

Stacie studied Madison, making a frank and speedy assessment. "Bet you're learning a lot in a short time. Bet it's more than you want to learn, too."

Madison looked directly into Stacie's brown eyes. Attorney or not, vampire or not, Madison's gut was telling her to like and trust the woman. She could see that Dodie did. "When it's TMI, I'll let you know."

"TMI?" asked Dodie.

"Too much information," Madison and Stacie answered in quick unison.

The attorney smiled at Madison. "I think I'm going to like you, Madison Rose." Before Madison could answer, Stacie shifted her brain into a higher gear. "So tell me what happened Saturday night. What do you remember? Did you see anyone besides the creep who grabbed you?"

"I've already told Detective Notchey everything," Madison answered.

"So now tell me," Stacie pressed. "Everything."

Madison looked over at Dodie. The older woman smiled and gave her an assuring nod.

"Like I told Notchey, I came out of the diner where I work. I was alone and it was late, after one in the morning. We stay open late on Saturday nights to feed the club crowd. It was very dark in the parking lot." Madison scrunched her eyes in thought. "Now that I think of it, it was darker than usual, like the light back there was burned out or something."

"See," Stacie said, "sometimes new details crop up in the retelling. Things you might have forgotten before."

Before continuing, Madison took a drink from her coffee, which was now cool. "I was about to get into my car when I felt someone come up from behind and hit me hard. It happened fast, too fast for me to react. I must have blacked out, because when I came to, I was tied and gagged and in the trunk of a car. Turned out to be my own car." Madison focused on the tabletop to keep her concentration. "When the car stopped, he dragged me out of the trunk and into a small clearing. He smacked me around a bit, then threw me to the ground. Then ... nothing."

"Nothing?" Stacie asked. She frowned, causing her bangs to fall farther over her eyebrows.

"Nothing," Madison repeated. "After dumping me on the ground, he grabbed a beer and sat down against a tree, like he was waiting for someone. When I started to struggle, he moved over to me. That's when ... that's when ..." Madison looked over at Dodie.

"That's when," Dodie finished for her, "Doug and I arrived. We were taking a moonlight stroll through the woods when we saw that Bobby person crouched over her and thought he was going to kill her."

Stacie aimed her frown at Dodie. "Too bad you two didn't take this guy alive. We could have gotten some answers out of him."

Dodie straightened her shoulders. "I'm afraid Douglas got a little carried away," she said in defense of her husband. "But his heart was in the right place. Our only thought at the time was to save the girl, not to capture her assailant."

"Then I hope the creep was at least tasty." Stacie delivered the line in a well-timed one-two sarcastic punch.

"I can assure you, Stacie," Dodie told her, her lips pursed in displeasure at being chastised, "Samuel gave us a thorough and well-deserved tongue lashing last night."

Turning back to Madison, Stacie prodded further. "You saw no one else?"

"No one, except for Doug and Dodie. But Bobby did seem to be nervous, and whoever it was he was waiting for seemed to be late."

"You knew this Bobby guy?" Stacie asked as if grilling a witness in court.

"Not really," Madison answered. "Like I told Notchey, he'd come into the diner a few times. Tried to chat me up in the last few weeks, but he didn't appear nuts or anything."

A waitress brought Madison another coffee drink. When she started to protest, Dodie said, "Don't worry, I asked them to make it with decaf. Can't have you up all night like us."

Madison gave Dodie a small smile and wrapped her hands around the warm mug. The restaurant was chilly, but no one seemed to notice but her. She looked from Dodie to Stacie and continued her story. "Today Mike Notchey brought some photos by for me to look at. He said they were people who had vampire clubs or cults here in LA. Asked me if I'd ever seen any of them before."

Stacie sat erect with interest. "And had you?"

Madison shook her head. "Nope, not unless they looked different from the photos when I did. Several were in goth makeup in the pictures."

Madison paused to take a drink. She started to say something else, then took another drink. Finally, she took a deep breath and continued. "He also showed me other photos ... photos taken of the dead women." When she started to say something else, a choked sob came out of her mouth, but her eyes remained dry. Slapping her right hand over her mouth, she squelched further sobs and fought to control her emotions.

Without warning and without regard to Madison's distress, Stacie grabbed at Madison's left hand, which was nearest to her. Madison instinctively pulled it back.

"Let me see your hand, Madison," Stacie insisted.

After a slight hesitation, Madison let Stacie take her left hand. The attorney examined it closely.

"What's with all the hand grabbing?" Madison asked after taking several deep, cleansing breaths. "Notchey did the same thing today. And last night I had a dream about a guy checking out my hand."

Dodie looked at Madison with concern but leaned toward Stacie, who was still scrutinizing Madison's left palm. "We told you, Stacie, she doesn't have the bloodline."

Madison snatched her hand back from Stacie. "What in the hell is a bloodline?"

"TMI?" Dodie asked Stacie.

"No," Madison said before Stacie could reply. "In this case, it's not *enough* information. So what's with my hand?"

Instead of answering, Stacie pumped Madison for more answers. "You dreamed about someone looking at your hand?

What did the guy look like? Maybe you did see someone and it's buried in your subconscious."

"He was a black man," Madison answered. She dug back into the part of her brain that stored dreams. "And bald, I think. But he didn't grab my hand rudely, like you and Notchey. He held it gently, like a boyfriend, and traced the lines on my palm." She took a drink of coffee. "Oddest thing," she continued. "Even though it was night, he was wearing sunglasses."

Stacie swung her head in Dodie's direction, the end of her long ponytail nearly hitting Madison. "That true?" she demanded.

Dodie nodded. "Yes. He came by last night to see her and to discuss what's happening."

"Okay, guys," Madison said, holding up both of her hands in protest. "Just hold on a minute." She turned to Dodie. "Are you telling me that I didn't dream that guy holding my hand?"

Dodie squirmed a bit. "Technically, dear, you did dream it. You were asleep when it happened. But, yes, someone came by last night, and he checked your hand. And he looks exactly as you described him."

"Whoa!" Madison pushed back from the table. A few people nearby turned to look at them, but one steely look from Stacie Neroni sent them back to their own business.

Madison shook her head to clear it. "Just when I'm thinking I can go along with this whole vampire thing, something even creepier happens." When neither woman said anything, Madison asked again, "So what's with my left hand?"

When Dodie started to answer, Stacie stopped her. "I'll handle this."

Stacie turned her attention to Madison and held out her hand. "Give me your left hand again."

Madison hesitated, then scooted back to the table and put her left hand into Stacie's cold right one.

"First," Stacie began, "you have to understand that vampires aren't created randomly. You don't become one simply by being bitten by a vampire or by drinking a vampire's blood. If that were true, there would be a lot more of us running around. Certain people are predisposed to becoming vampires. Only they can become vampires and only if a certain action occurs between them and another vampire. People not predisposed will never become vampires, no matter what happens."

Stacie looked at Madison to see if she was following. Assured she had the girl's full attention and understanding, Stacie continued. "There is only one way to tell if a person is predisposed toward immortality—a mark, so to speak."

"And that mark is on a person's left palm?" Madison asked.

"Yes."

Madison looked down in horror at her left palm resting in Stacie's hand. "And am I marked?"

"No, that's the thing," Stacie explained. "We were able to view the bodies of all the other victims, or at least the ones we know of, and they were." Stacie traced several of Madison's lines with a fingertip. Madison wiggled her fingers when it tickled.

"You see," Stacie said, showing Madison, "people who are marked for becoming vampires have an extra lifeline. It doesn't always show up in the same place on the palm like the usual lifeline, but it's there. Usually, it's a dark brownish red, like brick red, but not always. And it's not always obvious, but it is noticeable to someone who knows what they're looking for. We call it a bloodline."

Madison pulled her hand away and studied it before looking up again at Dodie and Stacie. "So you two have this bloodline on your hands?"

"Not anymore," Dodie answered.

"Once someone becomes a vampire," Stacie continued, "the bloodline disappears. It's only noticeable on people who have the potential of becoming vampires." She shrugged. "Who knows, maybe it was put there so we could identify those who could become vampires, then it disappears so others can't identify us after we've turned."

"And my *not* having this bloodline is big news to you guys?"

"It was unexpected," Stacie told her. "Like I said, so far, all the victims seem to have been vampires-in-waiting."

Madison gave it some heavy thought. "You think someone is trying to kill off these marked people before they become vampires, so more vampires can't be … well, born?"

"Originally," Stacie answered with a shrug, "we thought it might be something like that. But so far, it has only been women who have been killed—again, that we know of. And now, with you not fitting the profile, maybe that's *not* what's happening here."

Dodie sighed. "Then again, maybe what happened to Madison had nothing to do with those other poor women. Maybe Bobby Piper took her for another reason, totally unrelated."

"Hmmm, that's what I'm beginning to wonder." Stacie looked at Madison. "Could be, Madison, you got mixed up with us in error."

"Lucky me." Madison drowned the rest of her sarcasm by taking a big gulp from her mug.

"And if we're thinking that…," Dodie said, catching Stacie's eye.

"So is Samuel," Stacie finished. "Shit!"

Something jolted Madison's internal awareness. "Samuel? Is that who looked at my hand last night?"

The two vampires exchanged concerned looks, but it was Dodie who answered. "Yes, dear, Samuel was the man you saw in your dream."

"How did you know that?" Stacie asked, her eyes boring into Madison's face, looking for unspoken answers.

"I…I don't know, exactly," Madison answered truthfully. "But as soon as you said his name, I felt something moving around deep inside me, like a mouse looking for a way out."

Again, the two vampires looked at each other. Their unspoken dialog was making Madison even more nervous. "What?" she asked them, her voice raising a notch in frustration and fear.

Dodie turned her attention back to Madison. "Samuel La Croix is the chairman of the California Vampire Council. The council governs the vampire community in the state much as a homeowners' association would govern a neighborhood or condo development."

"So he's the big cheese here in vampire world?" Madison knitted her brows, absorbing the information.

"The biggest of cheeses," answered Dodie. "Before he came and set up the council, it was like the Wild West. Many vampires were out of control; it was total anarchy. Samuel came in, brought order—often through very violent means—then set up the council to keep things running smoothly. Doug and Stacie both sit on the council board."

"One of the ways Samuel keeps everything running well," Stacie added, "is by keeping outsiders from learning about us." She gave Madison another intense study. "He's not going to like it that you know so much without a good reason for it."

Madison's hands started to tremble as her earlier fears rose up and took on renewed life. "So is this where you decide to kill me?"

"Now, now," said Dodie, trying to comfort Madison. "The council will not vote to kill you without a good reason. Not even Samuel will overrule his own council. He can be terrifying, but he's fair. Just don't give him or the council a reason to doubt your loyalty."

"Loyalty?" Madison asked, incredulous. "To a group of dead people I didn't even think existed a few days ago?"

She started to take a drink of coffee to steady herself but stopped and put the mug back down on the table with a decided thud. "Look, I'm not going to tell anyone anything about vampires. No one would believe me if I tried. But that's also not my style." She glared at Dodie, summoning the courage to break through the thickness of her fear. "While I appreciate you saving my life, you and Doug put me into this situation. Now I expect you to do your best to make sure I come out of it in one piece."

Dodie shook her head. "It's not that simple, Madison."

TEN

"Wake up, Madison." A hand gently shook Madison, rousing her from her slumber.

It had been a long night. After returning home from their girls' night out, Madison had been agitated and unable to sleep, partially from the coffee but mostly from everything she was learning about the vampires. Dodie again offered some medicinal help, but this time Madison rejected it. For hours she'd turned over all the information that had been thrown at her in the last couple of days until her brain finally gave in and turned off for the night.

"Come on," the voice told her. "You need to get up." The bed-side lamp snapped on as the hand shook her again.

Shielding her eyes from the light, Madison slowly opened one eye. Standing over her was Dodie. "What's going on?"

"I need you to get up right now."

Madison glanced at the clock. It was 4:20; she'd only been asleep for three hours. She turned over. "Just give me another hour."

"We don't have an hour."

Dodie threw back the covers, letting the chilly air hit the girl's body. Madison shivered and started moving to get out of bed. Now that she had some of her own clothes, she'd returned to wearing oversized tee shirts to bed.

"You need to come downstairs right this minute," Dodie insisted.

"Can't I pee first?"

Dodie hesitated, weighing the request. "Yes, but hurry. Use the bathroom, then slip into some jeans."

It was then that Madison heard voices coming from downstairs. Again, she glanced at the bedside clock, letting the time register in her exhausted brain. "Shouldn't you be getting ready to go to bed and not entertaining?"

"Hurry!" Dodie hissed. "The council is downstairs waiting for you."

The news hit Madison like a cold shower. She backed away from Dodie and looked around for something to use as a weapon. "You are going to kill me, aren't you?"

"This isn't about you, Madison." From the back of the desk chair, Dodie plucked the jeans Madison had worn just a few hours earlier and shook them out. "It's an emergency meeting. Mike Notchey's downstairs, too." She looked up at Madison. "Another girl's been found dead."

The memory of the horrible photos exploded in Madison's head. "But—," Madison started to say.

Dodie cut her off. "Madison, please. Samuel does not like to be kept waiting. And he gets more surly as the sun comes up."

Letting the urgency in Dodie's voice guide her, Madison buttoned her lip and dashed into the bathroom. A minute later, she came out, face washed, teeth and hair hastily brushed, and pulled on the jeans Dodie handed her.

"What about this?" Madison asked, indicating the tee shirt she'd worn to bed.

"It's fine," Dodie said, then hesitated. Taking in the seductive way the shirt outlined Madison's bare breasts, she remembered how Samuel had looked at the girl. "On second thought, you'd better put on a bra."

As Madison pulled off the tee shirt and slipped into a bra, Dodie went to the closet and sifted through the few items she'd brought over from Madison's apartment. Settling on a loose and shapeless sweater in a dull brown, she brought it to Madison. "Here, put this on, and pull your hair back into a ponytail. And don't cover your bruises."

Even though her head was full of questions, Madison quickly did as she was told, ending with slipping her feet into a pair of basic sneakers.

"Come on now," Dodie called over her shoulder as she headed for the door.

As she followed Dodie down the staircase, Madison could hear the voices better. They were coming from the great room, the spacious living area that served as a living room and dining room located to the right of the stairs. Several people were talking at once. As she got closer, Madison realized an argument was in progress. She recognized Stacie Neroni's voice immediately, as well as Mike Notchey's, but she couldn't tell if they were arguing with each other or in favor of the same issue.

At the bottom of the stairs, Madison could see a group of people gathered around the Dedhams' large dining table. When Dodie led her to the table, everyone stopped talking and turned to stare at her. Madison shifted from one foot to the other in discomfort.

In all, there were six people at the table. On one side sat Stacie Neroni and a middle-aged woman with short blond hair and a friendly, open face. Across from them sat Doug and a very good-looking man dressed in black, with thick, black hair combed back and curling at his collar. He had an angular face partially covered by a close-cropped black beard. His nose was straight, his lips full. Black eyebrows bunched in displeasure above dark, intense eyes. Seated at the end closest to her was Mike Notchey. He was dressed in his off-duty uniform of jeans and sweatshirt, but the dark circles under his eyes and gauntness of his face suggested he hadn't been to bed all night. They all looked at her with furrowed brows of concern, except for the blond woman, who gave her a small smile of encouragement.

Madison gasped softly as her eyes traveled the length of the heavy wooden table to the far end. Seated at the head was the man Madison had seen in her dream. He wore a fine-knit sweater the color of fresh salmon, which played beautifully against his espresso skin, and sunglasses even though they were inside and it was only early morning.

A small, slow smile crossed his lips as he rose to greet her. "Miss Rose, we're very sorry we disturbed your sleep."

His voice was earthy and exotic, almost hypnotic. Hearing it, Madison fought the urge to ignore the others and go to him—to put her hand in his so she could once again feel the stroke of his fingers against her palm. But something inside her snapped her out of it. Instead, Madison crossed her arms in front of her, now glad Dodie had made her put on a bra and the bulky sweater.

Stretching out a long arm, the man at the end of the table indicated Stacie. "I believe you already know Stacie Neroni. Next to her is Kate Thornton."

The man next to Doug interrupted the introductions. "It is not necessary that she know our names, Samuel," he said in a voice with a cultured British accent.

Samuel turned his head toward the man who spoke. "Considering what we're going to ask of her, I think it's only courteous."

"I agree with Samuel," added Stacie, glaring at the man who'd interrupted.

"But of course you would," the man shot back at her in a snide tone. "You have your fangs so far up his arse, you can taste the O negative he had for breakfast."

Stacie stood up, fangs bared, and leaned across the table. "I'll show you fangs, you little pissant."

Terrified, Madison jumped back.

The man waved Stacie off like an annoying gnat. "Puritanical do-gooder."

Samuel rapped his knuckles on the table. "That's enough, you two. This is not the time and place for your petty mutual loathing." His voice was authoritative but not loud.

Stacie sheathed her fangs and sat down, but she remained ruffled and wary of her opponent, who seemed bored with the whole transaction.

After a moment's pause, Samuel continued his introductions. "The man, Miss Rose, who does not want you to know his name, is Colin Reddy." Colin glared at Madison, causing her to back up several more steps until she felt Dodie's hand on the small of her back, encouraging her to stand her ground.

"And, of course," Samuel continued, "you already know Doug and Mike."

Samuel placed his hand against his own chest. "And I am Samuel La Croix. With the exception of two members who were not able to be here this morning and Detective Notchey, this," he announced, with a small sweep of his hand, "is the governing board of the California Vampire Council." His smile widened. "Not a glamorous name, but I can assure you we get the job done when it comes to monitoring activities that concern the local vampire community, including internal grievances." He shot a stern look first at Colin, then at Stacie.

Mike Notchey indicated an empty chair next to him. "Sit down, Madison, here—next to me."

"Yes, please sit down, Madison," Samuel said, then paused. "I hope you don't mind me calling you Madison."

Madison looked back at Dodie, who encouraged her with a little nod to take a seat. As soon as she did, Samuel took his own again.

"Good," Samuel commented. He studied some papers before him. "We have a lot to discuss." He looked up at Madison. "I understand Mike told you about the rash of murders concerning young women?"

Unbidden, the photos Notchey had shown her came to mind. Madison shoved them aside and nodded. "Yes, I'm aware of them."

"We were beginning to think these had nothing to do with you," Samuel went on, "that maybe what happened to you was just a random occurrence, a coincidence. After all, you don't have a bloodline, and the other women did." He stopped and looked at her. His forehead furrowed in question, relaying the emotion his sunglasses kept hidden. "I've been told you know about bloodlines."

Madison looked down at her left palm. "Yes," she replied, looking back up. "I know what it means." She found it easier to speak to Samuel without seeing his eyes, as if she were speaking to his back instead of his face.

"Now we're not so sure," Samuel went on, "that it *doesn't* have something to do with you."

Colin, slouched in his chair, caught Madison's eye and sent her a grimace, purposefully showing his fangs. He licked his lips. Madison shivered and hugged herself again.

"Stop it, Colin," demanded Samuel. "Grow up or leave. We'll still have a quorum without you."

Like a bad child only temporarily chastised, Colin rolled his eyes and put his fangs away.

"There's been another murder," Mike told her.

"Another?" Madison felt herself grow cold at the idea of another young woman ravaged by a monster.

"This one," added Stacie, "makes us think that what happened to you is definitely connected."

"I … I don't understand," Madison stammered. "I don't have that thing on my hand."

With a small jerk of his chin, Samuel sent an order to Mike Notchey. Mike pulled out a large brown envelope like the one he'd brought over the day before and opened it.

Madison looked in horror at the envelope. "No! I won't look at those again." She started to get up, but Dodie came up behind her and put her hands on Madison's shoulders. With a light touch but surprising strength, she kept Madison in her chair.

"Madison," Dodie said in a gentle voice, "these aren't the same photos. Just as disturbing, but we need you to see them."

Madison shut her eyes tight. Next to her, she felt Mike moving.

"Madison," Mike asked. "Do you know this woman?" When Madison didn't answer, he added, "It is very important."

From across the table, Madison heard Samuel say, "Please, Madison, we need your help." His voice wasn't a plea as much as a command. "These women need your help."

Madison opened her eyes, but she didn't look down. Instead, she looked across the table at Samuel. He was sitting back in his chair looking straight at her, watching her from behind his glasses. His dark face was still as stone. His full lips were relaxed with neither smile nor scorn.

She swallowed and looked from Samuel to each of the others around the table. They were all watching her: Stacie with impatience, Doug with concern, Colin with boredom. Kate put a hand on Madison's hand and leaned forward. "You can do this, Madison," she whispered. "You're stronger than you realize."

Madison glanced at Mike. His anger and brusqueness of the day before was gone. On his weary face was sorrow.

Steeling her shoulders, Madison looked down at the photos. Like the women in the other photos, this woman was dead. She was pale as fog, but instead of being cut ear to ear, her throat had received short cuts in several spots. Her torso also showed a few short, deep gashes. And both wrists had been neatly slit.

"No! This can't be!" she shouted. Madison looked into Mike's eyes. "This is some trick, isn't it?"

"Do you know this woman?" Mike asked the question in a deadpan voice, even though he already knew the answer.

ELEVEN

odie escorted Madison to the den and told her to wait. There was already a man there. He was sitting on the sofa, his nose stuck in a book. He looked up when they came into the room. Dodie introduced him as Jerry Lerma, Kate Thornton's husband.

Madison gave him a curt nod and plopped herself down into the leather side chair. She didn't want to talk to anyone; she was too shaken. She did know the dead woman in the photos Mike had just shown her. At first, she'd been sure there had been a mistake, but Mike had confirmed the woman's identity.

The dead woman's name was Evie Banks, the waitress who'd been on the schedule to work both Friday and Saturday nights. The waitress who'd left Auntie Em's just weeks before, leaving a spot for Madison to switch from a day shift in order to take a class.

Even more startling to Madison, Evie had had a bloodline. The sweet but often ditzy woman with the long brown hair and soulful brown eyes had been marked to become a vampire; now she was dead. According to Mike Notchey, Evie had died last night, possibly around the time Madison had been in the vampire restaurant. But Evie's death had been different from the others. She hadn't been torn apart in a fit of animal rage but had died of blood loss. While she was still alive, her main arteries had been cut, and she'd been allowed to bleed out. Even more startling, there had been no sign of blood at the dump site of the body, which had been in Angeles National Forest.

Madison had stared at the photos of Evie in disbelief. Her eyes were closed, her body naked. Madison had worked with her a few times when shifts had overlapped. Evie was only twenty-four, just one year older than Madison. Evie Banks had not been the sharpest tool in the shed, nor one of the prettiest, but she had been one of the nicest.

Mike, in front of the council, had questioned Madison about Evie's life, such as boyfriends, family, or any customers who might have bothered her. When the police identified her, they'd learned she'd worked at Auntie Em's. That led Mike right back to Madison. Madison didn't have much to tell them. She knew Evie and had worked with her, but because their shifts were different, she hadn't learned much about Evie's personal life. Madison only knew that during the week she worked as a secretary for one of the Culver City studios—not one of the big ones like Sony, but one of the minor studios that seemed to crop up like weeds in the shadow of the giants. The weekend gig at Auntie Em's had only been to earn some extra money. She had been there just under a year.

"So you two weren't friends," Stacie had asked, questioning Madison in her blunt attorney style.

"We weren't enemies," Madison had shot back. "We were friendly coworkers, but we didn't hang out or anything like that.

With Evie working two jobs and me on days and going to school, our paths didn't cross very often."

"When did they cross?" Stacie pressed.

Madison shrugged, trying to give helpful answers while working through the trauma of seeing Evie dead. "If someone called in sick on Friday or Saturday nights, sometimes Kyle—he's the owner of Auntie Em's—would ask me to work a double shift. Then I might work with Evie." Madison thought of something else. "I'm also the one who trained Evie when she first started."

"Are you sure she didn't have a boyfriend?" asked Kate. "Or maybe a former one who didn't treat her right?"

Madison looked at Kate when she answered. "You're looking for a reason not to connect Evie's death to the others, aren't you?"

"We're looking at all possibilities, Madison," Samuel answered. "Before moving forward, we need to make sure this wasn't something else entirely, like a lover's quarrel."

"Angry lovers don't usually drain off their girlfriend's blood, do they?" Madison asked the question of Notchey, her voice tinged with anger.

Instead of answering her question, Mike said, "Answer the question, Madison. Do you recall Evie having a boyfriend?"

Madison turned back to Kate. "She never said anything specific to me, but I got the feeling she didn't date much. She was kind of quiet and shy—a good waitress, though. She did say she was saving her money to travel. I got the feeling from Kyle that she'd quit to do just that."

She turned in her seat to address Mike Notchey again. "Aren't these the same questions the police will be asking?"

"Yes, pretty much," the detective told her. "At least in their official capacity. And I'm sure Mr. Patterson will fill them in on everything concerning Evie that he can." Mike rubbed a hand up and down his face in exhaustion. "Thing is, now we believe you were taken by accident—that it was probably Evie the killer was after, and Bobby Piper screwed up and grabbed the wrong woman, especially since you changed shifts so recently. While you and Evie look different, you both have long dark hair, the same build, and are about the same age. If Bobby was just given a description, he might not have known he had the wrong person. When Bobby failed to show up with Evie, someone else might have tracked her down."

Madison had another thought. "The guy that the police are holding—the one who's confessed to killing the earlier women—what about him? If Evie's death is connected to those other women and to my kidnapping, won't the police realize they have the wrong guy? That the killer is still on the loose?" She looked at Mike.

"Right now," Mike answered, "they think it's a different matter or a very bad copycat, because the neck cuts are different."

"Madison," Samuel said from the far end of the table. "The police will, of course, be looking into the death of this unfortunate girl, and I'm sure they will consider that the man in custody isn't the real killer or wasn't acting alone, but we have our own reasons to look into it. Detective Notchey is helping us avoid a potentially dangerous public situation."

"He told me," Madison said, looking at Samuel and fighting the pull he had on her. "You think the people doing this are suffering from vampire envy."

A few of the vampires seated around the table chuckled. Colin eyed Madison with barely disguised scorn.

Samuel flashed Madison a quick white smile. "That's a colorful way of putting it, but yes." The smile vanished as he continued. "We think the person or people responsible for these unfortunate deaths know about the bloodlines and are killing women who have them. At least so far, no men that we know of have been murdered. We're not sure why this is happening, but one theory is that whoever is doing this is trying to become a vampire by using the blood or flesh of the bloodline carriers."

"One theory?" Madison looked straight at Samuel when she spoke, as if he were the only other person in the room. "What are some of the others?"

"There's really only one other, Madison," Samuel replied. "And that's that the murderers are trying to destroy all potential vampires, or at least the women."

"That maybe," Doug interjected, "they are trying to make sure no new vampires are created."

Madison thought about that. "Then why just women?"

"Because they make easier targets, why else?" said Colin.

"Not always," Stacie shot back.

Colin was about to fire off a retort when Samuel gently rapped his knuckles on the table, bringing the meeting back to order.

"Maybe," Madison said, frowning in concentration, "they think the bloodline is passed along through the female. Kill the future mothers and you eliminate future vampires."

Samuel smiled at her. "Good thinking, Madison, but bloodlines aren't genetic. We're not sure why certain people have them and others do not, but it seems random. Most people with bloodlines don't even realize they have them or even necessarily believe in the existence of vampires."

Madison's mind kneaded the puzzle like bread dough. "But the killer may not know that. Whoever it is could be shooting in the dark, hoping to stumble on the right combination." Madison paused. She had another question but wasn't sure if asking it would be the smart thing to do.

"What is it, Madison?" asked Samuel. "I sense there's something else on your mind."

Madison took a deep breath and avoided eye contact with the vampires. "There is a third possibility. Are you sure it's not a vampire doing this? I mean, maybe one of your own is trying to slow down the vampire population growth. Or maybe they're just doing it for sport."

All at once, the vampires were voicing protests, except Samuel. And for once, Colin seemed in agreement with Stacie.

"It is possible," Samuel said with a slow, steady voice. "But unlikely. Vampires usually know when a kill has been done by another vampire. We have examined the bodies and found no evidence of that."

"Doing your own vampire DNA swabs?" Madison didn't know why all of a sudden she had dropped her fear and had returned to her usual smart-mouthed self. Half of her begged her to stop. The other half was tired of running scared.

Colin leaned toward Madison and flashed his fangs. "Remember who you're talking to, beater."

Mike, sitting between Madison and Colin, wedged his upper body between the girl and the vampire. "Back it up, Reddy."

Samuel jumped to his feet. "Enough!"

Everyone went still.

Samuel looked at his watch, then at Madison. "Would you excuse us a bit, Madison? We need to discuss some details."

TWELVE

So you're the reason for all the fuss."

Madison came out of her thoughts and looked at the small, dark man on the sofa. She'd forgotten he was there. He smiled at her and picked up a large teapot that rested on the coffee table next to a couple of mugs and a plate of cookies.

"You look quite shaken," Jerry said, pouring her a cup of tea and handing it to her. "Here, this will make you feel better. It's chamomile."

Without a word, Madison took the cup and clutched the warmth between her trembling hands. She took a sip, her mind still turning over Evie's death and the possible reasons for it. Bloodlines, vampires, vampire wannabes—it was all too much. She wanted to turn back the clock to last Saturday morning, when the only thing on her mind was reading an assignment for school before her shift at the diner.

A sip of the tea brought Madison back to the den and its coziness. Samuel had asked her to leave the meeting because they had confidential things to discuss. Fine by her, but what she really wanted to do was go back to bed—maybe for a week or two.

"Usually during these meetings," Jerry told her, "I'm stuck making small talk with Samuel's latest fling, but he came solo this time." Jerry looked Madison over. "He has quite a taste for young mortal women who are a feast for the eyes."

Madison studied Jerry Lerma over the rim of the teacup. "You're drinking tea." It was a statement, not a question.

He nodded at her and raised his own cup in salute, knowing what her next question would probably be.

Lowering her cup away from her face, Madison asked, "You're not a vampire?"

Jerry shook his head and smiled. "No, I'm not. You might say Kate and I have a mixed marriage."

"Is that possible?"

"Very, as long as I learn to be a night owl and she doesn't mind my growing older while she doesn't. We've been married a couple of years now."

He picked up the plate of cookies with his left hand and held it out to Madison. "How about a cookie to tide you over until breakfast?"

Madison shook her head, then spotted another interesting detail about Jerry Lerma. It looked like he had a bloodline. At least, that's what she thought the odd line stretched across his palm might be. It was separate from his lifeline yet distinctly different than the other creases on the palm.

"You have a bloodline?" This time it was a question and not a statement.

Jerry put down the plate and studied his own hand. "Yes, I do."

"Then why aren't you a vampire? You're married to one."

Picking up his own cup, Jerry took a long sip before answering. "While I'd love to spend eternity with Kate, I'm not so sure immortality is such a good thing for anyone. And it's certainly not natural. Kate has offered to turn me many times, but from what I've observed, living forever is more of a curse than a blessing." He took another sip. "No, I'm content to live the life I have and be done with it." He gave Madison a wide, warm smile. "Quality over quantity, you might say."

"But what about Kate?"

"Kate was turned in Paris in the 1920s, quite against her will. At the time she was a budding writer, keeping company with the likes of Gertrude Stein and Hemingway, and having the time of her life. After, she had to build a new life, which has been quite colorful but bumpy. I'm one of the many rest stops she's made along the way." He smiled a knowing smile. "We met when I was lecturing on, of all things, vampire legends and myths. She came to my lecture and heckled me. After, I invited her to join me for a drink, my intent being to convince her my lecture was sound. Of course, I didn't know at the time she was a real vampire." Jerry winked at Madison. "Turns out my lecture was rubbish, after all."

Madison leaned forward, getting closer to Jerry. "Does ... does she bite you?" she whispered.

Jerry tilted his head back and laughed. "Yes, on occasion, but mostly in the throes of passion."

Madison blushed and considered shouting TMI.

"But am I a food source?" Jerry continued, smiling at Madison. "No, I am not. Like the Dedhams, Kate is mostly into animal blood, but human blood is better for them, so once in a while I oblige her."

Madison thought about the human blood Dodie had enjoyed the night before and the animal blood in the fridge.

"It's quite stimulating, you know," Jerry added. "Being bitten, I mean. Nothing quite like it."

Madison shuddered and leaned back in her chair with her tea, trying hard not to think about anyone's teeth embedded in her flesh.

The two were quietly sipping tea when the door to the den opened. Kate Thornton and Dodie came in. Kate settled next to Jerry and slipped an arm through one of his with affection. "I'm exhausted, dear," she said to him. "Let's go home and go to bed."

Madison looked at the middle-aged couple and tried to push the thought of comfy Kate feasting on the neck of the professorial Jerry. She shook her head like a wet dog and looked away.

Dodie's attention was on Madison. "They'd like to see you again, Madison."

"Why?" Madison wasn't sure she wanted to face the council again.

"Come along," Dodie encouraged. She turned to Jerry and Kate and smiled. "We'll see you two soon." She returned to Madison. "Kate and Jerry are two of our best friends. We play bridge with them every week."

Madison put down her teacup and got to her feet. Kate and Jerry stood up along with her. Kate took Madison's hands in her own. "We are so counting on you to help us out. But don't let Colin frighten you. He's like most young men, more bark than bite. Though you're so pretty, I'm sure he'd love to sink his fangs into you."

"Is that supposed to make me feel better?" Madison asked.

Kate gave her a throaty laugh. "Colin's been perfecting that bad-boy routine for hundreds of years. But don't worry, you'll do fine." She turned to her husband. "Won't she, dear?" Jerry agreed, and the two of them took their leave.

When Dodie and Madison were alone, Madison stalled by picking up her teacup again. She took a big swallow of tea. "Something tells me," she said, glancing at Dodie, "that I'm going to need something a lot stronger than tea to get through this."

When she took her seat back at the dining table, Madison was surprised to see that along with Kate, Stacie and Mike had also left. Dodie took the seat Kate had vacated. Doug was in his same seat and so was Samuel. Colin was pacing, agitated, and in an even more foul mood than when she'd last seen him.

THIRTEEN

I am not going to be bait for some psycho!" Madison yelled, jumping to her feet.

After she'd returned and taken her place back at the table, Samuel had told Madison their plan. It hadn't gone over well.

"We just want you to visit a few of the vampire-themed groups and nose around," Samuel explained to the frightened woman as she moved to and fro like a caged animal. He got up from his chair and moved to her end of the table, taking Colin's former seat. "Get to know the people involved, Madison. Many of these groups are just harmless clubs populated by people romanticizing vampires. But some, we know, dabble in very dark things. Based on the recent murders, somehow someone found out about bloodlines and for whatever reason is killing women who have them. They have to be stopped. We're not even sure it's someone from one of the covens, but it's a good place to start."

Madison paced on the side of the room opposite Colin. "So you're just going to send me in there to ask questions, hoping I stumble on something?" She stopped long enough to put her hands on her hips and stare at each of them, particularly the Dedhams. "Guess the life of a beater doesn't mean shit to you deadbeats. And why should it? In relation to your sense of time, my little life is nothing but that of a flea's, if even that."

"Madison, dear," started Dodie, "it's not like that, really."

"Then what *is* it like, Dodie? You're sending me into a hornet's nest of lunatics I know nothing about, and without protection."

"That's not true, Madison," Doug threw out. "Colin's going with you."

Madison stopped in her tracks and pointed at the sullen Colin. "Him? He doesn't even like me. What's to stop him from killing me himself?"

"Bloody perfect." Colin leaned against the back of the sofa, his arms crossed in front of him. "I told you this would never work. I should just handle this alone."

"You can't, Colin," Samuel told him. "They are targeting women. You can only go as her escort."

Madison stalked back to the table and looked down at Samuel. "They are targeting women with bloodlines." She held her left palm out like a stop sign. "In case you've forgotten, I don't have one."

Samuel leaned back in his chair. "You will have," he announced casually. "At least a temporary one."

Madison exploded with frustration and anger. "So you're going to give me a fake bloodline and send me out to meet a killer?" When Samuel said nothing, Madison continued her rant. "At least have the balls to look me in the eye when you sentence me to death." She snatched Samuel's sunglasses off his face and slammed them down on the table.

Everyone in the room caught their breath in shock, except Samuel. Like lightning, he grabbed Madison's wrist and pulled her to him until they were nearly nose to nose. Her breath hit his face heavy and fast, but no breath escaped his lips or nostrils. She turned her head rather than look into his cloudy eyes.

"Look into my dead eyes, Madison," the head vampire ordered, his fangs unfurled and menacing. "Look, I said." He jerked her wrist. "You can die now or you can take your chances. It's entirely up to you."

Against her will, Madison turned to look into Samuel's eyes, blue-white with hints of fire, like opals. She stared into them, mustering her inner core to hold strong. "Most of my life," she told him, eyes locked onto his, "people have threatened me to get me to do what they've wanted. Bullies at school, other kids in the foster homes. No one ever gave me a choice except between doing what I didn't want to do or receiving beatings for not doing it."

She wrenched her arm free from Samuel's grasp and rubbed her wrist. Walking over to the wall, Madison leaned against it and addressed the vampires, who were watching her with intense interest. "Ever since I came into this house, I've been battered around like a rowboat in a hurricane. One minute I feel safe; the next, my life is on the line. Same shit I've put up with since I was eight."

Leaning against the wall, an exhausted Madison slid downward until she was sitting on the floor with her back against the hard surface. Her body may have surrendered, but not her spirit. "Well, that shit's stopping here and now."

"See here," Colin started to say, but Samuel stopped him with a hand gesture.

Madison drew her knees up to her chest and wrapped her arms around them. Locking her eyes back on to Samuel's face, she said, "Give me a real reason why I should help you, then let *me* make the choice whether I do it or not. My life, my decision. If you don't, you're no different from the bastard who raped me from the time I was ten until I was nearly twelve. He told me he'd kill me, too."

No one moved. Except for the sound of the wind in the trees outside, the room was silent.

"Come on, vampire," Madison taunted, her voice beginning to crack as a tear ran from her left eye down her cheek. "Give it your best shot."

Both Doug and Samuel got to their feet. Doug went to stand behind Dodie, resting his hands on her shoulders. She reached up one hand and covered one of his.

Samuel walked up to Madison. Squatting in front of her, he studied her, taking in her scrapes and bruises and staring deep into her wet brown eyes without speaking. She never took her eyes off his face. The pull he had on her was strong, but so was her resolve. Taking each of her hands in his, he unwrapped them from her knees and held them while he continued to look at her.

After a few moments, Samuel said in a low but strong voice, "We need your help, Madison. We'd like you to help us stop the killings. We need a live woman to infiltrate these groups and see if one of them might be responsible for these deaths. Colin knows enough of these people to get you inside. They don't know he's a real vampire, and he's a man and has no bloodline, so I doubt he would attract much attention from the perpetrator." Samuel paused. "But you might." He squeezed her hands gently.

"Please help us. It could mean saving a lot of lives. Think about what happened to Evie."

Madison removed one of her hands and wiped her wet face and nose on the sleeve of her sweater. She sniffed back more tears. "And if I say no?"

Again, the room went deathly silent, everyone waiting for Samuel's determination.

"If you say no," Samuel replied, "we will return you to your prior life … unharmed."

Colin took a step forward. "You can't be serious, Samuel. This beater knows way too much about us."

Samuel didn't turn to look at Colin but continued staring into Madison's eyes. "I believe, Colin, that whatever decision Miss Rose makes, she will keep silent about us. Won't you, Madison?"

Madison nodded, then squeaked out a yes. She cleared her throat. "Yes, I will never tell anyone. On that you have my word."

Samuel raised the hand he still held and kissed the knuckles lightly. Then he let it go and stood up, still looking at Madison's face. He returned to the table. "She's telling the truth." He turned to look back again at Madison, still crouched on the floor. "About everything."

After returning to his seat at the head of the table, Samuel glanced at his watch. They'd been handling the issues at hand for three hours. "The sun is up," he told everyone. "We need to finish and go home. We need our rest."

Samuel addressed Madison. "I'm afraid we'll need your answer right now, Madison. We'd hoped to put our plan into action tonight."

Madison got to her feet and walked to the table, standing at the end opposite Samuel. She was emotionally and physically exhausted but had been thinking about Evie Banks and the other women, those in the police photos. She wanted to go back to bed—her cramped bed in her tiny apartment. But she also didn't want any more women to die. She could easily have been one of them—had nearly been one of them but for Doug and Dodie's intervention.

She looked at the Dedhams. Doug was still standing behind his wife, his hands protectively on her shoulders. His face was kind and encouraging. Dodie looked concerned and sad. Madison glanced at Colin. The young-looking, arrogant man still leaned against the back of the sofa with his arms crossed. He was dressed in black jeans and a black turtleneck sweater, his pale skin a stark contrast to his dark hair and clothing. Watching Madison as she watched him, he left his post by the sofa and walked back to the table.

"What's it to be, Madison?" he asked her, his tone a bit more civilized than before. "You in or not?"

"You'll have my back?" she asked Colin.

He nodded.

Madison closed her eyes. When she did, she saw the raw wounds of the dead women. "I'm in."

"Hold still, Madison," Pauline told her. "We want to get this right."

Madison and Pauline were seated at the Dedham kitchen table. Pauline, with an iron grip on Madison's left hand, was using a henna tattoo kit to make a bloodline on the palm. Spying exactly the spot she wanted to target, Pauline drew a thin and slightly curved fine line between Madison's real lifeline and one of her other palm lines. Madison squirmed.

"I can't help it," she said to Pauline. "It tickles."

Pauline let go of Madison's hand. "There." She consulted the package instructions, peering through the reading glasses perched at the end of her nose. "It says you have to let that dry for six hours."

"Six hours!"

"That's what it says." Pauline showed Madison the box. "So no washing that hand. Good thing you're right-handed."

It was now eleven. Madison did the math. "That means not until at least five. I wanted to go back to bed. I hardly got any sleep last night."

"You can go to bed as soon as that stuff is off—maybe a little sooner. We don't want it to get too dark. Meanwhile, take it easy. From what I understand, you've got a big night ahead of you."

"How did you even know to bring henna?"

"Mrs. D left me a voice mail to pick it up on my way in. That's why I was late. I had to wait for the beauty supply shop to open. That's how we mostly communicate, by texting and voice mail," Pauline explained, "since they're usually in bed by the time I get here. Today her message said to bring henna and give you a bloodline. Mrs. D also told me what's going on—about a new dead girl and her being your friend and all."

Madison studied the line of thick paste drying on her hand. "I must be out of my mind, going along with this."

Pauline put the cap back on the applicator. "You're doing a good thing, Madison. A very good thing."

"But what about Mike Notchey? Shouldn't *he* be doing stuff like this? He wasn't even there when they told me about it."

"He's really not working these murders officially."

"He's a cop, isn't he?"

"Oh, yes. Definitely. But these aren't his cases or his jurisdiction. He's sort of the vampires' man on the inside."

Madison frowned with understanding. "You mean he's on their payroll."

Pauline shook her head and laughed. "No, nothing like that. He's a clean cop, but over the years he's become close to the Dedhams and to the vampire community, as many of us have. He keeps their secrets and helps them out, and sometimes they help him out. These murders are something he's nosing about on his own time. Not to mention the cops already think they have the guy who did the earlier killings." She paused and looked off toward the wall while she gave it more thought. "Mike's a complicated guy who has seen more than his share of personal tragedy. He can be crotchety, but he's one of the good guys."

Pauline looked at the henna instructions again. "Says it will stay good for four weeks in the fridge." She headed for the refrigerator with the leftover henna dye. "Good. That way, if we need to, we can refresh that line."

"Four weeks?" Madison's jaw dropped. "You really think it will take that long?"

Pauline shrugged. "Who knows?"

An extended time frame gave Madison a whole new worry. She couldn't stay with the Dedhams for four weeks. She had a life to get back to, not to mention a job. Kyle had said he'd only hold her job for a week. She decided to address that in a couple of days. Certainly, no one expected her to be here indefinitely. Then she remembered that the concept of time to the vampires was different than it was to her. She had a finite allotment of it. They didn't.

After a few minutes, Madison addressed something else on her mind. "Have you met the vampires on the council, Pauline?"

Pauline gathered up the henna package and put it aside on the counter, then washed her hands. "Yes, I've met the present council and most of those who served on past councils. Mr. D has been on the council only for about six or seven years. Some of the others were on it from the start, like Stacie Neroni and Colin Reddy."

"Why do Stacie and Colin hate each other?"

"Fighting, were they?"

Madison nodded.

Pauline shook her head and made a clucking noise. "It's something that happened several years ago involving a mutual friend of theirs named Julie—Julie Argudo."

Madison's curiosity perked up. "Another vampire—or a beater?"

"A vampire. A very new one." Pauline paused, trying to remember. "I don't know exactly what happened, but Julie was tried and convicted by the council. Stacie and Colin blame each other for it."

"What happened to Julie?"

Pauline shrugged. "Not sure. Suddenly, she was gone—like she never existed."

"What did she do to get into so much trouble?"

Pauline gave another shrug. "No one talks about it."

A buzzer sounded, and Pauline went to the laundry room off the kitchen and returned with a basket of freshly washed and dried towels. She put the basket down on the table and started folding the towels. Madison started to help, but Pauline stopped her. "Your hand," she reminded her.

Frustrated, Madison put the warm towel down. "How boring is it going to be to sit here and do nothing all day?"

Pauline smiled. "When I think of a one-handed job, I'll give you a holler."

After folding a couple of towels, Pauline continued telling Madison about the council. "The Dedhams are thick as thieves with Kate Thornton and her husband. The four of them do a lot together—bridge, opera, stuff like that. Colin does a good impression of an English James Dean—sullen, brooding, and angry—but he must be solid or Samuel wouldn't have him on the council. Eddie Gonzales is a small, paunchy man with a big brain for business."

"I didn't meet him," Madison said. "Samuel said two of the members weren't there, but he didn't give names."

Pauline again paused to think. "Stacie handles most of the domestic legal work for vampires in this area. When people live for hundreds of years, things like estates, taxes, and property can get pretty complicated, not to mention people start to notice when someone doesn't age over twenty or thirty years. She makes sure no red flags are flying. She and Eddie work together a lot to protect the assets of their vampire clients."

"Colin called her a 'puritanical do-gooder.' What did he mean by that?"

"Stacie also runs a weekly legal-aid clinic for the homeless."

"There are vampire homeless?"

"No," Pauline laughed. "She does it for the living, for beaters. She believes in giving back to the community, as does Mrs. D.

Stacie brings her old clothing she collects, and Mrs. D mends and fixes them so they can be redistributed to the needy."

"That's a far cry from the vampires on TV."

"There are some out there like that—selfish and brutal—but Samuel La Croix keeps a tight rein on them." Pauline paused to think, counting the council members on her fingers. "Oh yeah, there's also Isabella Claussen. Did you meet her?"

Madison shook her head.

"I'm not sure what Isabella does," Pauline continued, "but I've heard she runs a lot of errands for Samuel all over the world—sort of like an ambassador for the council with other vampire groups. Can't miss her. She looks like a high-class runway model."

Madison looked up at Pauline with rapt interest. "Tell me about Samuel."

Pauline stopped folding towels. "Child, that man's a puzzle—both dangerous and kind in one handsome, elegant box. He can charm the pants off you, as well as scare them off, simultaneously."

"So I noticed." Madison fingered the edge of the plastic clothes basket. "Is he really blind?"

"You saw his eyes?"

Madison nodded, leaving out the part where she had stupidly snatched Samuel's sunglasses from his face.

"Physically," Pauline continued, "his eyes are as useless as Stevie Wonder's, but he can see as good as the two of us, maybe better." Pauline started back on the towels. "Strange things happen to people when they turn, physical things. A lot of their senses increase, like hearing, strength, speed. Other times they are returned to better health. Mr. D tells it that he was bent from arthritis. But look at him now, tall and straight as a pine tree.

Well, Samuel's eyesight was returned, even though his eyes still appear blind." She put the folded towel aside. "Some people say Samuel La Croix can see right through to a person's soul."

At this, Madison shuddered, remembering how Samuel's blind eyes had pierced her own, digging for the foundation of her existence, as if he could read her life story like a paperback novel.

"He's not African-American," Madison said. "Where is he from?"

"The way I hear it, he was sold into slavery as a young boy in Africa, eventually ending up in Egypt. It was during the time Rome ruled Egypt."

"Rome? You mean like during the time of Cleopatra?"

"No, after that. It was in Egypt that his master blinded him. Never heard why, but he was a young man by then. He was turned into a vampire several years later." Pauline stopped folding and looked around, then bent toward Madison. "I heard," she whispered, "that Samuel tracked down the man who blinded him and drank the blood of each of his three daughters until they died, forcing the man to watch."

Again, Madison shuddered. "Then he killed the man?"

Pauline shook her head. "Samuel spared his life, forcing him to live with the horror. The man ended up taking his own life." She paused. "At least that's what I've heard."

FOURTEEN

olin Reddy came by to pick Madison up around nine thirty. He was dressed all in black again, with a black leather jacket. Madison was wearing jeans and boots, with a long-sleeved cardigan sweater over a tee shirt. When she came down the stairs, he and the Dedhams were waiting for her.

Colin looked her over with a critical eye. "Is that what you're wearing?"

"What's wrong with what I'm wearing?"

"You look straight off a farm in Iowa."

"Well, excuuuuuse me," Madison snarled.

"I'm afraid that's my fault, Colin," Dodie told him. "I didn't bring many of Madison's things over."

Madison looked at Dodie. "You could have brought my entire closet and it wouldn't have mattered." She turned to Colin. "I'm a little too busy in my life to worry about club fashion, let alone have the money to buy it."

"I anticipated that." Colin held out a bag he was holding in one hand. "Go back up and put these on. I think I got the sizes right." He studied her again. "The boots and hair are perfect, but put on a lot more makeup."

Madison snatched the bag from his hands, gave him a salute, and started back up the stairs.

Dodie followed her up. "I'll help you, Madison."

When she came back down the stairs thirty minutes later, Madison was dressed in a short black leather skirt, her boots, and a tight black sleeveless tee shirt with a skull printed on the front. The skull had a tiny pink bow jauntily stuck to the side of its head. With Dodie's help, Madison had applied thick eyeliner, dark eye shadow, and extra mascara. She topped it off with lipstick borrowed from Dodie. She wore her long hair loose.

This time when Madison came downstairs, Colin gave her a thumbs up.

Doug looked at Colin and Madison, then said to Dodie, "Don't you feel like we're sending them off to their prom?"

"A prom with a Halloween hooker theme, maybe," Madison quipped. Looking at Colin, she pointed to the skull on her shirt. "Nice touch with the bow," she told him.

He gave her a half grin. "I thought so." He held out a hand to her. "Let's see your hand." Madison put her left hand in his, palm up, for inspection. "Looks real," he said, then dropped it.

Madison donned her jacket and slung her bag over her shoulder. Colin reached out and took the bag away. "Leave this," he told her, handing the bag to Dodie.

"But I might need it."

"Stick some emergency money in your skirt pocket if it makes you feel better," he told her. "But I don't want you carrying anything that might identify you."

"What if I'm carded at the door?"

"You won't be. You're with me."

Outside in the Dedham driveway stood a Harley. Colin handed her a helmet.

"We're going on that?" she asked.

Without answering, Colin straddled the bike. "Get on," he ordered as he started it up.

"Why in the hell did you get me a skirt if you knew I would be on a motorcycle?"

Again, a slight grin. "I thought it would be interesting. Now put your helmet on." As he put on his, Madison followed suit with her own.

"Now hold on," he called over his shoulder.

As the bike took off, Madison wrapped her arms around Colin Reddy, noticing against her will the muscles of his back against her. She also noted that as the cool wind whipped by them, Colin gave off no body heat.

Their first stop was in a seedy area of Sherman Oaks. Colin pulled into a lot near an alley. He got off the bike and helped Madison dismount.

She took off her helmet and looked around, confused. "There's a nightclub around here?"

"Yes. But since it's Tuesday night, it will be low-key."

"Maybe we should come back on Friday or Saturday."

Colin took off his helmet and shook his head, running a hand through his thick hair. "During the weekend, places like this get packed with kids from the suburbs playing dress-up. The weekends bring in enough money to keep the doors open the rest of the time. Tonight, the real members of the coven will be here. They're the ones we're interested in."

"Coven? As in witches?" Madison remembered Samuel referring to the vampire clubs as covens and wasn't sure she liked the idea of witches mixing in with the vampires.

"Similar meaning, in this case. Stands for a group of people organized for a common purpose. The physical clubs, or locations where they meet, are called havens." He started off for the alley. "Come on," he called over his shoulder, "and bring your helmet. Don't want it stolen."

They walked halfway down the alley until they came to a door painted red, with shiny black trim. It reminded Madison of the entrance to the restaurant called Scarlet. There was a light above the door, shining on a sign. Madison read the sign and rolled her eyes.

"This place is called *Fang Me*?" she said to Colin. "Give me a break."

Colin took her by the upper arm and hissed into her ear, "Keep smart-ass remarks like that to yourself in these places. These people are serious about their beliefs."

"Any other orders?"

"Only give them your first name, nothing else."

"Should I give my real first name or a fake one?"

Colin gave it quick thought. "Your real one. We don't want them to sniff out a lie the first time they meet you, not even a small one. But just give your first name. They aren't big on last names anyway. I'll do most of the talking. But make sure you don't hide that bloodline."

Colin knocked at the door. It was opened by an average-looking guy in his twenties, dressed in black. When he saw Colin, he nodded to him and let them in.

Inside, the walls were painted black. Dim track lighting cast shadows throughout the place. As soon as Madison's eyes adjusted, she saw clusters of chairs around small wooden tables scattered across the floor, and tall tables without chairs along the walls. Toward the far end was a riser holding sound equipment, and in front of the riser was a dance floor. Against the right wall was a short bar with stools. The place wasn't large, and tonight there were only a few people seated at the bar and two occupied tables. Everyone was dressed in black. Haunting rock music played over the sound system.

Madison followed Colin as he walked over to the bar and addressed the bartender, a scrawny, tall guy in a black tee shirt with *Fang Me* printed in bright red across the front. "Kind of quiet in here tonight, huh, Bernard?"

The bartender shrugged. "Been like this a lot lately, except on weekends."

"Where are the regular members? They used to be here all during the week."

The bartender leaned in close. "A lot of the coven have defected. Gone over to Bloodlust."

"That's the new place in Hollywood, isn't it?"

"Yeah, over on Gower, near Hollywood Boulevard."

"I was there once," Colin told him. "Didn't look like much. Just an old warehouse turned into a club."

"It's become the rage all of a sudden. The leader of the Bloodlust coven isn't shy about marketing. Heard they redid the place and even bought celebrity endorsements."

"Where's Lilith?" Colin asked the bartender.

"Right behind you, handsome."

Colin and Madison both turned at the sound of the voice. Standing just behind them was a tall, slender woman with severely short, dyed black hair and ice blue eyes made more prominent by the heavy black eye makeup she wore. She had on skin-tight leather pants and a leather halter top. Her skin was pale, her cheeks high and sculpted above full lips stained dark red.

Colin leaned over and gave her a light kiss on the cheek. "Nice to see you, Lilith."

"It'd be nicer if you came around more." Lilith wrapped her arms around Colin's waist and let one hand drop down to cup his ass.

Madison cleared her throat.

Lilith turned slowly toward Madison. "What's this, Colin, you dating your little brother's babysitter?" She laughed, turning her attention back to Colin.

Colin disentangled himself from Lilith's clutches and held out a hand to Madison. She took it and moved in close to him.

"Well," Colin said to Lilith, "if I did have a little brother, she'd make a damn cute nanny, wouldn't she?" Before anyone said anything more, Colin introduced the two women. "Lilith," he said, dropping Madison's hand and putting an arm protectively around her shoulders, "this is Madison. Madison, this is Lilith, the high priestess of this coven."

Madison was stunned by Colin's lightness. She didn't know he had it in him. As she turned her face from him to Lilith, she plastered on a strained smile.

"So," Lilith said to Madison, "you're the reason we never see Colin around anymore." The tone was accusatory, not friendly.

"You are a pretty little thing. You interested in the vampire culture?"

"Colin has been teaching me about it," Madison answered, keeping her eyes pinned on Lilith, letting her know she was no pushover.

Lilith met Madison's visual challenge. "Maybe the two of you will join the coven together. It's been years and we've never been able to convince Colin to join us officially."

Colin shrugged. "I'm not much of a joiner. I prefer to keep my options open."

Lilith placed a hand on Colin's chest. "I hope that goes for women, too. I always promised you a trip to a real blood bar. The invitation's still open." She gave Madison a sideways glance. "But it's only good for one guest."

———————————

Once outside Fang Me, Madison stomped to the motorcycle. "I can't believe that woman. She came on to you right in front of me."

"What's your problem?" asked Colin. "It's not like we're really seeing each other."

Madison pointed back down the alley. "But she doesn't know that. She wouldn't have cared if we were married and had three kids."

Colin was amused. "You're jealous. It's rather cute."

"I am not jealous. I'm just pissed that she dismissed me like … like some inconvenient child who got to stay up past her bedtime."

"Come on, we got what we came for—information."

Madison started to put on her helmet but stopped. "You think any of it will be helpful?"

Colin shrugged. "Hard to say."

After the touchy introductions had been made, the three of them—Lilith, Colin, and Madison—had sat down at a table on the far side, away from the bar and the few customers.

"What can I get you to drink," she asked Madison in a flat, bored tone.

"Thanks, but I don't drink," Madison replied.

A catty smile spread across Lilith's face. She turned to Colin. "As I recall, you don't drink either, Colin. Now I see the attraction. You're just a couple of straight-laced goths."

Lilith caught Bernard's eye. "A couple of Cokes for the kiddies and the usual for me. And bring some butts."

"So what's going on with Bloodlust?" Colin asked, getting the ball rolling.

Lilith casually waved a slim hand with long, tapered fingers capped with bright scarlet lacquer. "Bloodlust is the flavor of the moment, that's all. Give it a few weeks, maybe a month, and the hype will fade."

Colin pushed for clarification. "Are you talking about the nightclub or the coven?"

The drinks came. Bernard put down two glasses of soda and one short glass filled with an amber liquid but no ice. He left and returned with a pack of cigarettes, some matches, and a small, clear glass ashtray.

Lilith picked up the cigarettes, pulled one out, and stuck it between her crimson lips. Then she waited, an eyebrow cocked in Colin's direction, until Colin picked up the matches. He struck one, the smell of sulfur momentarily invading the table space.

Cupping the lit match, he held it out toward Lilith, who cradled the hand holding the match while she took her time lighting her cigarette. Colin pulled his hand away and shook the match until it went out. Lilith chuckled deep in her throat.

Taking a deep drag off of her cigarette, Lilith arched her neck, sending the smoke toward the ceiling. She turned to Madison. "I do hope you're not going to lecture me on how smoking is illegal in bars. You seem the type."

"None of my business," Madison replied, picking up her soda and smiling at Lilith. It was then that Madison realized she had seen Lilith before. Her photo had been among those shown to her by Mike Notchey. Lilith hadn't been as heavily made up in the photo, but Madison was sure one of the women in the group had been her.

Colin got back down to business. "Who's the leader of the Bloodlust coven?"

Lilith took another drag from her cigarette. "Some guy named Ethan Young."

Colin frowned. "I've never heard of him. He new to the area?"

"Not sure," Lilith said, raising her angular shoulders. "Seemed like one day he started coming around to the various covens, next thing he had his own. Doesn't believe in keeping it low-key, either. A lot of the local covens have lost members to Bloodlust, not just ours."

"Maybe cranking up the name of this place would help," Madison threw out. Lilith glared at her.

"What's he like?" Colin asked after sending Madison a look of warning. "You have met him, haven't you?"

"Yes." Lilith took another puff. "We even had a fling when he first starting coming to Fang Me." Lilith shot Madison a scowl as she took a sip of her drink. "Ethan is very *virile*." She emphasized the word, hoping to get a reaction from Colin, but was disappointed when he remained impassive. "Powerful body, about average height," she continued. "Bald, goatee, fabulous scrolling tattoo across his back and down over his shoulder, toward his stomach."

"Charismatic?" Madison asked, remembering what Notchey had said about whoever was calling the shots in the murders possibly being able to control people.

"What makes you say that? Have you met Ethan?" Lilith looked at Madison with real interest for the first time. "He'd probably find you quite fetching."

"No, I haven't, but he must have some sort of personal magnetism to rise as quickly as he did."

Lilith took a final puff and stubbed out her cigarette. She looked at Colin. "Your lady's quite perceptive."

Colin was about to say something when his cell phone rang. He looked at the display, then said, "I have to take this. I'll be right back." Before leaving the table, he gave Madison a look that ordered her to behave herself.

"How did you and Colin meet?" Lilith asked as soon as the two women were alone.

"Mutual friends introduced us."

"He's never talked about himself, except to say he's originally from England and his mother was Indian." Lilith gave off another throaty chuckle. "Of course, when we were together, we didn't talk much."

Madison ignored the innuendo. "Colin is a very private person. Another reason we get along so well."

"Definitely an enigma." Lilith squinted in the dim light at Madison. "Did Colin give you that black eye—the one you're trying to hide under all that foundation?"

Madison's hand shot up to gently touch the bruise just below her right eye. "No, he didn't."

"I knew he liked it rough." Lilith smiled a private smile. "But I thought he was more into biting than hitting."

"I assure you, Lilith, Colin did not give me this shiner."

Lilith pulled another cigarette from the pack, but when she started for the matches to light it herself, Madison reached for them first. "Here, allow me," she told Lilith.

Madison lit the match, holding it with her right hand. Putting down the matchbook, she leaned forward to light Lilith's cigarette, cupping it with her left palm. As Lilith put the cigarette end to the flame, Madison was sure she saw Lilith's eyes go wide when they caught on the bloodline.

Lilith took a big drag off the cigarette, holding it in her lungs for several beats. When she finally expelled it, she aimed it directly at Madison.

FIFTEEN

When they got to their next destination, Madison was surprised. "I thought after what we learned from Lilith, you'd want to head toward Hollywood and to Bloodlust. We're almost in downtown LA."

Colin shook his head. "Too late tonight, at least for a Tuesday night. I want to save Bloodlust for tomorrow night and make it our only stop. Bernard told me after I took that call that a lot of Fang Me's members go there on Wednesday night. Apparently they offer some sort of special. We'll fit in better if we know people."

"You mean if *you* know people."

"Exactly."

They were parked on a small, dingy side street where most of the businesses were boarded up. The others had metal grates protecting their storefronts. A few doors down, a yellow light showed off a sign for a place called Bat Beauty. A few people were gathered in front of the place, smoking.

"At least here," Madison observed, "they follow the no-smoking law." She started off toward the light, but Colin stopped her.

"By the way, that call was from Samuel. He's calling another meeting." When Madison groaned, Colin added, "It's for tomorrow night. Actually, that would be tonight, since it's already past midnight. Around eight at the Dedhams' again. We'll head out to Bloodlust right after the meeting."

Madison was curious. "Why another meeting? He expecting a report already?"

"He said Notchey might have found something, but he needs to check his sources before telling us. He should have the information confirmed by tonight."

"Well, I have a by-the-way thing for you, too."

Colin looked at her, waiting.

"While you were taking the call," Madison told him, "I made sure Lilith saw my bloodline. When she did, her eyes nearly popped out of her head."

Colin put a firm hand on each of Madison's upper arms. "You sure about that?"

She nodded. "Pretty sure. I lit her next cigarette. Just about put my palm into her face. It definitely got a reaction."

Colin didn't seem pleased by the news.

Madison studied his face. "You had a thing with her."

He looked away in thought. "Not a thing, no."

"But you had sex with her, didn't you?"

Colin looked directly back at Madison, his nostrils slightly flared. "Yes, Lilith and I had sex. Once." He paused. "Maybe twice."

"And she has no idea that you're a real vampire?"

"No."

"Are you sure? Because she mentioned something about you liking to bite while doing the deed."

Colin didn't look happy at the information Lilith had disclosed, but he also didn't seem embarrassed. "A lot of coven members bite during intercourse," he explained. "It's quite common in vampirism. And I didn't use my fangs."

"Okay," Madison said, accepting his response. "But here's another issue worth exploring. I've never seen a vampire naked, so I don't know this for sure, but I'm assuming you guys have all the same equipment as when you were alive."

Colin's eyes bore into her. "Get to your point."

"Well, even if all the parts worked the same, wouldn't a live woman notice how cold your body is?" Madison put a hand on one leather-covered hip. "I mean, you're like walking, talking blocks of ice. Or does your internal heat rise during passion?"

"Maybe Lilith didn't notice because I had gotten her internal heat so high." He shot a cocky grin at Madison.

"Maybe," Madison conceded in a businesslike manner. "But then there's the sweating. Vampires don't sweat, do they? Every living man sweats during sex. Even Eskimos sweat during sex."

"And how many Eskimos have you slept with, Madison?"

"I'm just saying, it's possible she has an inkling. Or maybe she thought you just had bad circulation."

Without another word, Colin started for Bat Beauty.

The inside of Bat Beauty was very much like the inside of Fang Me. The walls were painted black, the lighting subdued, the tables and chairs the same. But instead of being a long, narrow room, Bat Beauty was a square venue. The bar was at the far back, with the dance floor and DJ area situated halfway down the right side. Another difference was that this place was fairly busy—not full, but it hummed with moderate activity. A DJ played while a handful of people gyrated to the ear-splitting music. Most of the clientele were dressed in the goth style. The rest wore mostly jeans and dark tee shirts, with some of the women in short black skirts and fishnet stockings. Madison said a silent word of thanks that Colin hadn't provided her with fishnets.

As Colin and Madison worked their way around the dance floor, several people nodded a welcome to Colin. Once they reached the bar, he asked the bartender, a tall, husky black woman with exploding cleavage, a question Madison couldn't hear over the music. The bartender nodded and, with a jerk of her head, directed Colin to the far side of the bar. Taking Madison's hand, Colin headed off in that direction.

As they approached a thick curtain of black beads, a large man stopped them. Colin said a few words to him, and the man disappeared through a door behind the beads. A few seconds later, he returned and let them enter. They found themselves in a room a little better lit than the main room. Sofas and several chairs in the Victorian style, with red velvet upholstery, were grouped around the room in conversational settings. Sconces on the walls supported tall lit candles. Occasional tables and other furnishings were heavy and dark.

A man approached them, holding out his arms in warm greeting to Colin. He was of slim build, with silver hair that hung to his shoulders. His face was handsome, his large, dark eyes lined in black. He moved with a dancer's grace. Colin dropped Madison's hand and entered the man's embrace.

When they stepped back, the man noticed Madison. "And who is this charming creature?"

"Wilhelm, I would like to present my friend Madison." Colin turned to Madison. "This is Lord Wilhelm, Madison, high priest of the Bat Beauty coven."

Wilhelm smiled and held out his right hand to Madison. With some hesitation, she placed her own right hand into his. After a courtly bow, Wilhelm raised her hand to his black painted lips and lightly kissed it. Madison reflected that she'd never had her hand kissed in her life, and today it had happened twice.

"You are quite welcome here, Madison. Colin is a very special friend to the coven."

"Thank you," she said softly. As she studied Wilhelm more closely, Madison saw that he had fangs. At first she thought he might be a vampire, but his hand had been warm.

Wilhelm walked over to a sofa and indicated for them to follow. "Come, join us."

Two young men rose from the sofa and gave their seats to Madison and Colin. As soon as Wilhelm sat down, one of the young men, attired in a loose buccaneer-type shirt and tight black pants, sat at his feet, a look of genuine adoration stamped upon his smooth face. The other went to join a group of men and women clustered and chatting in low voices in another area of the room. Colin motioned for Madison to sit between him and Wilhelm.

As Madison sat down, her eye caught on a coffin positioned at an angle in a corner of the room. Its lid was up, the inside lined with what looked like quilted red satin. Next to it was a tall wrought-iron candle holder on which stood a lit red pillar candle. She wanted to look inside the coffin but took her place on the sofa instead.

"It has been a long time, Colin," Wilhelm said, leaning against the back of the ornate sofa in a relaxed and regal manner.

"I've been traveling a lot this year," Colin answered.

Wilhelm caught the eye of a young woman dressed in a scooped-neck, long black gown. She was leaning against the wall staring at Colin with cow eyes. "Miriam, refreshments for our friends, perhaps a glass of wine." He looked at Colin, a memory crossing his pale face. "Oh, I'm sorry. As I recall, you don't drink spirits. That still correct?"

"Excellent memory, Wilhelm. Madison does not drink them either."

"A pair of teetotalers. Whatever are we to do with you?" He turned back to Miriam, who waited patiently for her orders, still eyeing Colin with expectation. "Miriam, bring them a pot of my special tea. Tea for the teetotalers." He laughed at his own joke. With a smile to Colin and a slight bow to Wilhelm, Miriam went off to fetch the tea.

"Looks like business is good," Colin said, also relaxing on the sofa. Between them, Madison sat almost rigid, her hands resting in her lap, left palm upward.

"Can't complain," Wilhelm responded. "Well, I could, but who'd listen? Right?" He laughed again. "Actually, it's been down a bit, but that's to be expected in this economy."

"We just paid a visit to Fang Me," Colin told him. "It's dead over there. No more than six to eight people at the most. I've heard several of their coven members have left."

"No big surprise there, the way Lilith runs things." Wilhelm waved a hand in disgust. "The only reason she can keep her doors open is because the boys and girls in the valley are too lazy to travel to other clubs on the weekends."

"She said that new place, Bloodlust, has been attracting both customers and coven members."

Wilhelm gave the comment some thought. "It probably has something to do with it, but a loyal coven stays loyal if they're treated correctly." He smiled at the young man at his feet.

Colin leaned forward. "So you haven't lost anyone to Bloodlust?"

Wilhelm dismissed the idea. "We've only lost one member that I know of to Bloodlust. We've lost some of our weekend business, too, but we're not concerned. Once the shininess wears off, they'll be back."

"Lilith felt that way, too." Colin paused. "What about their leader, Ethan Young? What do you know about him?"

A wide smile crossed Wilhelm's face just as the tea was served. Miriam poured tea for Madison and Colin, serving them in delicate china cups with matching saucers. When she presented Madison with her cup of tea, Madison held out her left hand, palm up, to take it. Glancing at Wilhelm to her left, she didn't notice any reaction, if he noticed her hand at all. What Madison did notice was how much lower Miriam's dress bodice had gotten. As she leaned over to present Colin with his tea, her breasts nearly spilled into his cup. To Madison's side, Wilhelm noticed and chuckled.

"Ethan Young," Wilhelm began, as soon as Miriam was out of the way, "is quite delicious. He's in his prime and quite the stud." Wilhelm sighed. "Unfortunately, he's only into females." He grinned at Colin and flashed Madison a wink. "Like you."

"Is he a good coven leader?" Madison asked.

Wilhelm screwed up his face as he thought about it. "I suppose so. A bad leader can't keep a coven together. He's a bit too rah-rah for my taste, but he has certainly shot to the top quickly."

Colin played with his tea, pretending to drink it. "That was also something Lilith said, that Ethan had pretty much come out of nowhere."

Wilhelm picked up a glass of wine from the table beside him and swirled the red liquid in the glass. "It might have seemed that way, but I don't think he was new to the vampire culture. He knew too much about it, even a lot of the inner workings—things even someone like you wouldn't know, no matter how close you are to us, because you don't belong." Wilhelm took a drink of wine. "He might have been new to the area, but he was not new to vampirism. Or he had a very good and informed mentor." He paused. "Personally, I think he came to LA with the intention of starting his own group. He did his networking with us, got to know the lay of the land, then started his own group. His coven is more modern. More flash than velvet. More black and silver than black and red."

Wilhelm took another drink of his wine. "Ethan Young is more *Twilight*. We're more Bram Stoker."

After Bat Beauty, Colin headed to a house in Mar Vista, a neighborhood not far from Culver City, where Madison lived and worked. It was an unassuming but large ranch-style home on a double lot at the top of a hill. The house and the neighborhood were quiet. The circular driveway held four or five cars.

"This," he explained to Madison, "is the coven known as Dark Tidings."

"There's a club here?"

"Not all covens operate clubs," Colin whispered to her as they parked the bike and made their way up the driveway to the house. "Though many do. They raise money by catering to the goth music and dance scene. That's how the leaders support themselves. Others hold salons a few nights a week, where their members can gather and discuss poetry, literature, and things concerning their lifestyle. Dark Tidings is one of those. It is very serious in its pursuit of the intellectual side of vampirism."

At the door, Colin rang the bell. The chimes were soft and heavy, like a gong muffled by pillows. A few moments later, the door was opened by a short, plump, middle-aged woman wearing a flowing velvet caftan in dark burgundy, with black velvet side panels. Her faded red hair was streaked with gray and worn in a braid that hung almost to her waist. Circling her head was a wreath made of black silk roses. When she saw Colin, her dour face remained immobile but her eyes crinkled noticeably around the edges.

Although Madison had found Colin annoying and aloof, it wasn't lost on her that the people they'd met tonight each adored him in their own way. He'd made friends with these people, or at least had them thinking he was a friend.

Colin smiled at the woman. "Greetings, m'lady. I've brought you a young friend to meet. This is Madison." He turned to Madison.

The woman looked Madison up and down like a school teacher appraising a pupil. Upon reaching a verdict, she held out both hands to Madison and said warmly, "Welcome to Dark Tidings, Madison. I am Lady Harriet."

As Madison took Lady Harriet's hands, she saw that the woman had a bloodline across her left palm.

SIXTEEN

It was almost four in the morning when Colin and Madison returned to the Dedham house. Doug and Dodie were waiting for them like anxious parents.

"Did you learn anything?" Doug asked as soon as they came through the door.

"A bit," Colin answered, settling on the sofa in the den. "We visited three havens and talked to the leaders of each. Seems there's a new coven with a hot new club in Hollywood."

"That would be Bloodlust," Doug said, taking a seat in the leather chair. Madison sat next to Colin. Dodie excused herself. "Mike told us about that place. He says it's growing like crazy."

Colin nodded. "Seems it has pulled members from the three covens we visited, as well as clientele from the two with nightclubs."

Before the conversation went any further, Madison asked a question that had been haunting her since Dark Tidings. "Are you," she asked Colin, "like an underground spy for the vampires? Everyone seemed to know you, but from what I saw, they had no idea that you're a real vampire." She paused. "Except maybe my theory about Lilith."

"And what theory is that, dear?" asked Dodie, who'd returned with a tray of refreshments—tall glasses of blood for them and tea and cookies for Madison. "Here," she said, urging Colin to take a glass of blood. "You look positively peaked. This will help."

"It's just her nonsense, Dodie," Colin said, taking the glass. He pressed his lips together, then his mouth contorted, bunching his bearded cheeks up on one side as he thought of what to tell Madison. "I keep an eye on things for the council," he finally explained to her. "I monitor these groups, making sure our way of life is safe and that these folks don't get too close to the truth."

"Do they really believe that vampires exist?"

"Some do," Colin answered after taking a big swig from his glass. "Others follow what they believe is a vampire lifestyle, like drinking blood, coming out only at night, sleeping in coffins. And still others believe that they are vampires themselves." He looked over at Dodie, raised his glass, and smiled, his perfect teeth gleaming white against his black beard. "First-rate, Dodie."

"That's my Dodie," Doug said with pride. "The Julia Child of blood."

Dodie beamed and hoisted her own glass.

Madison looked up at Colin and tried to forget that the others were dining on blood. She took a quick sip of her hot tea to wash the imagined taste from her mouth. "Wilhelm had fangs," she said after swallowing. "Does he believe he is really a vampire?"

"What do you think?" Colin asked her.

"I'm not sure if he's playing a part or believes the part he's playing. I know he's not a real vampire like the three of you."

Madison paused to consider her answer. "Fangs or no fangs, his hands were warm, and he was drinking and eating."

"Some people," Dodie told her, "have fang dental implants inserted."

"For real?" Madison shuddered at the thought. She hated going to the dentist for any reason.

"Yep," confirmed Doug with a short laugh. "And they aren't retractable like ours."

"Wilhelm," began Colin, "believes that he was born to be a vampire. He drinks human blood from time to time and even sleeps in a coffin on occasion—a coffin with air holes drilled into it."

"I bet he'd freak if he knew you were a real one." Madison leaned back on the sofa. She was tired and wanted to go to bed but knew they needed to talk about the evening.

"My guess is that he'd be insufferable, pestering me all the time to become one." Colin said the words with a slight smile.

"Yes, it was quite obvious he had a crush on you." It was Madison's turn to laugh. "Maybe you should fix him up with a gay vampire and see what happens." She gave some thought to what she'd just said. "Are there gay vampires?"

Dodie was the first to answer. "Yes, of course, just as in real life. Eddie Gonzales is gay. He's on the council but wasn't here for the meeting."

Madison turned to Colin. "Why don't you introduce Eddie to Wilhelm?"

"They've met." Colin's answer was chopped. "Eddie has gone to Bat Beauty a number of times. It has a large gay following due to Wilhelm. Eddie has even done some financial consulting for Wilhelm on my referral."

Doug shook his head with amusement. "Two vampires so close to Wilhelm, and he didn't have a clue."

"There's more than that," Madison said. The three of them looked at her with curiosity. She looked at Colin when she spoke. "You didn't see the bloodline on Geoff's hand?" When he looked blank, she continued. "Geoff was the cute young guy sitting on the floor at Wilhelm's feet most of the night. The one in the loose white shirt."

Colin looked at her, his dark brows a solid black line across his forehead. "Are you sure that bloke had a bloodline?" Even the Dedhams leaned in, their attention sharpened.

"Positive," Madison said. "After you went off to talk to those people over in the corner, Geoff took the seat next to me. He's quite nice, but rather shy. He told me he came here from Nebraska just six months ago. We got to talking, and he noticed the line on my hand and showed me his. Said I'm the only person he's met with the same birthmark."

Doug zeroed in on Madison. "He called it a birthmark?"

"Yes. Said he'd had it all his life. Was surprised to see I had one, too."

Colin drained his glass before turning to Madison with serious concentration. "Did anyone else hear this conversation?"

"Probably. Wilhelm was nearby and some of the others, like Miriam." Madison looked quizzically at Colin. "You've never seen any bloodlines on anyone at these covens?"

He shrugged, half lost in his own thoughts. "Once or twice over the years, but that's it. There was a woman in Wilhelm's coven with one a few years ago. She called herself Sylvia; I'm not sure if that was her real name or not. I kept an eye on her, but last year she stopped showing up. I asked Wilhelm about her. He laughed and said she had gone off to marry some executive and have a normal life."

"Did you believe him, Colin?" The question came from Dodie.

"At the time, yes. It didn't seem odd at all. To a lot of these kids it's just a phase, not a true lifestyle. But now, with these killings, who knows."

"How old was Sylvia?" asked Madison.

Colin thought about it. "About your age, maybe a bit older, but not much. She was rather plain in the looks department, but a pleasant sort." He smiled. "What I remember most was her incredible hair. Tiny, tight natural blond curls all over her head."

Dodie didn't look happy. "You think she might have ended up like the others, but her body was never found?"

Colin shrugged, his leather jacket making a soft sighing sound as he did. "It's possible."

"Well, Geoff wasn't the only one with a bloodline," Madison announced. Dodie and Doug looked at her with surprise, but not Colin. "Lady Harriet had one, too."

"Lady Harriet of Dark Tidings?" Doug asked.

Madison nodded, then looked at Colin. "You knew that, didn't you?"

"Of course. I've known her for years."

"And she doesn't know what it means?" Madison looked down at her own fake bloodline.

"Not that I know of. Did she notice yours?"

"I don't think so."

Madison then remembered something from the evening. "When I was at Dark Tidings, I asked to use the bathroom.

When I came out, a man was waiting in the hall to use it next. I recognized him, but I'm not sure from where."

"Was he among the photos Mike Notchey showed you?" Doug asked.

Madison shook her head. "I recognized Lilith and Wilhelm from the photos. I didn't recognize Lady Harriet at first. She's aged some and gained weight; Mike must have an old photo. This guy's picture could have been there and he's changed since then. But I have a gut feeling I know him from somewhere else."

Doug cocked his head with interest. "From the diner, maybe? Or from school?"

"Hard to say. He was wearing dark glasses, which I noticed several people wearing inside at all the havens."

"Yes," Colin confirmed. "Many people don't want to be recognized as coven members. Others think it is rather cool and mysterious." He sounded amused at the idea.

"Well," Madison continued, "if he has been at the diner, I don't think he's a regular. Could be from school. He looked to be around thirty or so. People of all ages attend night classes."

Doug finished his drink and put the glass back on the tray. "I'm sure you'll think of it, Madison. You're probably too bushed right now to think straight." He stood up. "In fact, it's time for all of us to turn in. Colin, you're welcome to stay here today if you like, which makes sense if you're coming back later."

Colin stood up. "Thanks, Doug, but I'm going to head home. I always sleep better in my own coffin." He gave Madison an uncharacteristic wink.

"You don't sleep in a coffin," she said in disgust, then hesitated. "Do you?"

The three vampires laughed.

"No, Madison," Colin told her with a smirk. "I stopped doing that over three hundred years ago."

Dodie and Madison also got to their feet as the men headed out the door to the foyer. "Is he kidding about the 'three hundred years' thing?" Madison whispered to Dodie.

Dodie smiled. "No, dear, I don't think so."

SEVENTEEN

When Madison woke up, she had an idea. While at Bat Beauty, Wilhelm had given her his card. It was almost noon, and she knew the Dedhams would be sleeping for another five or six hours. After taking a shower and dressing, she went downstairs to find Pauline dusting in the living room.

"Pauline, I'm going out for a bit."

"Where're you off to?"

"We get paid every Wednesday at the diner. I want to stop by and pick up my check and say hello."

"Wednesday's an odd pay day, isn't it?"

"Yeah, but that's Kyle." Madison wasn't lying. The owner of Auntie Em's did pay them on Wednesday. "I also want to drop by my place and check the mail and pick up a few more things. That's okay, isn't it?"

"I don't see why not." Pauline stopped her work. "Just don't linger in either place—a quick in and out. And take your cell phone in case someone needs you."

In response, Madison held up her phone.

Pauline returned to her task, then shot back at Madison, "But eat something first. You're as thin as a baby bird."

Madison headed out the front door. "I'll grab something at Auntie Em's. I miss their cheeseburgers." Before Pauline could protest, Madison was in her car and heading out of the Dedham driveway.

During the drive to Culver City, Madison thought about the changes in her life in just a few days. No one had ever cared before where she was going or if she had her phone. Pauline and the Dedhams seemed genuinely interested in her, but a mile later, self-doubt rose like bile. They needed her. When they didn't, she'd be back to her old life. The idea both pleased and disturbed her.

Auntie Em's was bustling even though it was near the end of the lunch crowd. All the tables were full, so Madison grabbed a stool on the far end of the long lunch counter.

A couple of regulars had nodded to her when she came in. "You still working here?" one of them had asked on his way out. She recognized him as a studio suit—one of the buttoned-up, conservative business types who handled the purse strings and decision making behind the artists and tinsel-town glamour. He always ordered the Cobb salad, no bacon, dressing on the side.

"Yes," Madison had answered. "Just took a couple of days off." When he seemed to expect more of an explanation, she added, "Family stuff." It felt like he thought she worked for him and not the diner.

"Time off is good. Family stuff, not always." His face contorted into a half frown, like he'd seen more than his share of unpleasant family drama. "Come back soon, you're missed. Had to send my salad back two days this week." He'd said the last few words like it was her fault and an apology was in order.

Sandra, Kyle's wife, always worked the counter and often the cash register. She stepped in front of Madison. She was a thick, tall woman with bleached hair, a big mouth, and an even larger personality—at least in the diner. When waiting on customers, Sandra liked to give them a loud, colorful show reminiscent of Flo, a waitress from an old TV sitcom. Off work, she was low-key. "Nice to see you, Madison. Hope everything's okay with your grandparents."

"My grandparents?" Madison caught herself. That was the story she had handed Kyle when she'd called him, a health problem with her grandfather. "Yeah, they're fine. Thought my grandfather had a heart attack, but it was just a scare. I've been staying with them this week, helping out until everyone and everything settles down." She smiled at Sandra. "Thanks for asking."

Sandra cocked her head and studied Madison. "What happened to your face?"

Madison groaned. So much for the artful use of makeup. "I fell at my grandparents' place," she lied. "On the back patio, moving stuff around for them. I was lucky I didn't break my nose. But it should be gone by the time I come back to work."

"Hope so. You're far too pretty to look like you went the distance with Mike Tyson," Sandra laughed. "You come in for your pay?"

"Yeah, and a cheeseburger." Madison rolled her eyes. "You wouldn't believe what my grandparents eat. It's disgusting."

"Old-people food," Sandra said knowingly. "Same thing with my folks."

Madison gave her a mild grin, thinking if Sandra only knew exactly what her 'grandparents' ate, she'd swoon.

Sandra put Madison's order in, then served food to a customer near the middle of the counter. When she returned, she had a tall glass of Coke. When she put the soda down in front of Madison, she lowered her head and whispered, "Did you hear about Evie Banks?"

"Evie? No, what?" Madison concentrated on unwrapping her straw. She didn't look up until after she'd stuck it into the liquid and took a long pull.

"It was all over the news last night and this morning." Sandra paused for effect, then looked around before lowering her voice even more. "She was murdered."

Madison faked surprise by popping her eyes wide with astonishment. "Murdered? You sure?"

"Dead as a doornail. Her body was found in Angeles National Forest. She was *naked*. Can you imagine?"

Sadly, Madison could.

"The cops came in early this morning asking about her."

Sandra left to cash out a customer. When she returned, she had Madison's food.

While she poured ketchup onto her plate, Madison asked, "I thought Evie left Auntie Em's to travel or something like that?"

"That's what we all thought." Sandra leaned back against the counter behind her. "Isn't that shocking?"

Madison picked up her burger. Before she took a bite, she asked, "Do they know who did it?" Her teeth dug into the perfectly cooked burger and chewed with delight. It was heaven.

"Not a clue that I know of. Poor girl." Sandra picked up the coffeepot to go refresh someone's cup. "Her parents must be beside themselves with grief. You know, her father's a Baptist minister in some little town up by Sacramento."

"I didn't know that." Madison stuck a fry into her mouth and wondered what it was like for Evie's parents, mourning a daughter killed so brutally. She'd mourned a mother killed senselessly, but she'd been a child when it had happened. Most of her grieving had happened later, as she got older and realized more clearly what she'd lost. She'd almost been killed like Evie and the other girls, yet no one would have mourned her. She thought about the Dedhams and wondered if they would be sorry if she died while helping them. Or would they just chalk it up to one beater down, plenty more to go?

After taking another bite, Madison pushed her plate away, her burger half eaten, and concentrated on drinking her soda.

"Not hungry?" It was Kyle Patterson, her boss, asking.

Madison shrugged. "Guess not."

Kyle took the stool next to her. As much as his wife's diner persona was loud and brassy, Kyle's was quiet and behind the scenes. He was not as tall as his wife and of an average build, except for the soft belly that hung over his belt from eating too much of his own diner's good food. "Sandra told me you'd come in. You coming back?"

"Monday, as planned," Madison told him. She wiped her mouth on a paper napkin. "Sandra just told me about Evie. Pretty awful, isn't it?"

Kyle nodded and looked off, his eyes not focusing on anything in particular. "Yes. She was a nice girl." He refocused his attention back on Madison. "Here's your check," he said, handing her an envelope.

When Madison held out her left hand to receive her pay, Kyle noticed the bogus bloodline. "What's that on your hand?" he asked, examining it. "An ink stain?"

Madison wasn't sure what to say, then decided to throw out another lie. "I'm thinking I must have broken a blood vessel or something when I fell." She pointed at her face. "Landed face first on my grandparents' patio like a klutzy dork." She took the pay envelope and stuffed it into her purse.

"Your grandparents live in the area?" Kyle asked. "You've never mentioned them before."

"They have a place in Topanga. I never saw them growing up, not until I moved here. Still don't see them much. They're retired and travel a lot." Madison was surprised at how easily the lies fell from her lips. Maybe if she said it often enough, she'd start believing it, too.

"Topanga's nice."

"Yeah, they have a cool place. Almost like being on a real vacation."

Sandra finished with a customer and came over. She looked at her husband. "You convince Madison to come back sooner than later?"

Kyle laughed. "Never even brought it up. Girl's worked hard for us. She's entitled to time off." He turned to Madison. "We do need you back, Madison. You're my best waitress. Even better than the old lady here."

Madison laughed softly and felt a low-level blush start. "I'm not sure about that."

"It's true, Madison," Sandra told her. "I'm not as young as I used to be, and neither are my feet."

Madison glanced at her watch. She still had things to do. "Guess I'd better be going." She dug in her purse for her wallet, but Kyle stopped her.

"You still work here, Madison," he told her. "Lunch is included, as always."

Madison's next stop was her apartment. Her only mail was a utility bill. She looked around the place, realizing now, after spending time with the Dedhams, how shabby it was. She wondered what the Dedhams had thought when they came to pick up her things, then dismissed her concern. It was hers. Everything was paid for, and there was nothing wrong with it. She went to the closet and pulled out a couple of tops that she thought might pass muster with Colin. There was no way she was going to wear that tee shirt with the stupid girly skull again. Pulling out a duffle bag, she folded the tops into it, along with her bathing suit and a few other favorite items of clothing. With one last glance at the tidy but meager apartment, she left, thinking that maybe it was time to upgrade a bit.

Madison had gone halfway down the stairs when she had a thought. Returning to her apartment, she headed straight for the cabinet under the bathroom sink and pulled out two boxes of tampons. Stuffing the boxes into the duffle, she headed back out and down to her car.

EIGHTEEN

Before she'd gone to her apartment, Madison had called Wilhelm. After identifying herself, she'd asked if he would meet with her.

Madison had the address of Bat Beauty and remembered vaguely where it was from her visit with Colin. She headed east on the 10 Freeway and exited on Vermont, the same exit she remembered Colin taking. It took her several wrong turns, but eventually she found the club.

During the day, the neighborhood was even seedier than at night, but not as foreboding. The few businesses in the area had their security gates up, but none looked very busy. When she tried the door to Bat Beauty, it was unlocked.

Inside, the club was just as dark as it had been before, but there was no deafening music, just a soft, eerie instrumental piece being piped over the sound system. There were a few people having drinks at or near the bar, but they weren't the dancing, heavily made-up revelers of the night before. Today's patrons looked run over by life and left for roadkill, and Madison wondered if it was the neighborhood crowd.

Walking up to the bar, Madison caught the eye of the bartender, a guy easily in his sixties, with broad shoulders and a slight paunch, wearing jeans and a tee shirt.

"I'm here to see Wilhelm," she told him. "He's expecting me."

"Wait here," the guy told her. He headed for the end of the bar, where he picked up a phone.

Madison wasn't exactly sure what she was doing in Bat Beauty, but after hearing about Sylvia's disappearance, she felt compelled to find out if the woman had left the Bat Beauty coven to get married, as Wilhelm had said, or was missing for some sinister reason. She knew if she'd told the Dedhams or Colin, or especially Mike Notchey, that she wanted to talk to Wilhelm alone, they would not have allowed it. She also knew on another level that contacting Wilhelm was stupid from a security standpoint. But if the vamps wanted to use her as bait, then she was damn well going to call some of the shots on her own. The sooner all this was over, the sooner she could return to her life. She'd promised Kyle she'd be back to the diner on Monday, and she intended to do her best to move things along.

The bartender returned and pointed toward the door with the beaded covering. "He's in his office. Go right through there."

"Thanks."

There was no one in the room when Madison entered. The candles were unlit and the lights were up, casting a harsh reality on the furnishings. In the better light, Madison could see that the sofas and chairs were old, the area carpets threadbare. It looked more like a warehouse for used, battered furniture than the meeting place of an active coven of vampire worshipers she'd seen just a few hours earlier.

She stepped over to the coffin in the corner. The lid was still up. The coffin appeared to be fairly new and was easily the nicest thing in the room.

"Ever get inside one?" a voice asked.

Madison spun around to find Wilhelm just a few feet behind her. She placed a hand over her thumping heart. "Oh, I'm sorry, Lord Wilhelm. I didn't know you were there."

His face was washed of its makeup, and he wore a long black Indian-style cotton tunic over loose black cotton pants. An ornate clasp held his silver hair in place at the nape of his neck. On his feet were huaraches. He looked healthier but older than he had the night before.

"So, have you?" he asked again. He put out a hand and caressed the smooth outside of the coffin.

Madison looked at the casket and did her best not to shudder noticeably. "No, never."

"Every now and then I'll sleep in it," he admitted. "It's a little snug, but emotionally it's rather liberating." He stroked the shiny box with love and respect. "Kind of a sneak preview of coming attractions, you might say."

"But I thought you were a vampire?" Madison gave him what she hoped was a look of doe-eyed innocence. "Don't they live forever?"

"There are immortal vampires—those who live forever until killed by certain means—and mortal vampires, like myself." He touched his chest with a finger adorned with a heavy silver ring. "Both enjoy darkness and the blood of innocents." Noticing Madison's bewildered look, he smiled. "You have much to learn, little one." He moved toward the sofa. "Come, sit with me." His words were smooth and inviting.

With very little hesitation, Madison took a seat on the sofa she'd occupied earlier.

"Isn't Colin teaching you any of this?" When she didn't answer, Wilhelm laughed. "Or is he just fucking you like a wild stallion?" He looked Madison over, taking in her form-fitting sweater and tight jeans. "I know I would, were I so inclined that way." He sighed. "As it is, I'm very jealous of you. I've wanted him for years, but he won't let me have so much as a nibble, the cruel boy."

Until now, Madison had never thought of Colin Reddy as a sexual partner, not even when she was teasing him about Lilith. But now, sitting with Wilhelm and listening to his lusty talk, it was all Madison could think about—as if Wilhelm's lascivious suggestion had implanted the idea in her brain with mere words spoken in dulcet tones.

Wilhelm reached out and touched Madison's neck with a fingertip. "I'll bet Colin's feasting on you, both sexually and otherwise, like an all-you-can-eat buffet—and from the look of your unblemished neck, he's being very discreet."

"Colin is teaching me about vampirism," she told Wilhelm, shaking off the cloudiness of desire. "But he's not into the drinking of blood."

"Oh, no?" Again, Wilhelm laughed and continued to stroke Madison's graceful neck. "Once a mortal vampire gets a taste for human blood, he or she must have it. And Colin Reddy thirsts for blood. I know, I've seen it."

Madison pushed his hand away. "What do you mean?"

Wilhelm leaned back and gave Madison a thin-lipped smile. "The last time any of us saw Colin was on a holy day, a day of feasting, about ten months ago. On feast days, one or two of our acolytes sacrifice themselves to the rest of us."

"You kill them?" Madison started to get to her feet, but Wilhelm moved forward to prevent her.

"No, dear girl, nothing like that at all. Relax and let me tell you what happened. It may increase your appetite for the worthy Colin."

When Madison leaned back again on the sofa, Wilhelm continued. "That feast day, only one acolyte was being presented. We dressed her in a white and gold chiffon Grecian-style gown and laid her on a table in a circle of flowers. It was a beautiful sight. Throughout the day, members and special guests could partake of her blood."

"She let them?" Madison was shocked.

"No," Wilhelm corrected, "she *wanted* them to do it. It was her privilege as an acolyte and servant of the coven."

"People bit her and sucked her blood?" Madison fought the urge to be sick.

Wilhelm had closed his eyes, fondly remembering the event. When he opened them, he reached over to the table next to the sofa and opened a small drawer, retrieving a tiny packet. He opened it and held its contents up for Madison's inspection. "Know what this is?"

"Yes. They use those at the doctor's office when they stick your finger for blood."

Wilhelm nodded. "They're called lancets. Diabetics also use them. And so do we. Generally, when we partake of another's blood, we stick them with one of these. We don't bite them. On feast days, members prick the acolyte and suck the blood from the tiny incisions."

Unbidden, the photos of Evie Banks invaded Madison's mind. Evie's body had received multiple small cuts. Had Evie been a sacrificial killing?

Madison pushed the memory of the photo aside, but not the thought. "And they don't mind being stuck over and over?"

"On the contrary, they go into another realm of being," Wilhelm explained with enthusiasm. "They are actually transported into a state of nirvana as the feasting continues."

"So what does this have to do with Colin?"

Wilhelm put the lancet on the table and turned back to her. "On that particular day, everyone was taking their turn feasting on the girl, except for Colin. He hung back, but I could see in his eyes that he wanted to devour her ... to suck her dry. Finally, I handed him a new lancet and pushed him toward the table. He looked the woman over for a moment, then drove the lancet into her neck, right about here." Wilhelm reached out a hand and touched Madison right where her neck and shoulder connected. Her sweater had a boat neck, and his fingers were hot on her skin. Mesmerized by the story and his voice, she didn't push them away.

"So he drank her blood?"

"Oh, my, it was much more than that. As soon as Colin's lips touched the girl's neck and started sucking, she let out this moan, guttural and deep, from some dark, untouched place inside her." Wilhelm continued fingering Madison's neck. "It was beastly and absolutely fabulous. We all stopped our own feasting and merrymaking and gathered around the table, positively awestruck."

Wilhelm withdrew his fingers from Madison's neck and stroked his own neck as he spoke, as if sensing it himself. "But Colin didn't stop with that one snack. Like a man possessed, he kept sucking on her. Cutting her over and over with the lancet when the wound he was drinking closed up. Blood dripped from his mouth and over that sexy black beard of his. And all the while she kept moaning and writhing on the table in ecstasy. Finally, right there in front of us all, she had this mind-blowing orgasm."

When Wilhelm stopped talking, Madison had to remind herself to breathe. "The woman was Miriam, wasn't it?"

He nodded. "Until last night, we never saw Colin again. I daresay Miriam would follow him to the ends of the earth for a rematch."

Wilhelm studied Madison. "And you're saying he's never sucked your blood?"

"Never." Though after that story, Madison wasn't so sure she didn't want Colin to try.

"Then he's a man scared of his true identity. Pity. He has such potential."

Madison almost laughed, thinking about Colin's true identity and how it would shock Wilhelm. Then she sobered up, thinking about how close Colin had come to being discovered, and Miriam possibly killed, in his uncontrolled bloodlust.

Pushing blood sucking and orgasms aside, Madison fought to put her priorities in line. She'd come to Wilhelm with a purpose.

"Although Colin is teaching me a lot," she told Wilhelm, getting things back to her purpose, "I first learned about the lifestyle from a friend of mine a few years ago. A friend you might know."

"Oh, really?" Wilhelm arched one eyebrow. "Who, pray tell?"

"A couple of years ago, I met a girl named Sylvia. I never knew her last name. She was the one who first told me about vampirism. She was really into it."

"Sylvia?" Wilhelm gave the name some thought. "I don't recall a Sylvia, but then I seldom become acquainted with the young people who come here to party."

"No, she was a member of your coven. I'm sure of it."

Wilhelm gave her the cocked eyebrow again.

"I lost touch with Sylvia. Then this morning, when I was looking at your card, I remembered that it was the Bat Beauty coven that she belonged to, but I don't recall seeing her here last night."

"You're sure it was Bat Beauty?"

"Yes. She was about my age, with very, very curly blond hair."

Wilhelm gave it more thought. "I do remember a girl with rather gorgeous untamed blond hair."

"I'd really like to contact her again."

"Tell you what, let me go into the office and see if I can find her name on our past members lists. If I do, I can at least give you the information we had on her at the time. Although we don't use last names in the coven, we do keep rosters for some purposes."

While Wilhelm was gone, Madison tried hard to erase the image of Colin sucking on Miriam's neck from her mind, but the harder she tried, the clearer it appeared, like a permanent stain no amount of scrubbing would remove. She clamped her eyes shut but only succeeded in replacing Miriam's face with her own.

"You can't stop thinking about it, can you?"

Madison gasped in surprise. Wilhelm had quietly returned, startling her once again.

She shook her head. "No, that's not it. I didn't get much sleep last night. I'm afraid I was dozing off."

From the smirk Wilhelm gave her, she knew he wasn't buying her bullshit.

"I found her information." Wilhelm held a piece of paper in his hand. "I wrote it down for you. According to our membership notes, she left the coven about a year or so ago to get married, so she might not have the same last name."

Madison thanked him and held out her hand for the paper, but Wilhelm didn't give it to her. Instead, he sat back down on the sofa, closer to Madison.

Wilhelm looked into Madison's eyes while his fingers stroked her neck again. Her brain told her to get up and leave, but her body wasn't listening. She was getting lost in Wilhelm's eyes, just like she'd gotten lost in Samuel's.

"I gave you what you want," Wilhelm told her in a lullaby of words, never taking his eyes off of hers, "now it's your turn to help me."

"What do you want?" In spite of her resolve being sapped, her words challenged him.

"Every day when I wake up," Wilhelm explained, "I feed off an acolyte. It's my privilege as high priest. Today, Geoff was to serve me, but he didn't show up." His fingers played with her hair, using it to tickle her neck. "Today, I shall feed off of you."

She shook her head, both to dispel the trance and to say no.

"Yes, my girl, today you're not Colin's. Today you're mine. I'll be your first."

Keeping his eyes glued to Madison's, Wilhelm reached back and picked up the lancet. He held it up in front of her face, its sharp point bright and inviting. "This is just the beginning to new worlds for you, Madison," he said in hypnotic words of seduction. "Just the beginning. Embrace it."

NINETEEN

When Madison came to, she was stretched out on the red velvet sofa in the back room of Bat Beauty. She was alone. Her sweater had been pulled up from behind. Her arms were still encased in the sleeves, but the neck had been pulled up and over her head, exposing her entire back. She sat upright and pulled her sweater back over her head, covering herself. Next to her on the sofa was a piece of paper. She picked it up. It contained the contact information for Sylvia Hannaford.

Leaning back against the sofa, she felt a stinging on the upper part of her shoulder, near the back of her neck. Reaching back, she felt a bandage. She also smelled alcohol. At least Wilhelm had sanitized the wounds.

A fuzzy glance at her watch told Madison she'd been at Bat Beauty for almost two hours. How much of that time was spent passed out or being sucked on by a gay vampire wannabe, she wasn't sure.

Taking the paper, she looked around for her bag before remembering that she'd left it locked in the trunk of her car. She headed out the door and through the bar while fishing her car keys out of the pocket of her jeans. She didn't look at the people at the bar, nor did she look for Wilhelm. She just wanted to get the hell out of Bat Beauty.

When Madison returned to the Dedham home, she went straight upstairs to her room. She wanted to plug into her computer and see if she could find anything on Sylvia Hannaford.

Once upstairs, she noticed the door at the end of the hallway was open. It was the door to the master suite. Thinking Doug and Dodie were up already, she went to the doorway and knocked. When she didn't get an answer, she stepped inside the dark room.

A gasp escaped Madison's lips before she could clasp a hand over her mouth to muffle the scream. On the bed were the Dedhams—side by side cadavers. Doug was on his side, one arm thrown across Dodie. Dodie was on her back, her hands folded ladylike across her chest like a relief on a sarcophagus. Her eyes were closed, but Doug's were open, staring without seeing. Dodie wore a nightgown; Doug, pajamas. Neither were covered by a sheet or blanket. Notwithstanding their spray tans, they were deathly white and waxy. And stiff.

"What are you doing in here?" a voice behind her demanded. Madison jumped. It was Pauline, standing in the doorway. In one arm she cradled folded laundry. The hand of her free arm was glued to her thick hip in annoyance. "You were told not to come in here."

"I … I … ," Madison stammered, her voice shaking. "I saw the door open and thought they might be up." She looked back at the bed. "They're dead," she whispered, a catch in her voice.

"Of course they're dead," Pauline said, not keeping her voice down. She snapped on the light, making the death scene on the bed even more ghastly. "They're vampires. What did you expect?"

Pauline pushed by Madison and walked to the triple dresser. Opening a drawer, she placed some of the clean clothing inside and closed it. She repeated the process with the remaining clothing in the next drawer down.

"But they're really dead, not sleeping." Madison inched back toward the door.

"Vampires don't sleep." Pauline took Madison firmly by the arm and guided her out of the room. On the way out, she snapped off the light and closed the door behind them. "Every day when they go to bed, they die. If you called in the coroner right now," Pauline explained, "he'd examine them, then call the meat wagon. And they can't be woken up like you and me. Shaking, noise—nothing brings them out of it until their bodies come back to life on their own. It's just the way it is." Pauline squeezed Madison's arm until it hurt. "It's also the only time they're vulnerable to attack, so it's important that no one goes in there while they're like that. They trust you, Madison. That means you must keep them safe, just like I do."

"There's no way to wake them?" Madison asked, looking back at the closed door.

"Only one way," Pauline said, her face close to Madison's. "Blood. The smell of fresh blood is the only thing that will snap them out of it."

Pauline let go of Madison's arm when they were in front of the guest room. "The Dedhams will be up soon enough." Pauline started down the stairs. "I'm heading home now, so you keep your nose out of their business and don't go in there again." She shook a finger at Madison. "You hear?"

Madison looked at the closed door to the master suite and shivered. She had no intention of going in there again.

The sun was almost down as Madison started up her computer and connected to the Internet. She checked her e-mail account. Nothing. There was never much, except spam. She started by Googling the name Sylvia Hannaford. Quite a few references popped up. She was starting to work her way through them, looking for something that might connect her to the right Sylvia Hannaford, when the wounds on her shoulder started throbbing.

As she reached over her shoulder to touch the place were Wilhelm had fed off of her, tears welled in her eyes. When it became difficult for her to see the computer screen, she got up and went to the window.

Twilight was upon the canyon, settling over it like a soft veil. Madison fixed her eyes on the house across the street, on the corner of the roof that peeked at her through the trees. In a few minutes it would be too dark for her to see it. Her tears came in earnest. Rolling down her cheeks, they dripped unchecked onto her sweater. She wiped them away with the back of her hand and went to the bed, where she'd tossed her duffle bag. Opening it, she started taking out the clothing, moving robotically as she hung the items in the closet.

Grabbing the tampon boxes, she headed into the bathroom to put them away, keeping busy to keep the memory of what had happened at Bat Beauty at bay. But when she saw her reflection in the mirror, a choking sob escaped her lips. Then another. She didn't look different, but she felt different. Wetting a facecloth with cool water, Madison pressed it against her swelling eyes.

Continuing to coo in a rhythmic, spellbinding voice, Wilhelm had coaxed her into submission, even as her last shred of will had stood against him like the last soldier standing in a conflict.

"Turn around," he'd ordered gently. "Face away from me."

When she had turned on the sofa so that she was sitting with her back to him, he'd raised her sweater from behind and lifted it over her head, leaving her arms encased in the sleeves. She'd helped him, not understanding why. Once the sweater was off, Wilhelm had gathered up her long hair, sweeping it over her right shoulder. Then he had kissed her on her neck, on the left side, at the very place he sought to defile. It hadn't been a sexual kiss but one of preparation, almost of worship. Madison had relaxed, taking a deep breath. Soaking in his words of persuasion, she'd given in to Wilhelm like a drowning man who realizes he's too tired to thrash any longer and accepts his fate.

When the lancet first stuck, Madison had cried out in pain. It had been fast, and the instrument had penetrated surprisingly deep for such a small blade. Almost immediately, Wilhelm had encircled her waist with one arm and clamped his mouth down on the wound, making gleeful sucking noises like a babe to a breast. Beneath his grasp, Madison had whimpered.

When Wilhelm pulled away, she'd thought it was over, but the lancet had struck again, and again she'd cried in pain. By the time the tiny blade had ripped into her skin for a fourth time, an emotionally and mentally exhausted Madison had passed out.

Lifting her face to the bathroom mirror, she lowered the facecloth and studied her reflection again. What horrified her wasn't what had happened but the fact that, if she were honest with herself, she'd liked it or had found it stimulating on some bizarre level. Jerry Lerma had called being bitten just that—stimulating.

Madison felt ashamed.

Turning her back to the mirror, Madison slid to the bathroom floor until she was sitting with her long legs straight out and her back against the cabinet. She tried to focus on the bathtub across from her, using the clean white porcelain to cleanse her mind.

"Madison, are you all right?"

Madison didn't move, just continued to stare glassy-eyed at the tub while she sniffed back tears.

Dodie Dedham, dressed in her nightgown and robe, stepped into the bathroom and looked down at the devastated young woman. "What is it, dear? We could hear you crying."

When Madison started weeping harder, Dodie slipped down on the tile floor next to her and took her in her arms. Madison gave in to the comfort of the older woman and nestled against her soft but cold body, clinging to her as the tears continued to flow.

Doug Dedham appeared in the doorway in his pajamas and looked down at the two women, a look of concern stamped on his face. Cradling the crying Madison, Dodie looked up at her husband and indicated for him to leave them alone for a bit. He tiptoed away without Madison ever noticing he was there.

For the next several minutes, Dodie held Madison, whispering words of comfort as she rocked her gently.

"I let him do it," Madison finally choked out without looking at Dodie. "I'm so stupid."

Keeping her voice soft and even, Dodie asked, "Who did what, Madison?"

"Wilhelm. I let … I let him suck my blood."

The rocking stopped as Dodie stiffened. "Wilhelm? The high priest at Bat Beauty? He attacked you?"

Still weeping, Madison shook her head against Dodie's shoulder. "He didn't attack me. I let him."

With ragged words, Madison gave Dodie a summary of what had happened at Bat Beauty and why she'd gone there. When Madison was done, her tears again flowed heavily. Dodie continued rocking and murmuring words of comfort, but her face was hard and her eyes flashed with anger.

"Someone will deal with Lord Wilhelm," she told Madison. "I can assure you."

"No." Madison turned her puffy face toward Dodie. "You don't understand. I *let* him. I bartered with him for the information about Sylvia. It was no different than if I'd dropped my pants and spread my legs." A sob from deep in her gut tore through Madison. "At least it felt no different." She pulled back a few inches and wiped her face with her hand. "Mike's right—I *am* a whore."

Dodie grabbed Madison by her shoulders and gently shook her, staring into her wet eyes. "You are no such thing, Madison Rose. No such thing. You hear me?"

"But … but …," Madison stammered. "I think I wanted him to do it. I think I liked it. I …"

Dodie's face softened as she tried to find words that would teach and comfort the girl at the same time. She moved her hands from Madison's shoulders and brought the girl back into her embrace.

"Being bitten or having your blood sucked is a very intimate act, Madison, as you've just learned. It's a lot like sex in that way. While it can be painful, it can also bring intense physical pleasure. We're not sure why, but it does. I think that's why so many of the living are into it, and why so many of the vampire movies and shows have sexual themes."

"It felt as if … as if he'd screwed me." Madison's voice was small and edged with disgust. "And I let him."

"Emotionally, Madison, he did. But you were also seduced, and by a man, it seems, well versed in mind control. Most of the coven leaders are very skilled at that. It's how some keep many of their followers loyal for so long. They mentally enslave them, especially the younger ones."

Dodie released Madison and held her so she could look into her face. "You are a good person, Madison. I know that, even if you don't. No matter what you've been through—no matter what you will go through in the future—never lose sight of the fact that you are a good and valuable human being." Dodie lightly touched Madison's chest, directly over her heart. "In here, pure gold. And don't you ever let anyone tell you otherwise."

Madison started crying again. No one had ever said anything like that to her before.

"I know it, and so does Samuel," Dodie continued. "Don't think for a moment that Samuel La Croix would have spared you had he thought you weren't worthy."

Madison remained quiet, trying to believe what Dodie was telling her about herself.

Dodie touched Madison's cheek with a fingertip. "Wilhelm should never have done this to you, and he knows it. Especially since he was under the impression that you're with Colin. There are certain codes within covens, even for the high priest."

Madison took a deep breath. "I think that's one of the reasons he *did* do it, because he thought Colin and I …," her words drifted off. "He has a thing for Colin."

"That may be, but it's still no excuse. Lord Wilhelm has lots of pretty and willing followers he can suck from without seducing you." Dodie's voice turned harsh before she caught herself and toned it down.

Dodie stood up and smoothed out her long robe. "Let me see the wound. I want to make sure it doesn't get infected."

While Dodie went to get her first-aid kit, Madison slipped off her top and studied her neck wounds in the mirror. They were larger than she expected, and she asked Dodie about it.

"Didn't you say Lord Wilhelm had fangs?" Dodie asked, cleaning the wounds.

Madison flinched as the alcohol hit the raw openings. "Yes. Dental implants that look like real fangs."

"Then I'd say that after he made the cuts, he inserted his fangs, making the openings larger so he could suck more."

Madison's stomach lurched at the thought.

Dodie readied a needle and swabbed Madison's upper arm with more alcohol.

"What's that for?" Madison asked.

"It's a tetanus shot," Dodie explained as she jabbed Madison with the disposable syringe. "I want to make sure you stay well."

"A tetanus shot? You just happen to have one laying around?"

"This might hurt for a day or so." Dodie put a small bandage on the puncture. "From time to time, vampires bring their human lovers to me for first aid. Even in a mutual consent relationship," Dodie told her, "things can get carried away. And it's not as if they can go to a doctor without raising questions." When she saw Madison's face go pale, Dodie added, "Don't worry, it doesn't happen often."

When Dodie was satisfied with the state of the wounds on Madison's neck, she said, "Come on now, let's both get moving. Before long, Samuel and the others will be here."

Madison groaned as she slipped her sweater back on. "Another council meeting. Dodie, I'm really not up for it tonight. Or for going out with Colin to Bloodlust—especially not that."

"Yes, dear, you are up to it." Dodie smiled at her. "I know you are. Besides, it's not a council meeting, it's just Samuel, Colin, Mike, Doug, and me. Mike has some more information on your friend Evie."

Dodie started to leave, but Madison stopped her. "Dodie," she began, struggling to find the words. "Thanks. For everything."

Dodie smiled at the hurt young woman and opened her arms. Madison fell into them again, this time not in despair but in relief.

Doug, now dressed, poked his head back into Madison's room. "Everything okay?" When Dodie gave him a positive nod, he entered. In his hands were two pieces of fruit.

"Here, Madison," he said, holding them out to her. "You'll need to eat something."

"Thanks, Doug, but I'm not hungry."

He pushed them on her. "We don't know how much blood the bastard took from you. Probably not much, but you still should eat a little something."

Madison took the fruit. "You heard?" she asked Doug.

Doug gave her a sheepish grin. "Unless we're asleep, we hear everything." He looked at Madison with compassion. "However you came to us, Madison, you'll always have a safe haven here. Know that."

Still clutching the fruit, Madison walked up to Doug and put her arms around him. She buried herself against his strength while his wife looked on with a smile.

"Thank you," Madison murmured.

Doug Dedham gently wrapped his arms around the young woman and gave her a tender squeeze. "You know," he told her quietly, "I once had two daughters. One was about your age when I was turned. Abigail and Caroline. I still miss them every day. Every year. Hell, every century." Madison looked up at Doug. He looked down into her face with warmth. "Maybe one day you'll let this old man tell you about them."

Madison eased herself out of his arms. "I'd like that, Doug. Truly."

Dodie beamed with happiness. "You like lasagna?" she asked Madison, who nodded with a slight smile. "Good, because I'm going to make it for your supper tonight before the meeting. Mike will be joining us."

TWENTY

I t seems that Evie Banks was involved with vampire covens," Mike Notchey told the group gathered around the Dedhams' formal dining table.

He'd announced the news earlier to Madison and the Dedhams over a dinner of lasagna and salad in the kitchen. Doug and Dodie had their usual animal blood—a new concoction Dodie had whipped up in the blender, mixing cow's blood with that of wild boar. At the last minute, she'd added a dash of sheep's blood for extra flavor.

Mike had seemed edgy during the meal and said he had other news that he didn't want to share until everyone was together. But whatever it was, it agitated him further, like a large splinter pushed deep under his skin, when Madison told him she'd visited Bat Beauty to get more information.

"Damn it, Madison," he'd barked after slapping his fork down on the table. "That was a very stupid and dangerous thing to do."

Madison shifted her left shoulder. She hadn't told Mike about Wilhelm, and she was pretty sure the Dedhams hadn't told him either. Doug had warned her, though, that Samuel would know just by looking at her and might bring it up at the meeting. Dodie confirmed that, saying Samuel could read a person's history as if it were stamped on their forehead. She also advised Madison that it would be best not to show fear if he questioned her about it. Show respect, Dodie had said, but not fear. Madison was not looking forward to the piercing stare of Samuel La Croix's dead eyes.

"It's not like I'm in prison here," Madison shot back at Mike. "I was told I could go anywhere I wanted."

"That doesn't mean you can behave stupidly. There's a reason why we sent Colin with you last night." Mike picked up his fork again but didn't go back to eating. He looked at Madison. "Are you at least going to tell me why you went back there?"

Madison rolled her eyes at him. "Colin remembered later that there was once a woman at Bat Beauty with a bloodline. Wilhelm said she'd left the coven to marry, but we wanted to make sure she didn't just disappear. I went to ask him for some information on her."

"And did Wilhelm give it to you?"

"Yes, he did." Madison looked down at the food on her plate and stuffed a forkful of pasta into her mouth before she said anything more. The Dedhams were silent.

"And?" Mike prodded.

Madison chewed, swallowed, and took a drink of the iced tea that had been freshly brewed by Pauline earlier in the day. "I did a search online using the information Wilhelm gave me. There were a lot of Sylvia Hannafords around the country, but I did find a wedding announcement for one here in California. Based on the photo I also found, I'm pretty sure it's the same one."

"So Wilhelm was telling the truth." Notchey went back to eating.

"The announcement was for several months ago, but I went on Facebook and found her. Lucky for me, she's using her maiden name of Hannaford as her middle name now." Madison played with her food. "As of this afternoon, she was posting to Facebook about her pregnancy. So there's one less dead girl with a bloodline."

"Good job," Mike said, half under his breath. "Stupid but productive."

Samuel listened intently while Mike continued filling them in on Evie Banks. Once in a while he jotted down some notes.

"They found more than just a little proof at her apartment," Mike continued. "Clothing, photos, books. She even had a small altar in a closet. Seems she was dabbling in witchcraft."

"Any particular coven?" asked Samuel from the head of the table. Colin was sitting to Samuel's left. Next to him was Madison. Doug and Dodie were on the other side of the table, to Samuel's right. Mike was seated at the opposite end, as before.

Mike shook his head. "Buddy on the case said there was no sign of any one specific coven, vampire or witch, but they did find photos of her taken at a party at Bloodlust. He recognized the setup in the background. But there was also a matchbook from Fang Me mixed in with her other trinkets."

"What about Bat Beauty?" asked Colin.

He was already dressed to go out to Bloodlust right after the meeting, and so was Madison. Tonight she was wearing snug black jeans and a black, clingy, sleeveless knit top with a mock turtleneck. The tiny bandage from the needle puncture was gone, and the turtleneck covered the larger bandage protecting the wounds Wilhelm had inflicted. Half of Madison's hair was piled on top of her head in a carefully disheveled manner, and she was wearing red lipstick so dark it was almost black. She'd purchased the lipstick and heavier eye makeup between her trip to her apartment and Bat Beauty. Dangling from her ears were large antique-looking earrings, another purchase made today at the drugstore where she'd bought the makeup. When she'd come downstairs for the meeting, every man but Doug had stared in fascination. It had made Madison uncomfortable, but judging from what she'd seen of the club scene so far, she was sure she'd fit right in at Bloodlust.

"So far," Notchey answered, "there's been no link to them or any of the other covens, but she was definitely into the vampire scene."

"But she seemed so shy and straight-laced," commented Madison, who was still having a difficult time believing that Evie had been involved with dark dealings. "Are you sure?" she asked Mike. "Isn't her father a minister or something like that?"

"They're often the worst—and the most vulnerable," scoffed Colin. "The more strict the upbringing, the wilder the kid once they get a taste of freedom."

"I'm afraid Colin is right. Not always, but often it's that way," Mike added. "Evie Banks was from a very strict home in a small town up north. Seems she moved here a couple of years ago against her family's wishes. At least that's what I've heard."

Madison thought of Geoff. "When Colin and I were at Bat Beauty last night," she told the group, "I met a young man who had just arrived from Nebraska a few months ago. He seemed awfully naïve to be in such fast company. And he had a bloodline."

Mike Notchey shifted in his chair and coughed. Samuel studied him, then said, "I sense Detective Notchey has some other unpleasant news for us. Might as well spill it, Mike."

Mike coughed again and rolled his neck to try and expel tension. Madison could hear the pops of his vertebrae with each head twist.

"Another body was found early this morning," Mike told them. "On a wooded jogging trail near Valencia. It was a young man." He glanced at Madison. "His name was Geoff Baxter."

Madison raised a hand to her mouth, then lowered it to squeak out, "Did he have a bloodline? The Geoff I met had a bloodline."

"Don't know about that yet, but I was told he was from Nebraska. At least he still had a Nebraska driver's license."

"Wilhelm said Geoff didn't show up for … for a meeting they had scheduled today." As soon as Madison said it, Colin and Samuel turned to her—Colin with angry surprise, Samuel with his usual stone face from behind dark glasses.

"Seems Miss Rose also has something to tell us," announced Samuel.

"Go ahead, dear," coaxed Dodie. "Tell them what you learned."

As Madison told the group what she'd learned about Sylvia Hannaford, Samuel took his sunglasses off and stared at her. Madison avoided looking at him.

"What is it you're not telling us, Madison?" Samuel demanded.

"That's about it. Seems this Sylvia, who Colin had met, did leave the coven to marry. She lives in Thousand Oaks now. And

Geoff didn't come by Bat Beauty today for his meeting with Wilhelm."

"And?" pushed Samuel.

Madison stirred up the courage to look in Samuel's direction. "And what?"

In an instant, Samuel vanished from his seat and popped up directly behind Madison. Startled, her breath caught in her throat, and she put a hand over her heart. The others seemed less surprised.

"Don't you have more to tell us, Madison?" Samuel coaxed in a soothing voice, not unlike the tone Wilhelm had used. He placed his hands on Madison's shoulders at the base of her neck. Madison stifled a cry of pain as one of his hands squeezed the area where she'd been cut.

"Wilhelm—," she started, but stopped as she fought not to cry.

"Wilhelm—," Dodie jumped in, but was stopped short by a look from Samuel.

"Let the girl tell us." Samuel pressed harder over the bandaged area. Madison winced, her eyes watering.

Madison focused her attention on Dodie and remembered what she'd told her earlier: show respect but not fear. Madison took several breaths while everyone waited. Samuel kept his hands on her shoulders.

Madison turned slightly in her chair and looked up at Samuel with as steady an eye as she could command. "Wilhelm sucked my blood." Madison managed to say the words evenly and clearly. "Is that what you wanted to hear, Samuel?"

"He did what?" Colin was on his feet.

"Goddamn it!" yelled Mike. "I knew you couldn't be trusted out on your own."

Without a word, Samuel grabbed the collar of Madison's jersey and tore it away from her neck on the left side, from the collar right through to the sleeveless opening, exposing the bandaged area. She let out a soft cry of surprise and clutched her shirt in front of her to keep it from falling. Samuel ripped off the bandage. Although Madison couldn't see Samuel's face, every other eye at the table was on him, watching in serious contemplation of what would come next.

With one finger, Samuel lowered Madison's bra strap down off her shoulder. The area was showing signs of bruising from the earlier aggressive suction. Then he squeezed the large puncture wounds. A soft gasp of pain escaped Madison's lips.

"Did you like it?" Samuel asked Madison, continuing to speak in a soft, persuasive tone.

"Now see here, La Croix," said Mike in anger. "That's quite enough. Stop torturing the girl."

When Samuel pressed harder on Madison's shoulder, Mike reached out to grab Samuel's arm. The head vampire's fangs shot out as he bared them at the cop. "I wouldn't if I were you," he warned.

Colin moved to Notchey and pulled him back from the table. The Dedhams looked on in silence. Like Colin, they were totally obedient to Samuel and would not interfere.

Madison looked straight ahead, her eyes fixed on the sofa in the living area of the great room, trying to forget that anyone else was in the room. "I'm not sure," she said in a small voice, answering Samuel's question.

"And what does that mean?" Samuel asked, his fangs still exposed, long, sharp, and deadly.

"It means …," Madison paused. "It means I did not enjoy that it was Wilhelm doing it to me."

Samuel gathered Madison's hair, just as Wilhelm had, and tossed it over her right shoulder. Leaning close to Madison, he rubbed his fangs over her long, graceful neck, several inches above Wilhelm's marks. She could feel their sharpness against her flesh.

"Maybe you'd like me to bite you?" suggested Samuel. "Believe me, it would be much more satisfying than the sucking of an old, delusional man." For a brief moment, he closed his mouth over Madison's neck, but he didn't bite. "Would you like that?"

Madison relaxed in her chair, a feeling of unexplainable peace enveloping her for the first time since she'd met the vampires. "I don't know, Samuel," she answered honestly. "But if you wish it, you have my consent."

"No!" shouted Mike, still restrained by Colin.

"This doesn't concern you, Mike," Doug said in a firm voice.

As if they were alone, Samuel turned Madison around in her chair so that they were face to face, showing her his terrifying fangs. She displayed no fear.

Samuel leaned in close to her neck again. "And why would you let me bite you?" he whispered to her.

"Because I trust you," Madison whispered back. When Samuel pulled away to look into her eyes, she reached up and placed the palm of her hand against his cheek. "Because I trust everyone at this table more than I've ever trusted anyone."

TWENTY-ONE

For a few moments, Samuel was still, his fangs exposed and threatening. Then, as quickly as he had arrived at her side, he was back at the head of the table. He retracted his fangs, replaced his sunglasses, and sat down as if nothing beyond a little misunderstanding had occurred.

Samuel looked at Colin, signaling him to release Notchey. "So, Mike," Samuel said. "Any ideas on who killed this Geoff Baxter fellow?"

Mike Notchey shook off Colin and stood bewildered, like a man who'd entered a private party by mistake. He looked at Madison, then at Samuel, not happy with either the recent news or the dental display. Colin sat back down on the other side of Madison, studying her now-exposed neck as he walked behind her.

Dodie left the table and returned with the cardigan sweater Pauline kept in the kitchen. She placed it over Madison's shoulders as Madison pulled her bra strap back in place. After giving Madison a gentle pat of reassurance, Dodie returned to her spot next to Doug.

"Geoff Baxter died the same way Evie Banks did," Mike explained, taking his seat but still watching Madison. "He bled out after receiving small but accurately placed cuts. It happened elsewhere, and his body was dumped in the woods."

Doug scrunched his brows in thought. "First time it's been a man, correct?"

"That we know of," Mike answered.

Turning to Madison, Doug asked, "And you're sure this Geoff person had a bloodline?"

"Positive," she answered.

Samuel tapped his pen on the notepad in front of him. "Seems whoever is doing this is no longer gender specific."

"There's something else I'm wondering about," Madison said. When all eyes turned to her, she continued. "Wilhelm told me about a ceremony at Bat Beauty—something involving the coven cutting and sucking the blood of newer members, people who volunteered."

"It's done on feast days," Colin said, turning to look at her, his eyes bright with intensity.

"Yes," Madison continued. "That's it. Feast days." She looked away from Colin as the strong erotic memory of Wilhelm's description started to shroud her purpose. "Apparently, the members cut these volunteers and suck their blood over the course of several hours. Maybe that's what happened to these people."

"But no one dies from those ceremonies," Colin added. "I've seen them."

"Seen them, yes," Madison said, looking at Colin. "Wilhelm told me you attended one." She looked quickly away, mindful of Samuel's eyes on both of them. "But what if sometimes these ceremonies get carried away? What if not all the covens took the same care as Bat Beauty and the sacrifices of these members included death?"

Notchey leaned in closer to Madison, totally forgetting about the earlier drama. "It's possible you're onto something here, but I don't recall any evidence that the other women were into vampirism." He sorted through some of his notes as he spoke. "Did Wilhelm say anything about other types of ceremonies?"

Madison shook her head. "No, just that one."

Samuel looked to Colin. "How about you? Ever see or hear anything about members being bled to death?"

Colin also shook his head. "Never. I've witnessed feast days at most of the covens I've visited, and they are pretty much the same. Lilith at Fang Me has mentioned blood bars, but I've never seen concrete evidence that they exist outside of our own vampire culture. That doesn't mean they don't, of course."

Madison's eyes widened. "There really are such things as blood bars?" She turned to Colin. "I thought Lilith was just teasing you."

"No," said Dodie moving her head up and down with quick, short movements. "They exist. Scarlet, the place I took you on Monday, is a vampire blood bar."

Madison drew her lower lip into her mouth while she digested the information. She'd not given much thought to where the blood Dodie had ordered at Scarlet had come from, just that Dodie had assured her that no one had died to provide it. "So blood bars are places where vampires can get human blood by the glass, like ordering a merlot or chardonnay?"

The vampires all glanced at each other. Finally, Dodie cleared her throat and prepared to set the record straight. "That night I had a glass of human blood—blood that was donated by a willing human. It's like making a donation to a blood bank, but for money. As you may have already discovered, some vampires prefer blood fresh from the vein."

"Some?" Samuel said. "Don't sugarcoat it, Dodie. Tell the girl the truth. She needs to know."

"All right," Dodie said, not pleased with having to be so blunt. "Not some, Madison; all—all of us prefer blood straight from the vein. But that doesn't mean we run amok like savages—at least, most of us don't. In the back room at Scarlet, a vampire can go and get sustenance directly from a human who is paid to provide it."

"Paid well, I might add," commented Doug.

Madison frowned. "That sounds like a brothel."

Samuel tilted his head back and laughed heartily. "That it does, Madison. Though at Scarlet, sex isn't on the menu, just the blood. But there are places for both."

Madison looked at Samuel with confusion. "And there are beaters who do this, and you don't fear them telling anyone?"

It was Mike Notchey who continued her education. "There's a whole service industry out there that caters to vampires, Madison. People like Pauline who care for their homes and personal needs, those who provide human blood, deliver animal blood, take care of their business and finances. It's a small, tight, and very secretive service community."

"That's paid very well," repeated Doug.

"Yes," Mike conceded. "People who are paid well to do what they do and keep their mouths shut."

"And they know if they talk, they will die," added Samuel, the laughter gone from his voice.

"Okay," said Madison, ignoring the die part and turning the information around inside her head with the other stuff. "So if there are blood bars for vampires, then why can't there be blood bars for the covens?"

"There very well could be," agreed Mike. "And probably are. But they would be very deep underground—so underground that even Colin here hasn't seen them."

"That doesn't mean these people weren't killed at one," Madison persisted. She shivered at her next thought. "Maybe their blood was drained and stored to keep the covens provided with human blood for those who drink it or for special events. Like Dodie said, it's like making a donation to a blood bank, but in these cases it wasn't voluntary."

"But why only people with bloodlines?" Dodie asked. "Seems if these poor folks were killed during a ceremony or at a blood bar, the bloodline wouldn't matter."

Notchey leaned back in his chair. "Sorry to say this, but I think someone—a beater *outside* the service industry—knows about the bloodline and what it means. Could be, they think the blood of people with bloodlines is special."

Madison looked down at the fake bloodline in her own hand and rubbed it. It didn't go away. It felt like having a target on her back, but then it was meant to be exactly that.

"Outside of Geoff noticing my bloodline last night," she told the group, "only two other people have taken notice of it. Although she didn't say anything at the time, I'm sure Lilith at Fang Me was surprised by it." Madison didn't want to say the other name but knew she had to, and if she didn't, she knew Samuel would know by getting into her head like an unwelcome bed bug. "Kyle, my boss at the diner, noticed it when I was in there today."

Colin jerked his head in her direction. "What did he say? Did he seem surprised?"

"He just wondered what it was. I told him I thought I'd broken a blood vessel or something like that and it was starting to go away." Madison shrugged. "That was it."

Samuel's jaw was tight. "He didn't say anything to you about Evie having one like it?"

"No. Nothing like that. He just seemed curious. But I thought I should mention that he'd noticed it."

"You did the right thing, Madison," Samuel told her. "Anytime anyone notices that bloodline, tell one of us, especially Colin if he's with you at the time. Your boss, does he work at the diner at night?"

"Sometimes."

"Do you know where he lives?"

Madison nodded.

Samuel paused before speaking again. Everyone waited. "Doug. Dodie," he finally said. "I want you to follow this Kyle person from sundown to sunup, starting immediately. I'll have Gordon take over from sunup to sundown."

Madison was puzzled. "Who's Gordon?"

"Gordon is Samuel's personal driver and bodyguard," Dodie explained. "He's waiting outside right now."

Curious, Madison got up and went to the window. Pulling back the drape, she spotted a dark sedan parked in front of the house. Leaning against the car was a tall, beefy man in a dark suit.

"What about that man you recognized at Dark Tidings?" Dodie asked Madison. "Have you placed him yet?"

"No, not yet. I keep thinking about it, but nothing comes to me."

"What man?" asked Mike.

"There was a guy at the Dark Tidings coven I thought I'd seen somewhere before, but I can't remember where."

"Was he in one of the photos I showed you?" Mike pulled a folder out of a case he'd brought with him. From it, he retrieved the photos of the coven leaders and spread them on the table for Madison to have another look.

Madison came back to the table. She pushed the photos of Lord Wilhelm, Lady Harriet, and Lilith to the side and studied the others. "No, he's not here. But this one," she tapped a photo in the pile. "He was tending bar at Bat Beauty today." She looked at Mike. "Do you have a photo of Ethan Young?" She shot a glance at Colin. "Wasn't that his name? The leader of Bloodlust?" Colin nodded.

Mike pulled a photo out of the pile and showed it to her. "This is Ethan Young."

The man in the photo fit close to the description Lilith had given them. He wasn't a big guy but looked very built, with a shaved head and trimmed goatee. The wire-framed glasses perched on his nose gave him an intellectual air, while the tattoo Lilith described was nowhere to be seen in the photo.

"Colin," Samuel said, continuing to hand out further orders, "you keep making the rounds of the covens with Madison. Give her some room to roam without you, but not too far. Mike and I will work our respective contacts. I'll also get someone to cozy up to Lilith and see what she might know. Isabella Claussen just got back into town. I'll see if she can do it."

Samuel looked at Madison. "I also want you to go back to Bat Beauty tomorrow afternoon."

Both Colin and Mike started to say something, but Samuel stopped them. "Now that he's had her blood, he may not be suspicious of her intentions," he explained. "He might think she's coming back for more." He looked at Mike. "Will the news about Geoff Baxter be in the paper or on local TV news?"

"Some information was on TV tonight."

"Good." Samuel returned his attention to Madison. "Show up under the pretense of seeing it on the news and offer your condolences."

Madison spoke up. "I don't think Wilhelm killed Geoff. He seemed genuinely pissed that Geoff didn't show up today. He would never have mentioned him if he'd killed Geoff himself, would he?"

"Probably not," Mike told her. "Unless it was an act to throw suspicion away from him once the death was discovered."

"Mike's right," said Doug. "So be very careful. But if Wilhelm is grieving, he might want to talk about Geoff. You may be able to find out if Geoff was hanging out at other covens in addition to Bat Beauty. Just don't stay long."

"And for bloody sake," Colin barked, "don't let the bastard drink your blood!"

Everyone turned to stare at Madison. Unperturbed, she scowled back in return.

Samuel started gathering his notes, signaling that the meeting was almost over. "We have to find out who is doing this and stop them. If Mike is right and this person knows about bloodlines, then he knows that we really exist. We've got to nip this in the bud before everyone knows."

Madison chuckled.

Colin glared at her. "You find this amusing?"

"No, I don't," she answered truthfully. "I just thought of something one of my foster mothers, a religious nut, used to say all the time." She clutched the sweater together in the front of her with one hand. "Something like, 'the devil's greatest trick was convincing the world he didn't exist.' Seems to me it's the vampire's greatest trick, too."

TWENTY-TWO

Madison was upstairs going through her closet, looking for something to wear now that her top had been torn to pieces. She didn't own many trendy things to start with, and now she was down one garment—a favorite top she'd purchased only after patiently waiting for it to go on sale. She'd wanted to say something to Samuel but thought better of it, under the circumstances. She'd meant what she said about trusting him and the others, but she didn't want to push her luck when it came to ruined clothing. She didn't know what any of the vampires did for a living except for Stacie and Eddie, but they all seemed flush with cash and oblivious to those who weren't.

An idea struck Madison as her eye caught on the tee shirt she'd worn to bed. It was a favorite of hers that she'd picked up in a used clothing store when she'd first come to Los Angeles. The faded black tee shirt, size men's large, hung on her and came well past her hips. It was a souvenir shirt from the Rolling Stones' 1972 US Tour, touting big red lips, white teeth, and a huge red tongue on the front. As she held it up in front of herself and looked in the mirror, a knock sounded on her closed door.

"Madison," asked Dodie through the door, "may I come in?"

"Sure," Madison called to her, still studying the tee shirt in the mirror. It didn't look half bad with her jeans and boots.

Dodie came in and shut the door behind her. "I wanted to bandage those wounds before you got dressed." Dodie eyed the shirt. "That could look very cute with the right accessories. Very hip, isn't that what it's called?"

"Not sure it will cover the bandage, though. I don't have many things that will."

"Let's see what we can do after I patch you up." Dodie took Madison into the bathroom and washed the cuts. They weren't that bad, but Dodie knew that puncture wounds could get infected easily, and she didn't want to take any chances. "There," she announced when she was finished. "I think that will do. I used smaller bandages this time. Fortunately, Wilhelm cut you on the back of your shoulder instead of on your neck. Now let's try that shirt on."

Madison slipped the shirt on over her head. It hung like a sack on her, and the collar gapped. She started rolling up the sleeves. "I think this will help." Dodie helped her with the rolling. It did make it look better, but it was still just a man's tee shirt.

"Wait here," said Dodie. "I have just the thing." When Dodie returned, she was carrying a couple of items. One was a wide black leather belt with an ornate buckle. She handed the belt to Madison. "Here, try this."

Madison fastened the belt low on her slim hips. "That definitely helps. Thanks."

The other item Dodie had was a very long silk scarf in silver and black with fringe on the end. She loosely draped it around Madison's neck twice, leaving the long, feathery tails to hang in front. "There," she pronounced. "It completes the outfit, and it covers your neck in case the collar slips down."

Madison looked in the mirror. It was a doable club look, especially for a club with dark themes. Then suddenly she felt sad, wishing she'd had such moments with her mother.

Madison released the hair that had been pulled up and started brushing it out, leaving it loose. "This should help with the neckline, too."

Dodie looked at the young woman with pride. "You look quite fetching."

"Huh," Madison said as she stopped fussing with her hair. "That's what Lilith said yesterday."

"Lilith at Fang Me?"

"Yeah. She said something like how Ethan Young would find me fetching." Madison laughed. "Odd. I've never been called that before. It's such an old-fashioned term, and now two of you have said it almost back-to-back."

Dodie picked up some makeup and started dabbing at Madison's black eye, touching up the cover job. "Well, you are fetching. And there are three men downstairs who have noticed, so I'm sure Mr. Young will also."

Madison put down her brush. "Three men? You mean Mike, Colin, and Samuel?"

"I certainly don't mean Doug," said Dodie, feigning shock. "Though he does find you adorable, but only in a fatherly kind of way."

Madison shook her head. "Mike yells at me. Colin can't stand me. And Samuel was pissed enough to want to bite me. I hardly think I'm making a great impression." She paused as she reached for her leather jacket. "And I'm not sure I want to make that kind of impression. Mike's as big a mess as I am, and the others are ... well, vampires."

"I dated Doug before I was turned," Dodie pointed out. "And Jerry married Kate."

"Uh-huh," Madison said, heading for the door. "Thanks, but no thanks."

Colin was waiting outside on the motorcycle for Madison. Parked in front of his bike was Samuel's sedan. Gordon stood straight as an arrow next to the open rear passenger door. The two vampires were talking when Madison bounced out the front door and down the walk. The Dedhams came out behind her. Mike Notchey had already left.

Colin appraised her outfit. "Going grunge, are we?"

"It's my nightgown," Madison quipped.

Colin grinned. Samuel studied her in silence before walking to his car. Before climbing into the back seat, he turned to Dodie. "I thought about your request, Dodie. My answer is yes, providing circumstances play out as we expect."

Dodie slightly bowed her head toward the head vampire. "Thank you, Samuel."

TWENTY-THREE

Bloodlust was very different from Fang Me and Bat Beauty. For one, it was packed with people, even on a Wednesday night. The placard at the front door proclaimed Wednesday as fang night. Every person who wore fangs of one kind or another got half off the cover price, which was fairly steep to begin with.

After leaving the motorcycle and helmets with the valet, Madison and Colin stood in line behind scores of young people mostly dressed in various shades of black, gray, and red. Most of them had wax fangs that they flashed at the person collecting the cover charge. Once at the head of the line, Colin paid the full price for the two of them.

Inside, the place was throbbing with energy, and the décor and music were glitzy goth, as opposed to dark and depressing goth. It was Transylvania gone Hollywood.

As the two of them entered the club, Colin took Madison's hand and guided her through the throngs of people. Along the way, several people said hello to Colin. There were even a couple of people they'd seen in the back room at Bat Beauty the night before, and Madison was surprised to receive greetings of her own.

"Colin," she whispered, getting close to him. "There are people here from Bat Beauty. Do you think they don't know about Geoff yet? Seems odd they would be here when their friend was murdered. I hardly knew him, and I feel funny about being out partying."

Colin shrugged, his face impassive. "Difficult to say. Maybe they weren't close."

The club was on two levels. The lower level was mainly for dancing, with tables and booths scattered around the edges on various levels to give people seated in the back a view of the dance floor. Upstairs, there was a large loft area with more booths and tables. The music was still loud upstairs but better for customers who wanted to have some shot at conversation.

"I don't have the same contacts here since it's fairly new," Colin said to her. "We'll just have to mingle like regular customers."

They were working their way toward the stairs to the loft when they heard someone call out Colin's name. Turning, both of them saw Miriam.

Wilhelm's handmaiden had left her long, dark frock at home and was dressed in a black leather-looking mini-dress and boots. Her hair, worn in a single, long, demure braid the night before, hung loose down her back. Her demeanor was also not as meek as it had been at Bat Beauty.

When Miriam reached Colin and Madison, she only had eyes for Colin. "I didn't know you came to Bloodlust." The girl spoke to Colin with shiny, eager eyes.

"I've only been here a couple of times before," he told her. He held up his hand, in which he still clutched Madison's. "You remember Madison, don't you?"

Miriam gave Madison a side glance and a perfunctory nod, then returned her adoring gaze to Colin. "There's, like, this huge multi-coven party going on upstairs. Follow me."

They followed Miriam through the crowd and up the wide, curved staircase. A large group had commandeered the far corner of the loft area. Madison recognized a few of the people clustered around from the night before—some from Dark Tidings, some from Bat Beauty. She felt someone watching her and turned to see Lilith seated in the middle of everything, her eyes glued to Madison. Next to her was an attractive bald man with a goatee and glasses, whom Madison recognized as Ethan Young. With her eyes glued to Madison, Lilith's head was tilted toward Ethan and she was saying something to him. He turned to watch Colin and Madison, but Madison felt his attention riveted on her.

"Look who I found downstairs," gushed Miriam as she presented Madison and Colin to the main table, at which Ethan and Lilith sat like reigning royalty.

Ethan Young stood up and held out a hand to Colin. "You must be the Colin Reddy I've heard so much about. I'm Ethan Young, high priest of Bloodlust."

Ethan wore a loose white silk shirt only partially buttoned. As he bent to shake hands, it gapped enough to show off part of the large tattoo Lilith had mentioned.

"It's nice to finally make your acquaintance," Colin said, shaking Ethan's hand. "And this is Madison."

Ethan held his hand out to Madison, but not in shaking position. Instead, he held it out palm up. With a brief hesitation,

Madison placed her right hand palm down in Ethan's. He bent over it and kissed it gently. "Lilith was just telling me that she had the pleasure of meeting you last night," Ethan told her. "Welcome, both of you. Please join us. Here, Madison, sit next to me."

Following a jerk of Ethan's head, the others at the table cleared out, leaving it a private party. Ethan had Madison sit next to him on his right side. Lilith was on his left. But instead of sitting down himself, Ethan excused himself.

"Please pardon me for a moment," he told the table, "but I have to check on something." Ethan left, but he returned less than two minutes later.

"So what brings you two here tonight?" Ethan asked, settling himself back into his seat.

Colin leaned slightly toward Ethan to be heard over the music and other conversations. "We heard you attract quite a crowd on Wednesday."

Ethan looked out over the club and smiled. "The half price helps. Weekends, at full price, it's standing room only. Of course, the current frenzy over vampires is what really brings them in. Every time a new vampire movie or TV show comes out, my profits soar." Ethan picked up a bottle of beer from the table and hoisted it in the air. "May the fang fad last forever."

"Your coven as active as the club?" Colin asked.

Ethan nodded and cut his eyes back to Colin. "I'm happy to say both have been growing by leaps and bounds. A lot of people are curious about vampirism these days." He glanced at Lilith. "I was just trying to convince the Lady Lilith to merge her coven with mine. Together, we could bring true vampirism out into the open."

All eyes turned to Lilith, who was watching the exchange like a crouched black cat. "We'll see," she said with a sly smile.

Madison couldn't resist the urge to taunt Lilith. "I've heard that most of your coven's members have already moved over to Bloodlust." She made the comment with a straight face, as if delivering boring news about a traffic tie-up.

Lilith's eyes flashed. "Fang Me has been around a long time. Don't think it's dead quite yet."

Colin put his arm around Madison's shoulders and discreetly squeezed, signaling her to behave. Ethan's eyes danced from behind his glasses as he sensed and enjoyed the tension between the two women.

"There's champagne in the bucket next to the table," Ethan announced to them. "Grab a glass and help yourself. Me, I'm more of a beer drinker." He indicated the bottle in his hand.

"Neither of them drink, Ethan," Lilith informed him, taking a pointed gulp from her own champagne flute. "Maybe they should sit at the kiddie table?"

Ethan laughed. He had a thick, easy laugh. "Then what can I get you both?"

Colin stood up. "Thanks, but I'll get our drinks. I see someone at the bar I'd like to say hello to anyway." Before he left, Colin nuzzled Madison's ear and whispered, "Buddy up to Ethan. Find out what you can about him and his coven." Madison played along and let out a giggle as if he'd said something naughty.

As soon as Colin left, Ethan slid closer to Madison. "You're certainly a fresh face around here."

Madison looked him directly in the eye. "Fresh face or fresh blood?"

Again, Ethan laughed. He turned to Lilith. "You're right. I *am* going to enjoy this girl."

At his comment, Lilith aimed a smug smile past Ethan toward Madison, which put Madison on red alert.

Ethan turned his attention back to Madison. "You into that, Madison? You into having your blood sucked?"

His words woke the memory of Wilhelm nursing at her neck. She blushed, both in embarrassment and disgust.

The rise in her color was noticed by Ethan even in the dim light of the club. He leaned close to Madison. "Methinks the elegant Mr. Reddy already enjoys the fruit of your veins." Ethan chuckled and winked at her. "He may not drink spirits, but I'll bet he enjoys a fine red of another kind."

Madison almost laughed at the irony and wondered what they would think if they knew the truth about Colin. Knowing a real vampire was in their midst, would they be titillated—or scared out of their minds?

Lilith, overhearing, had her own comment. "Seems Mr. Reddy likes variety."

When Ethan and Madison looked her way, she tossed a glance at the bar, where Colin was chumming up to a very tall and willowy blond in tight leather pants and a black lace camisole. She was as drop-dead gorgeous as Colin, and together they made a striking couple. They had their heads together, talking discreetly. Colin's wavy black hair contrasted against her short platinum hair like piano keys. The woman said something to Colin that made him laugh and flash her a wide smile of white teeth.

"Stunning, isn't she?" Ethan's voice puffed with open appreciation.

"Who is she?" asked Lilith. "I've never seen her before."

"Name's Isabella Claussen," Ethan told them. "Comes around from time to time, but I haven't seen her in a while. Heard she travels a lot, something about international consulting work."

Madison knew the name. Isabella Claussen was on Samuel's vampire council. She was also the vampire he was going to assign to watch Lilith. Madison wondered if that was why Isabella was here tonight. She also wondered what kind of relationship she had with Colin to look so cozy.

"Looks like Colin's trading up," hissed Lilith with a look so smug, Madison wanted to slap it off her face.

Instead, Madison smiled at Ethan, knowing full well how to charm him. She'd made decent money conning lonely men in bars in and around Boise, batting her eyelashes and offering promises she never intended to keep. In the end, they wound up with their pants down, their wallets empty, unsatisfied and too embarrassed to call the cops. Except for one. That was the time she'd been arrested.

"Colin and I don't have an exclusive relationship," Madison said, keeping her eyes on Ethan.

"Well," he replied with an answering smile, "that's information worth having."

Turning to Lilith, Ethan said, "From what I hear, Isabella swings both ways, just like you, Lilith. Maybe the two of you can become BFFs? Or maybe Colin is trying to line up a threesome with Madison here." His grin was wide at the thought.

Lilith's eyes narrowed as she watched Colin and Isabella like a hungry tigress on the hunt. "If Colin and that woman have a threesome, it won't be with Alice in Wonderland here. It will be with me." She nearly smacked her lips at the thought.

"Well, here's your chance," Ethan announced as Colin, with a beverage in each hand, returned to the table with Isabella in tow. He made introductions. "I hope you don't mind, Ethan, if my friend Isabella joins us."

"Not at all." Ethan got up and gallantly welcomed Isabella as he had Madison. "Welcome, beautiful lady."

"Why don't you sit next to me," Lilith purred.

If Isabella Claussen had been sent by Samuel to keep an eye on Lilith, it was going to be easy pickings. Isabella gazed into Lilith's eyes, and the high priestess of Fang Me nearly drooled. With fascination, Madison watched Isabella work.

"Not to change the festive mood," Colin said, taking his seat next to Madison again, "but did you hear about that young bloke that was killed this morning?"

"This is Los Angeles, Colin," Ethan commented dryly. "Young men are killed here every day. So are young women."

"But this was one of Wilhelm's people," Madison added. "His name was Geoff Baxter. We met him last night at Bat Beauty."

Ethan and Lilith exchanged glances before Ethan answered. "Geoff? A young, good-looking kid from somewhere in the Midwest?"

Colin and Madison nodded almost in unison. "He come around here?" asked Colin.

"Yes," answered Ethan, the earlier mirth in his face now gone. "He was here quite often. Even talked to me about joining our coven."

"He was going to leave Bat Beauty?" Madison was surprised. "He seemed so devoted to Wilhelm."

Ethan took a drink from his beer before answering. "While Lord Wilhelm has his charms and his knowledge of vampirism is second to none in this town, he's not very progressive. Young people coming into the culture today want more than ancient rituals and feast days. They want fun. They want excitement." He took another drink.

Madison sipped her own drink. It was a combination of cranberry and orange juice with lime. Another just like it sat on the table in front of Colin. Across the table, Isabella played with a thin straw in a glass of clear liquid and lemon, but Madison never saw her take a drink. She wondered if the others noticed.

"Like Miriam over there," Ethan continued. "She's still an acolyte at Bat Beauty, but it's just a matter of time before she converts to Bloodlust. She's blossomed since coming here."

Miriam, sitting at a table across from them with several others, never took her eyes off of Colin. Whenever they looked her way, she would stretch her neck and lick her lips. Ethan caught it and laughed.

"Seems she's hot for you, Colin," Ethan said.

Lilith stopped mooning at Isabella long enough to snap with disdain, "She's hot for anything in pants with a taste for blood." She left off her seduction of Isabella to study Colin with amusement. "Though I do recall, Colin, that you're quite handy with a lancet. One of the best. Maybe you should do Miriam a favor and taste her before she explodes." She cackled. Ethan and Isabella joined in the laugh.

Madison reached up and touched the spot where she'd been sucked. She had no idea so many people were into it. She looked over at the cow-eyed Miriam. She'd been sucked on by Colin and craved more. Lilith wanted more of him, too. But it would be different between them if Madison allowed it to happen, because Colin wouldn't have to hide who he was with her. The thought frightened Madison to her core. She remembered his fangs and Samuel's ... and she remembered Dodie's first-aid kit. The vampires were wild wolves easily mistaken for well-behaved German shepherds.

"What about Dark Tidings?" Madison asked, getting her mind back in the groove. "Are its members coming here?"

"We get a lot fewer people from Dark Tidings," Ethan replied. "Mostly because that's more the intellectual, artsy set. Their members tend to be a bit older and more settled, less interested in dancing and drinking."

After a short lull in the conversation, Ethan stood up. "May I dance with your lady?" he asked Colin.

Colin looked at Madison. "If the lady would like that, certainly."

Ethan held out a hand to Madison. With a look of encouragement from Colin, she took it and followed him downstairs to the dance floor. The music was neither fast nor slow. Ethan gyrated to the beat, sometimes against her. She followed along. The band played something a little slower, and he took her into his arms and moved them through the music with ease.

"You should come around more often, Madison." He pulled her close so she could hear him. "Without Colin."

"To the coven or to the club?"

Ethan grinned. "To both. You belong to a coven?"

She shook her head. "I'm kind of new to the whole vampire scene."

"I thought you might be."

"Tell me, Ethan." Madison looked up at him. "Do you believe in real vampires? You know, the kind in the Dracula movies? Or just in the worship of blood and darkness?"

"How do you know I'm not a real vampire?"

"Vampires are dead. Do the dead drink beer?"

"Guess we'll never know until we die, will we?"

But Madison already knew the answer. The dead, or undead, didn't eat or drink.

"You didn't answer my question, Ethan. Do you believe that vampires exist or just that some people have a thirst for blood?"

He leaned in, his breath warm and damp against her ear. "More the latter, but if you repeat that, I'll deny it." He winked at her, gave her a spin, and brought her back close. "I'm a business-man, Madison. I've followed vampirism for years—long before it became the rage. But I'm a businessman first. I simply found a way to turn a passion into a gold mine."

When the song ended, a young man approached them and whispered something to Ethan, then melted back into the crowd.

"Seems someone is here to see me," Ethan explained to Madison.

"Go ahead. I'll find my way back upstairs."

"Not at all," he told her. "Come with me. Shouldn't take but a minute or two. Then I can show you the office and coven meet-ing room—give you the grand tour."

Taking her hand, Ethan directed her through the crowd as Colin had done earlier, but instead of heading upstairs, they went through a door to the right of the bar, marked Private. This led down a long corridor with other doors along both sides, all closed. They stopped in front of a door marked Office. Ethan opened this one and directed Madison inside.

Inside the room, pacing impatiently, was the man Madison had seen at Dark Tidings.

TWENTY-FOUR

Except for his clothing, the man looked exactly the same as he had in the hallway outside the bathroom at Lady Harriet's. He'd worn jeans and a dark turtleneck jersey that night. Tonight he had on nice slacks and a V-neck sweater, both in black. His brown hair was nearly to his shoulders, with one side caught behind an ear. When he saw Madison come through the door, his thin-lipped mouth dropped open slightly and his eyebrows shot up above the upper rim of his sunglasses. It was the only way Madison could tell he was surprised to see her.

"Madison, this is Ben," Ethan said once they were inside the office with the door shut.

Before Ben could say anything, Madison approached him. "We sort of met last night at Dark Tidings, but not officially." She held out her right hand to him and he took it, giving it a quick shake and a short grunt.

Madison was going to ask him where they might have met before, but Ben cut off any further pleasantries by jerking a thumb in her direction. "What's she doing here? This is a private meeting."

"And so it will be," Ethan assured him. "So stop being rude to my guest."

He turned to Madison with a smile and held out both hands to her, palms up. "This won't take long; please wait." Madison placed her hands in Ethan's. As he gave them a warm squeeze, he turned her hands over and released her right one, still holding her left. He took it in both hands and caressed it gently.

Madison glanced up at Ben. His mouth was still open slightly in surprise, but his brows had relaxed. In seconds, his mouth did, too, changing from a look of annoyance to a small, tight smile. Ethan was showing Ben her bloodline, she was sure of it.

Madison was on guard yet curious at the same time. Ethan had shown no interest in her hand before, but he'd obviously noticed it. And the bloodline meant something to both him and Ben. It occurred to Madison that Ethan had manipulated her down to his office for the purpose of meeting Ben. No, not to meet him, but to be seen by him. She had the strange sense of being on display, like a pork chop under plastic wrap at the supermarket.

"I have some business to attend to," Ethan told her as he squeezed her hand one last time and released it. "Why don't you go back upstairs and relax with the rest of them. When I'm done here, we can continue our dance. Shouldn't take too long."

Not wanting to show alarm, Madison smiled. Taking a step closer to Ethan, she placed a hand on his chest, over his heart, and poured on the charm. "Sounds good to me. Besides, you promised me the full personal tour."

Ethan flashed her a wide smile. Ben just stared at her from behind his sunglasses. As Madison headed out the door, the two men disappeared through an internal door marked with another Private sign and closed it behind them.

Madison wondered what to do. She wanted to hear what Ben and Ethan were discussing. She knew they saw her bloodline, and from their behavior, she was pretty sure they both knew what it meant, or thought they knew. She wanted to tell Colin about it, but if she left and went back upstairs now, she might not get the chance to eavesdrop.

The two men had been so sure she'd follow orders that they hadn't waited for her to leave and shut the outer office door before they went into the inner office. Madison waited a few moments before tiptoeing carefully back into the office and toward the closed private door.

Madison strained to hear something, wishing she had the vampires' keen hearing. It was then she realized she *could* hear a lot of what the men were saying. Snatches of conversation were finding their way under the wide gap at the bottom of the old door. The space between the door and the floor had probably been allowed for clearance over carpet. Now the floors were bare, but the door hadn't been replaced. Madison scooted closer and almost stopped breathing.

"How do you like your present?" she heard Ethan ask.

Ben chuckled. "She was right under my nose last night, but I never saw the bloodline. How'd you know?"

"Lilith told me when she saw the two of them walk in the door tonight. I called you immediately. One less you and your paid goons will have to find." Ethan paused. "You're sure it will work this time?"

"No, I'm not. All we know is that people with those blood-lines are key to turning vampires. Drinking the blood does it, but you need to drink a lot to turn yourself without an actual vampire doing it."

The hair on Madison's arms rose like spikes as she glanced down at the fake bloodline in her hand. That was it. These creeps thought that you could become a vampire by drinking the blood from a bloodline carrier. They had no idea that only those with bloodlines could become vampires. If she didn't get out of there, they would do to her what they'd done to Evie and Geoff. She swallowed back the memory of the photos.

"And if it doesn't work again?" asked Ethan. "Nothing happened after those first few."

"Then we'll keep trying till it does." Ben's voice was tinged with amusement. "The bloodline is the key. That we know for sure."

There was some mumbling that Madison couldn't hear, then she heard Ethan say, "Should be easy enough. She's a lightweight, and the music should cover any sounds of struggle. You have your van outside?" There was a slight pause and more mumbling before Ethan continued. "Good. I'll bring her down here for the tour." He laughed. "You be waiting with the chloroform."

"What about her boyfriend?" she heard Ben ask.

"There's a girl upstairs hot to trot for him. I slipped her some money and told her to keep him busy so I could put the moves on Madison. She was only too happy to do it, thinking I'm removing her competition. He's also a bloodsucker. Something tells me the offer of a piece of tail *and* a piece of neck will do the trick." This time both men laughed. "Miriam's one of Wilhelm's girls," Ethan continued. "Believe me, her talents are totally going to waste under the tutelage of that old fart." More chuckles.

Madison heard a drawer open, then close.

"Here's my share of the money for your people," Ethan said. "Between the last couple and this one, we might have enough blood for another try. Lilith's money is there, too. You might want to count that to be sure it's not light."

Careful her boots didn't make noise on the bare floor, Madison tiptoed back to the door. She had to be quiet but fast, not knowing how long before the two men would finish their business and Ethan would come looking for her. Once out the door, she gently closed it, but not all the way, fearing the latch would make too much noise. She ran toward the end of the corridor and entered the club, slowing down so she wouldn't cause any notice. Moving fast, she headed for the stairs, taking them two at a time to the loft.

Upstairs, things had changed. Colin was gone. So were Lilith and Isabella. Madison located her leather jacket and slipped it on.

"Do you know where Colin went?" she asked a man she'd seen at Bat Beauty the night before. He shrugged. She asked a couple more people, but no one knew.

Madison was about to descend the stairs when a young waitress balancing a tray of drinks stopped her. "You looking for that tall, dark-haired guy? The really good-looking one?"

"Yeah. Know where he is?"

The waitress made a face. "He left with that skank Miriam. She was throwing herself at him all night. Guess he finally gave in."

"Left? As in *gone*?" Madison couldn't believe Colin would go off and leave her behind.

"Not sure if they left the building or not, but they went downstairs and haven't come back." The waitress delivered drinks to a nearby table and returned to Madison. "You might try the catacombs," she said, signaling to another table that she'd be right there.

"What's the catacombs? Is that another club?"

The waitress leaned close to Madison. "Behind the bar, there's some stairs going down to some rooms the coven uses. Sometimes people go down there to suck blood on the sly or to fuck. Miriam might have taken him there."

Madison dug a few bills out of her pocket and dumped them on the waitress's tray. "Thanks." After a thought, she pulled out a ten and left that as well. "If anyone comes looking for me, you know nothing. And I mean *anyone*."

The waitress winked and moved on. Madison flew down the staircase. She had to find Colin and get them both the hell out of Bloodlust, hopefully before Miriam made him an offer he couldn't refuse.

Madison found the door leading to the lower level. It was located in a dark corner behind a heavy velvet drape. After making sure no one was watching, she slipped through the door and down a short flight of metal stairs. At the bottom was a good-size room with its lights on. At one end was a black altar. In front of it were an ornate table and lots of folding chairs set up in raggedy aisles. It was the Bloodlust coven's meeting room. Along one wall were a couple of drape-covered alcoves. From one of them came the unmistakable moans and grunts of sex in progress.

Madison wasn't sure what to do. She wasn't in the habit of breaking in on a couple, but she and Colin needed to get out of there. She listened just outside the drape but couldn't tell if it was Miriam and Colin. Finally, more worried about Ethan than delicacy, she peeked behind the drape.

The alcove was larger than she'd expected but still small. It held a small built-in bench with a pad and a chair. The space was dimly lit by a sconce. Inside were a couple in the throes of passion, but they were not the two she was looking for. Before they saw her, she discreetly let the drape drop and moved to the next alcove, which was empty. It was then her ears caught more moans. They sounded distant, like they were close but not in the immediate area.

Madison followed the sounds past the altar to a door that was ajar. Gently opening the door, she discovered a large storage room with boxes of supplies and unused furniture. A dirty overhead fixture cast a dull yellow glow over the room. Entering, Madison tread softly toward the sounds. She found the couple behind a tall stack of boxes containing paper goods. It was Miriam and Colin. As her eyes grew wide at the sight, Madison stepped behind the boxes, unsure of what to do.

Colin was seated in an old, beat-up chair, his pants around his ankles. Miriam, her dress hiked up to her waist, was impaled on his lap, her back to Colin. Moaning in jagged sobs, Miriam gyrated on top of Colin while he sucked on the back of her neck and made low growling sounds.

Unable to take her eyes off of them but unwilling to stay, Madison backed away. She'd retreated a couple of steps when she tripped and fell on her butt to the floor. In a trance, Miriam didn't notice, but Colin did. He turned toward Madison, fangs bared and bloody, his eyes glowing like embers.

Madison slowly got to her feet, her eyes riveted on Colin. While she watched, Colin raised his face toward the dim light and let out a low, guttural cry of primeval triumph. The girl in his arms joined him in his howl, then slumped against him with a whimper. Colin licked Miriam's neck clean while she released a chain of soft, satisfied moans.

Madison ran.

TWENTY-FIVE

When she reached the metal stairs leading back up to the club, Madison took two steps up, then paused. Ethan should be looking for her by now, so going through the club toward the main door could be dangerous. She contemplated going back to Colin, but that didn't seem appetizing either. She was deciding on the lesser of two evils when her eyes spotted a red light behind the stairs. It was an exit sign. It winked at her through the openings in the metal steps like an illuminated escape hatch.

Hopping off the steps, she ran to the exit. With her hand on the push bar, she hesitated again, worried that it was attached to an alarm. Above, the door to the stairwell opened a crack. Music drifted down into the bowels of the building.

"No one saw her leave," Madison heard someone say. It was Ethan's voice. "I'll check down here."

"Madison." It was a different voice speaking to her—one with an English accent. Standing at the threshold to the coven meeting room was Colin. The fangs were gone, his eyes back to their usual deep black. He was alone.

Madison didn't know if Ethan heard Colin above the loud music, but she wasn't taking any chances. With one last look at Colin, she gave the exit door a big push. No alarm sounded. On the other side was a short flight of dirty steps leading up to an alley. She flew up the steps and ran down the alley toward the busy boulevard at the end, hoping to lose herself in the crowds on the street.

She'd almost reached Hollywood Boulevard when Colin appeared beside her. He stopped her short with a strong grip on her upper arm.

"Madison, stop." He pulled her into the darkness of a doorway.

Madison jerked her arm away. "Go back to Miriam. I have more important things to do, like saving my skin."

"I'm sorry, Madison. I got carried away."

"Save it, Reddy."

She started running again. When she reached Hollywood Boulevard, she slowed down. Again, Colin was beside her in the blink of an eye.

"You have no way to get home," he pointed out. "Let's go back to Bloodlust and get the bike."

"No!"

After quickly looking around, Madison pulled Colin into another alley, away from the crowds. "This isn't about you, Colin." She grabbed both lapels of his jacket and shook him as she squeezed her words through clenched teeth. "Or about … about … what happened back there with Miriam. Ethan's going to turn me over to the killer. I heard him. Ethan and this guy Ben, the guy I saw at Dark Tidings, they're the ones killing people with bloodlines."

Colin stared at her for a second, then steered her behind a dumpster. "Wait here," he ordered.

"Not on your life." Madison kicked the dumpster with her booted foot. "I'm not staying in any dark alley alone, waiting for a psycho with a chloroform rag. Better I stay with lots of people. You know, safety in numbers."

With a nod of agreement, Colin escorted Madison out of the alley and walked her down the street away from Bloodlust. They stopped in front of a crowded Starbucks.

"Go inside," Colin told her. "But stay by the window and watch for me. I'll be back with the bike in just a minute." He took one last look at Madison, then vanished.

It seemed like an eternity before Madison spotted the motorcycle, but in truth it was just a few minutes. The bike came to a stop in a loading zone in front of the coffee shop. She ran out and hopped on the back, fastening her helmet as Colin took off.

They rode along for quite a while. Occasionally, Colin would weave in and out of side streets in case anyone was following them, but all the time they headed west, toward the ocean. Shortly after they hit Pacific Coast Highway, Colin turned into the underground garage of a high-rise condo. Pulling into a space near the back of the garage, he stopped the bike and motioned for Madison to dismount and follow him. They entered an elevator, where he used a key card to gain access to one of the top floors.

After what she'd seen, Madison wasn't sure she wanted to follow Colin anywhere, but she knew she didn't have many options. She'd tipped the waitress using most of her pocket cash and didn't have her cell phone. And even if she did, who would she call? She'd never bothered getting the telephone number for the

Dedhams. The only one she might be able to reach would be Mike Notchey. She could call his station and ask them to patch her through, telling them it was an emergency. She'd said back at the Dedhams that she trusted everyone seated at the table. Colin was one of those people. It was time for Madison to put her money where her mouth was.

"Who lives here?" Madison asked as they got off the elevator.

"I do."

Madison stopped in her tracks as Colin continued down the hallway lined with plush carpet and expensive wall sconces. He stopped in front of one of the doors and put a key in the lock.

"You coming?" he asked, opening the door.

Madison took a deep breath and trotted down the hallway toward him.

The door opened into a huge living room. The outside wall was a bank of windows. Madison walked to the windows and looked out. They were very high up. Below, she could see cars moving along Pacific Coast Highway like late-night beetles scurrying home. Looking forward, she saw black, some stars, and the moon high in the sky. Every now and then, moonlight would shimmer across the ocean like ribbons of liquid silver.

"Looking out makes me feel like I'm drifting in outer space," she said, not turning around. "Bet it's awesome in the daytime."

"It is," Colin replied, coming behind her to look out. "Though I've seldom seen it. But I love the night view. And you're right, it does feel like being in space."

He took her helmet from her and walked away, heading for the kitchen area, which was separated from the living room by a long stone counter, at which were positioned four tall stools. The apartment was incredible and sleek, but it was also stark and cold, with no personal touches whatsoever. The only color came from a large crystal bowl filled with oranges, tangerines, and lemons.

"I can offer you hot tea or water," Colin said to her as he put her helmet on the counter with his own.

"What's with the fruit?" Madison asked as she shed her jacket and hopped up on a stool.

"Or fruit. I have fruit." He grinned, then explained, "I love the smell of oranges, most citrus actually. So I keep it about." He filled a teakettle with water and placed it on the stove. It looked like the only cooking utensil he owned.

"And the tea?"

"Same thing. I like the comfort of it, even though I cannot drink it. Guess it's an English thing—or more likely an Indian thing. Though tea was just a novelty in England when I was … before I turned." The words were spoken with a touch of sadness. "Some evenings, especially if I'm reading, I'll brew a pot and hold the warm cup in my hands. It seems so …"

"Normal?" Madison ventured.

"Quite."

"The Dedhams do that, too. They have favorite smells around that remind them of the past. Dodie loves to bake just so the house smells good."

Colin picked up a navel orange and leaned against the counter. He started peeling it, sending a sweet, juicy scent into the air. When he was done, he handed it to Madison. "Please. I'd like to know someone can enjoy their flavor."

She took the peeled orange and broke it into sections, placing them on a napkin Colin provided. She took a bite. It was fresh and succulent. When the teakettle whistled, Colin placed a tea bag in a sturdy mug and filled it with hot water.

"If I were truly a proper Englishman," he told Madison as she watched, "I'd be making this with loose tea in a china teapot." He picked up a lemon and held it up in question. "I don't have any milk, I'm afraid."

"Lemon's fine," answered Madison, swallowing the orange in her mouth.

"If you like nice scents," she said, looking around, "then why don't you have flowers in here? I've noticed that Dodie loves fresh flowers in the house."

Colin smiled. "Dodie Dedham is the best homemaker I've ever come across—alive or dead." He removed the tea bag from Madison's mug and slid in a freshly cut lemon slice. "That should warm you up and calm you down," he said, pushing the mug in Madison's direction before turning to the sink to wash his hands.

"About tonight, Madison." He turned around while wiping his hands on a towel. Madison was blowing over the surface of her hot tea.

"Which part of tonight, Colin?" She put her mug down, lest she stop feeling so trusting and throw it at him. "The part where you boffed and devoured Miriam, or the part where someone wanted to kill me?"

"Let's start with Miriam and work our way up, shall we?" Colin put down the towel and leaned against the counter. "I was only doing what comes naturally to me, Madison. I am, after all, a vampire."

The calm, civil tone in Colin's voice annoyed Madison. "First of all," she said, holding up an index finger, "I thought you were avoiding Miriam."

"I was, it's just that she was … well, rather persuasive."

Madison slapped her hand on the counter. The tea in her mug jiggled. He might have had a jolly good vampire time, but she hadn't.

"It was a setup, Colin. Miriam was paid to seduce you to get you away from me." Madison rolled her eyes. "Not that she wouldn't have done it for free." She held up two fingers. "And, secondly, you were supposed to be keeping an eye on me, to some degree. If Ethan hadn't been so smug as to think he could entrap me later, I would be dead right now, or at least drugged in the back of a van."

Colin put both of his hands flat on the counter and leaned toward Madison without one shred of remorse on his handsome face. Instead, his face was pinched with anger. Madison wasn't sure if it was aimed at her, Miriam, or himself.

"I admit, I've made a right hash of it, Madison. But vampires suck blood. Miriam cut her own neck and paraded it in front of me. It also sounds like you might have been dead even if I had stayed upstairs with the rest of the party." He leaned back against the sink again, his face a dark bucket of brooding.

Madison became alarmed. "Miriam doesn't know you're a vampire, does she?"

"No, but she knows I have a thirst for blood, like many in the covens. And she has a desire to be … sucked."

Colin ran a hand through his thick black hair. "Vampires are like animals, Madison. Remember that. Most of the time we can control our urges, but sometimes we regress to our more primitive side. Remember Samuel tonight at the Dedhams'? When he saw the marks Wilhelm had left, he came dangerously close to savaging your neck for real."

"What?" Madison was shocked. "I thought he was just mad at me."

"He was, but he also wanted you—your blood and your body. Like an animal, he can smell fresh blood and open wounds. We all can."

Madison gave that serious thought. "But Dodie didn't mention that when she fixed Wilhelm's cuts."

"Trust me, Dodie covered those up and doused them with alcohol for a lot of reasons, one of which was to mask them from us and our natural tendencies."

"But what about Dodie? She didn't seem turned on by them. Nor did Doug."

"She's a younger vampire. She has less impulse along those lines. And both she and Doug have a protective instinct toward you. But if Samuel had bitten you, they would not have interfered."

Madison felt squeezed from both sides, as if two opposing walls were closing in on her—vampires on one side and those wanting to be vampires on the other. Pushing her tea away, she cradled her head in her arms on the counter. "What am I going to do?" she asked herself, not Colin.

"You're going to continue to assist us and stop whoever is doing these killings."

She shook her head in final surrender. "I'm going to die one way or the other. It's up to me to choose how, right?"

Colin arched an eyebrow at her. "You're not going to die, Madison. Not unless those bastards get their hands on you or unless you do something incredibly stupid. That's why I brought you here tonight. Doug and Dodie are on surveillance till morning. I didn't want you to be alone."

Silence fell between them. Colin pushed Madison's tea back in front of her. She picked it up and took several soothing swallows.

"Now," said Colin. "Tell me everything you found out. Then we're going to call Samuel."

Upon receiving the call, Samuel came straightaway to Colin's. He wanted to hear what had happened at the club personally from Madison. She told the two of them everything she had heard and seen at the club, over and over. Samuel questioned every detail, often asking the same question more than once but in a different way. She felt like she was being interrogated by the police or a lawyer.

"You're sure," Samuel pressed, "they mentioned Lilith as being involved?"

"Yes," Madison answered. "Both Ethan and Lilith gave money to Ben. Ethan said something about it being for Ben's people."

Colin glanced at Samuel. "Sounds like this Ben is the one hiring the guys grabbing the ones with bloodlines."

Samuel nodded but kept his eyes on Madison. "And you're sure Ben is the same man you saw at Dark Tidings? The one you think you know from somewhere else?"

"Yes." Madison squeezed her eyes shut in concentration. "Even his voice is familiar, but for the life of me, I still can't place from where."

"Did you see Ben?" Samuel asked Colin.

Colin shook his head. "Not tonight, but I vaguely remember him from Dark Tidings." He turned his eyes to Madison. "Long, light brown hair and dark glasses. Right?"

"That's him." A new thought crossed Madison's tired brain. "What about Lady Harriet?" she asked with some alarm. "She has a bloodline. If he's noticed, might he go after her?"

Colin's eyebrows raised at the thought. "There's a horrible thought."

"Makes you wonder," Samuel observed, "why he hasn't done it yet. He obviously knows what he's looking for."

"Perhaps it's because she's the leader of his coven," suggested Colin.

"But if he runs out of available bloodlines," added Madison, getting worried, "he might go after her. He started with young women, then killed Geoff. Doesn't sound like he has a preference anymore."

"True," agreed Colin. "He might just be going after what he believes to be easy targets. If he's desperate for a bloodline, he might overlook the fact that Lady Harriet is his superior at the coven."

Madison looked at Colin, then Samuel. "Shouldn't we warn her?"

Without answering, Samuel walked to the window and looked out into the darkness. "What concerns me is that these beaters have discovered that the bloodlines are connected to us."

"But they don't know how," Madison told him. "They think the blood from someone with a bloodline is special—that they just have to drink it to turn into vampires." She paused and looked at Colin. "That's not how it works, is it?"

"No," Colin confirmed. "Only a vampire can turn a blood-line holder into a vampire, and it's an involved and dangerous process."

"Still," said Samuel, facing the view, "this means they are sure we exist."

Madison was puzzled. "When we were dancing, Ethan told me he didn't believe vampires really existed ... or that's what it sounded like he meant."

"He could have been lying to keep you off guard." Samuel turned back to them. "He probably knew by then that he was going to turn you over to Ben."

Samuel walked back to the counter and took a stool next to Madison. "Did they say anything about where they were storing the blood from the bloodlines?"

Madison shook her head. "No, or they did and I didn't over-hear it. But it definitely sounded like Ben was in charge of getting the blood."

"Fresh blood doesn't have a long shelf life," Colin pointed out. "By tomorrow or the next day, they will be needing to replenish their stock. That means more deaths."

"We need to get to these men and make them talk," Samuel decided. "We have to find out if others are involved besides them and Lilith. Ben might be in charge or he might be just another paid employee like Piper and that bastard in jail."

A phone rang. Samuel pulled a cell phone from his pocket and looked at the display. "It's Isabella. Let's see how her evening went with Lilith." Taking the phone, he walked back toward the windows.

While Samuel spoke with Isabella, Madison folded her arms on the counter and lowered her head again. It wasn't until she woke while being carried by Colin that she realized she'd fallen asleep. He placed her on a bed.

"What are we going to do?" she asked him in a sleepy voice as he pulled off both her boots.

"*We're* doing nothing," he told her. He pulled a cover over her. "You're going back to sleep while Samuel and I figure this out. It will be morning soon. Then I'll take you back to the Dedhams'. And you are *not* to go to Wilhelm's today, as was planned. Is that clear?"

She gave him a sleepy nod in agreement.

TWENTY-SIX

Colin didn't take her back to the Dedhams', Samuel did. They left Colin's just before sunrise. Gordon and Samuel's black sedan were nowhere to be seen. Instead, she was guided to a sleek silver Mercedes sports coupe. Samuel settled in behind the wheel.

"You can drive?" she asked the blind vampire.

"My eyes may seem incapacitated," Samuel told her from behind his sunglasses, "but they see as well as yours. Maybe even better."

It was then Madison remembered what Pauline had told her about Samuel regaining his sight after he became a vampire. "It's still hard to believe someone gave you a driver's license."

"Who says I have one?"

Madison jerked her head in his direction but said nothing.

Samuel started the engine and pulled the car out of the parking spot. "Now buckle up."

Madison snapped the seat belt in place. "Just remember, you may not be able to die, but I can. Seems you vampires let that slip your minds on occasion."

Samuel chuckled softly.

They rode in silence for several minutes before Samuel glanced Madison's way. "Are you upset because you saw Colin biting that woman or because he wasn't biting you?"

"What?" Madison shifted in her seat to look at Samuel. He certainly wasn't one for beating around the bush. "I'm upset because I was nearly kidnapped—for a second time in less than a week, I might add. And Colin—who was supposed to have my back—was nowhere around."

They stopped at a red light. Samuel looked at her. She squirmed in her seat and looked away, knowing he could read her like a neon sign.

"That is a good reason to be upset, yes. But it's not what's on your mind right now, is it?"

Madison shrugged. It was dawn. The sky was gray but full of bright promise. They were driving along Pacific Coast Highway, with the ocean to their left. She concentrated on the sea, trying to replace the picture of Colin and Miriam in her mind with the serenity of the waves.

"It won't work, you know." Samuel moved the car forward when the light turned green.

"What won't work?"

"Trying to block me out. No matter what you're thinking now, I'll just skip over it and read your past thoughts."

"That's just plain annoying, you know that?" Madison crossed her arms and sulked.

"Maybe. But I find it very useful."

"Then why bother asking me anything?" Madison snapped. "Just read away."

"I'd rather hear it from you. I want you to express your feelings, not bottle them up. It's healthier for you and will help calm you down—which, in turn, will help our progress."

"Colin gave me a cup of tea to calm me down. He didn't try to play psychiatrist." She turned her head in Samuel's direction. "And considering I'm a sneeze away from death, who gives a rat's ass about what's healthier?" As a thought occurred to her, she added, "Can you also read Colin's thoughts?"

Samuel shook his head. "It's something I can only do with the living."

"Lucky us."

Again, Samuel let out a soft laugh. "You're avoiding my question."

"Which was? Oh yeah, the biting thing." Madison rolled her eyes. Samuel already knew the answer, but he was going to make her say it. "A little of both, I guess. I was upset about Colin biting Miriam and maybe I wanted to know what it felt like. You know, to be bitten for real."

"And what about the sex? Did you also want to have sex with Colin?"

"Yes," she answered with the bluntness of an axe hitting wood. "At least at the time I saw him with Miriam. It was a creepy sort of turn-on, although it repulsed me at the same time." She paused. "Does that make sense?"

Samuel nodded. "Yes. It's quite normal, in fact."

"I'm normal? Who knew?"

"The behavior is quite normal," Samuel clarified. "You, on the other hand, are a bundle of contradictions. Pain. Hope. Anger.

Vulnerable. Tough. Even sweet at times." He glanced at her. "Which is also quite normal, considering your background."

"When we get to the Dedhams', I'll stretch out on the sofa and you can analyze me for real. Do you charge by the hour or by the decade?"

"Sarcasm," Samuel added. "I forgot to list defensive sarcasm."

They had turned away from the ocean and were heading into the Topanga area, getting closer to the Dedhams'.

"You know, Madison," Samuel said after a few moments of silence. "If a vampire bites you, you won't die. Not unless the vampire wants to kill you."

"Like you killed those girls when you first turned?"

"Yes." Samuel's voice was solemn when he answered. "Who told you that? Dodie?"

"Pauline. She told me you killed the daughters of the man who blinded you. At least she said that's what people say about you."

"And what else has Mrs. Speakes told you?"

"That you were enslaved as a young boy and lived in Egypt during Roman times. That you were blinded by your master when you were a young man. It that true?"

"Mostly, except that I was blinded while very young." Samuel kept his eyes on the road while he talked. "The father of the girls I killed had raped and killed my mother, right in front of me, when I was a boy. He blinded me after making me watch, then he sold me into slavery."

Madison shivered at the thought, then sat silent for a moment. "You raped them, didn't you?" she asked, not looking at Samuel. "Pauline said you made the man watch while you killed his daughters. But you made him watch while you raped *and* killed them." Her tone was accusatory.

"Yes."

"So the daughters paid for their father's sins. Hardly seems fair."

"No, it wasn't fair, but life isn't about what's fair, anymore now than then. Was it fair that my mother was raped and murdered? Or that I was sold into slavery?" Samuel glanced at her. "Was it fair that you were raped repeatedly as a child?"

Madison didn't answer, just wrapped her arms around herself and squeezed.

"Fair is best left on the athletic field," Samuel continued. "Life isn't a game, Madison. Neither is an undead life."

Again, Madison was quiet with her thoughts.

"Yes," Samuel said, answering the unspoken question in Madison's head. "That is why I backed off that night at your first council meeting. In you I saw my mother and those girls. You have been harmed enough."

They rode the last few miles to the Dedham home in silence. Once in the driveway, Samuel turned off the car's engine. "They're not home yet. I have some things to tell them and you together. Things Colin and I decided."

"You're going to kill Ethan and Ben, aren't you?" In the shadowy light of the car, Madison studied Samuel, looking for nuances in his facial expressions. She found none.

"You already know the answer, Madison, so why ask the question?"

"Because *I* want hear to it from *you*."

Samuel took off his glasses and latched his murky eyes onto Madison's brown ones. She couldn't have looked away if she'd tried. "The council has already sentenced to death whoever is behind these killings. If Ethan Young, Lilith, and Ben are, in fact, the killers, then they will be dealt with by extermination."

"You make them sound like vermin."

"Aren't they?"

Remembering Geoff and the corpses of the dead women, Madison agreed. "Yes, they are."

Madison unbuckled her seat belt and started to open the car door. Samuel placed a hand on her arm, stopping her. "To answer your other question," he said to her. "Yes, I wanted you last night, Madison. But I would never again take a woman by force. I currently enjoy the social and sexual company—and, yes, even the blood—of a couple of young, beautiful women. They come to me willingly. I wouldn't have it any other way." The two of them looked into each other's eyes but said nothing until Samuel patted her arm and let it go. "You're cold. Let's get you inside."

When the Dedhams returned home from their surveillance job, they had nothing to report from their evening. Kyle Patterson went straight home after leaving the diner and stayed there all night. He and his wife had a mild fight, watched some TV, and went to bed shortly before eleven. He never left the house again until about daybreak, when they followed him back to the diner. Gordon took over the shadowing from there.

"But," said Dodie, "I did get an interesting call from Stacie while we were watching Mr. Patterson. She said one of her homeless clients was babbling about seeing people getting killed. He was telling everyone that vampires were running wild in Los Angeles."

The news got everyone's attention except for Doug, who'd heard the call in the car.

"Did Stacie find out anything more?" asked Samuel.

"She couldn't. She said there were too many people around. She said no one believed him, of course, and thought he was drunk. Before she could spend any time alone with him, he'd run off."

"We need to find that man," said Samuel, his voice thick with authority.

"Stacie thinks she knows where he stays," Dodie continued. "It's some alley not far from where they hold the legal clinic. She's going back there tonight when there are fewer people around."

"Good," Samuel said, his voice a little more relaxed. "I'll give her a call tonight and check in on it."

Samuel lifted the glass of blood Dodie served him and drained it. Dodie and Doug were still working on theirs. Madison was slowly munching her way through a bowl of cereal and milk. She was getting used to seeing glasses of dark red liquid. The four of them were seated at the Dedham kitchen table, going over the various events of the evening.

"Colin and Madison are going back to Bloodlust tonight," Samuel told them.

This was news to Madison. She dropped the spoon she was holding into the bowl. It hit the side of the stoneware with a clang. "Are you kidding?"

Samuel turned to her. "Pretend that you know nothing about their plans—that you left the club angry because you found Colin with Miriam."

Madison wasn't convinced it was a sound plan. "If we had a fight, won't they find it odd that we're there together again?"

Samuel shrugged. "You patched it up. Couples do that. Just don't seem overly lovey-dovey. Give Ethan the impression that you really returned to see him again."

"Colin and I were never very lovey-dovey."

Without comment, Samuel continued. "Colin will be watching you every second."

Madison started to say something snotty, but Samuel saw it coming and cut her off.

"Don't worry," Samuel assured her with a half grin. "He'll be covering you even if half the club slits their wrists in front of him." He turned to Doug. "You're to go to Bloodlust tonight, too, but separate from them. I want you to observe everything. Be a second set of eyes on Madison."

"Won't someone of my age seem out of place?"

Madison shook her head. "There were several old—I mean mature—guys there last night. Most of them hung out at the bar."

"Considering I'm over two hundred years old," Doug said with a wide smile, "you can say *old*."

"Isabella is back in town," Samuel continued. "She'll be covering Lilith at Fang Me."

"What about me?" asked Dodie, eager to get into the action.

"You're heading to Dark Tidings tonight," Samuel instructed Dodie. "Colin said that Tuesdays and Thursdays are when Lady Harriet conducts her coven meetings and poetry readings. I want to see if that Ben character shows up there again. Madison will give you a full description of him. Tell Lady Harriet that Colin referred you to the coven; that should get you in. Also keep an eye on Lady Harriet. Since she has a bloodline, she might be in danger, though I keep thinking they would have grabbed her by now, since she's so accessible to them."

Dodie nodded, her face set in determination.

Samuel leaned back in his chair. "By this time tomorrow, I want Ben, Ethan, and Lilith in our custody and answering questions."

"Why don't we just call Mike Notchey," Madison suggested, "and tell him what I heard?"

Samuel shook his head. "From this point on, Mike's out of this."

"But it's his job," Madison persisted.

Samuel leaned forward. "There are some things, Madison, that we can't involve Mike in. He already goes far out on a limb for us."

Madison still did not see his point. "But he can take them into custody and interrogate them."

"That's right," Doug said. "And maybe they will be brought to justice, but probably not. And if Ethan and Ben are *not* the ones pulling the strings, we might never find out who is. Remember the suspect the police already have in jail now? He's not talking. Ethan and Ben, even Lilith, might give the police the silent treatment, and then we'll learn nothing."

Samuel placed a hand on Madison's arm. "Remember what we talked about in the car, about the council's decision?" When a light of remembrance shone in Madison's eyes, Samuel knew she understood. "Mike can't be involved in that. He can't even know about it, at least not directly. He's not a stupid man. He'll know, I'm sure, but he cannot be involved."

Finally, Madison saw the situation through their eyes.

Doug lifted his head as if sniffing the air. "Do you hear that?" he asked Dodie. The Dedhams cocked their heads like dogs hearing a silent whistle. "I've heard it a couple of times now."

"It sounds like a cell phone ring," said Dodie. "It's coming from upstairs."

"That must be my phone," said Madison without concern. "Bet it's Kyle, asking me to come back to work before Monday."

Dodie asked, "Aren't you going to answer it?"

Madison shrugged. "Why? I'm not going back yet, and if I don't answer he'll find someone else to fill in. I'm really not in the mood to hear him beg this morning."

Doug was still listening for the phone. "It stopped, then started again. Someone is really trying to reach you, Madison."

"It might be Mike," suggested Dodie. "If he thinks we've gone to bed, he may be calling you with some news."

Realizing that might be true, Madison trotted upstairs to find her phone. Several minutes later she returned holding it, her face white.

"It wasn't Mike or Kyle," she told them. "It was my landlord. Someone has broken into my apartment and trashed it."

TWENTY-SEVEN

Everything in Madison's tiny apartment had been smashed and destroyed. Madison walked through the debris too stunned to speak. Tears rolled down her cheeks.

"It was all I had," she said to the Dedhams, who had insisted on accompanying her to see what had happened.

Dodie put her arm around Madison. "They were just things, dear. What's important is that you weren't here when it happened."

"You're right, Dodie, just things." Madison's voice was dull and lifeless. They were just things and not very elegant, but they were still *her* things, and the small, cramped apartment had been the first real home she'd made for herself. Before coming to Los Angeles, she'd only rented rooms after leaving foster care. Madison felt like she'd lost more than material items.

Almost as soon as she'd received the news about her apartment, Madison's mind had jumped to the tampon boxes. She had sighed in relief, remembering that they were upstairs in the Dedhams' guest room.

Madison's landlord, an old man bent like a shepherd's crook, hovered nearby. "Damn kids," he growled. "Like I told the police, I spotted your door open when I took Trixie out for a walk this morning. Had to be about 5 AM."

Doug approached the old man. "And no one heard anything?" He waved a hand in the direction of the damage. "All this and no one heard or saw anything?"

The landlord shook his head. "I'm deaf as a post without my hearing aid. The apartment below is vacant, and the other tenants keep to themselves. Everyone's afraid to get involved." He handed Doug a card. It was from the Culver City Police. "The police took my statement and left. They want Madison to call as soon as she can. Meanwhile, I'm having a new lock installed later today, though I doubt it will do any good."

The landlord started for the door. He stopped and looked back at Madison. "Come by this afternoon and get the new key." He took another step, then looked back again. "Almost seems like whoever did this knew you were off visiting your grandparents."

That theory was the opposite of the opinion that had gone around the Dedham table after Madison had received the call.

"Someone went looking for you," Samuel had decided. "Did you let your last name slip while at Bloodlust?"

"No," she'd answered, still in shock. "I'm sure of it. And Colin wouldn't let me take any ID."

"Then someone there knew you," Doug said. "Probably that Ben fellow you can't place."

Madison slumped into a kitchen chair, her closed cell phone still in her hand. "But that doesn't mean he'd know where I live."

Doug looked at everyone around the table. "It only takes a few clicks on a computer to find most addresses these days, especially if he knew her last name and the general area." The rest agreed.

Based on the new development, Samuel announced a change of plans. "Madison, you are not to go to Bloodlust tonight. You're to stick close to the Dedhams today. You're not to go out without one of them by your side. Understand?"

Madison nodded, eager to agree to anything that might save her neck.

"Doug," Samuel started, "I still want you and Colin at Bloodlust tonight. I want you both to keep an eye on Ethan Young. Don't let him out of your sight. One of you cover the front, one the back. If he leaves, follow him. If he makes a phone call, Doug, I want you to listen to it. If he goes to his office, eavesdrop. We want to know everything he does."

"You don't want him apprehended?" asked Doug.

"Yes, but use your judgment on the timing. I want to see if he can lead us to the others involved, but if an opportunity arises to grab him without being seen, do it. You know where to bring him when you do." Samuel paused and looked away, lost in his thoughts. "Even if he's afraid of someone higher up, believe me, he'll be more afraid of us when he's questioned."

"What about Ben?" Dodie asked.

"If Ben is at Bloodlust, we'll take him there. But just in case, stick with your plans to go to Dark Tidings." Samuel looked at Madison. "You'll be with me for the evening. Pack your toothbrush. It's going to be a very long night."

Their meeting was breaking up just as Pauline came in through the kitchen door. She was mildly surprised to see the vampires still up and very surprised to see Samuel La Croix at the table.

Samuel got up and went to her. "Mrs. Speakes, I have a favor to ask."

Pauline put her bag down on the kitchen counter. "Of course, Mr. La Croix, whatever I can do to help."

Noting the way the crusty Pauline was melting in the hands of Samuel's charm, Madison smiled to herself. He was charming when he wanted to be. Charming and deadly.

"We'll need you to stay a bit longer tonight," Samuel told her. "Will that be possible?"

Pauline gave him a sappy smile. "I think that can be arranged."

"We believe Madison here is in grave danger." Samuel took Pauline's hand and held it. "I've asked the Dedhams to do something for me tonight, and I don't want Madison left alone while they're gone. I'll be by to pick her up a little later, but until I do, could you stay with her?"

"Yes, I believe I can stay as long as it takes, Mr. La Croix."

"Wonderful." Samuel bent over Pauline's hand and kissed it. She nearly swooned.

After leaving Madison's apartment, Madison and the Dedhams went by the Culver City Police Department, where Madison checked in and gave her statement, which wasn't much. Nor did the police have much to tell her about the break-in, except to ask if she had any enemies who might have committed the vandalism. She told them not that she knew of, carefully editing out the part about vampire-crazed killers.

From there, the three of them stopped by Auntie Em's. Madison wanted to tell Kyle about her apartment and let him know she might not be returning until she could get resettled. She hoped he'd keep her job open a few more days. When the three of them entered the restaurant, it was just past noon and the place was already busy. At the counter sat Gordon, a plate of food in front of him, a newspaper folded next to him. Madison and the Dedhams exchanged looks as they spotted him. From the other end of the counter, Sandra waved to Madison.

Madison walked up to the counter. As she passed Gordon, she tried not to let recognition show. "I need to talk to Kyle," she told Sandra.

"He's in the back, on the phone," she told her. "Would you believe we were broken into last night?" Sandra made no attempt to keep her voice low.

Madison's mouth dropped. "What?" She glanced at the Dedhams and could tell they had their super hearing tuned in to the conversation. No doubt Gordon had his regular hearing plastered on it, too.

"Someone cut the alarm and broke in," Sandra continued, her eyes wide with excitement. "They didn't take much, just vandalized the office. Broke into the filing cabinets, messed up our records. Got a few dollars. But that's all."

"Wow," was all Madison could come up with.

"Why don't you take a seat at the counter and wait," Sandra suggested. "The special today is chicken pot pie. I know how you love it. I'll bring one out for you."

Madison indicated the Dedhams. "I'm here with my grandparents."

"Then grab a booth while one's available," Sandra instructed her. "You might as well have lunch while you wait."

Madison took a nearby booth and waved the Dedhams over. The three of them sat down—the Dedhams on one side, Madison on the other. When a waiter approached, Sandra intervened. "I've got this, Jack," she told him. The waiter gave Madison a quick wave hello and moved on to another table.

After introductions, Sandra asked what she could get them.

"My husband and I are on such restrictive diets," Dodie told Sandra with a smile. "So just a cup of coffee will do for us."

"You sure?" Sandra asked. "We make the best split pea soup in the city."

Doug brightened. "I'd like a cup of that, but just a small one, if you please."

Sandra beamed at him and turned to Madison. "Chicken pot pie? Ranch on the salad?" Madison nodded. Sandra looked at the Dedhams and winked. "I know all your girl's favorite dishes."

When Sandra left, Madison leaned toward Doug and whispered, "What are you going to do with that soup, Gramps?"

He smirked. "Stir it around and pretend I'm enjoying it like a normal person. Split pea used to be one of my favorites."

"Then it's too bad you can't taste it," Madison told him. "It's very good, just like she said."

Sandra came with two mugs of coffee and placed them in front of the Dedhams. She put a tall glass of soda and a straw in front of Madison. When she left, Dodie whispered, "Did we hear right? Was there a break-in here last night?"

"Yes," Madison confirmed as she took the wrapper from her straw and stuck it into the soft drink. "Sounds like they trashed the back office." She took a big thirsty drink.

"That's it," Doug exclaimed. "That's how they knew where you lived. I'll bet they rifled through the employee records, found yours, and went straight to your apartment."

"Makes sense," Dodie agreed, pretending to sip her coffee.

Madison wasn't happy with the conclusion they were reaching. "That means they knew I worked here. Ben has to be someone who comes in here, but for the life of me I can't place him."

A moment later, Jack delivered their food to the table. When he placed the chicken pot pie in front of Madison, he asked, "You coming back to work soon, Madison? We sure miss you around here."

"Probably next week," she told him.

"Good. The customers miss you, too. Especially that jerk with the Cobb salad fetish." He grinned and took off.

The three of them stared at each other, thinking the same thing. Madison looked over the crowd in the restaurant but didn't see the studio suit who always ordered the Cobb salad. She caught Jack's eye and called him over.

"Has that Cobb salad guy been in here today?" she asked him.

"Not yet, but maybe he's not coming. His usual group is here, but he's not with them." Jack indicated a large group in the back circular booth. Madison recognized them as the guy's regular lunch pals. She thanked Jack.

"Does that salad guy look like Ben?" Dodie asked Madison.

"Not at all," she answered. "But remember, Evie worked here, too, and I was grabbed by Bobby Piper from the parking lot in back of the restaurant."

Madison took a bite of her salad, followed by two bites of her chicken pot pie. While her jaw worked, so did her mind. The

Dedhams toyed with their coffee, and Doug did a bang-up job pretending to eat his soup, raising the spoon to his nose more often than his lips and sniffing appreciatively.

"Can't you just take a taste?" Madison asked as she stuffed more chicken and gravy into her mouth.

Doug shook his head sadly. "I tried that when I first turned, but while the smell is still the same to us, our tongues don't have the same taste buds. No matter how good this smells to me, it would taste nasty to my palate."

"You might say," Dodie added with a slight smile, "that we can now only eat with our noses."

Madison took a drink of soda, glad she could taste everything on her plate. "Colin keeps oranges and lemons in his apartment for the same reason."

After a few quiet moments, Madison looked from one Dedham to the other. "Are you guys okay? You seem a bit paler than usual—and droopy."

"It's the sun, dear," Dodie explained. "It saps our strength."

Madison became alarmed. "Then we should go right now and get you home."

"We're fine, Madison," Doug assured her. "Really. Once we're home, we'll recharge good as new. It's actually quite nice being out in the day for a change."

While she ate, Madison kept one eye on the Dedhams and one eye on the group in the corner. The latter had finished eating and were relaxing before paying their tab and going back to the office. The obnoxious salad guy had not shown. She wiped her mouth with a napkin and scooted out of the booth.

"It's a long shot," she told the Dedhams without explaining her plan, "but it's worth a try."

Grabbing a pitcher of iced tea from the back counter, Madison glided over to the corner booth. "Anyone need a refill?" she asked the group as she held out the pitcher. Two of them scooted their glasses forward and thanked her.

As she filled the glasses, Madison asked as nonchalantly as possible, "Where's your friend—the one who always orders the Cobb salad?"

"Con called in sick today," a woman with purple-rimmed glasses and short red hair answered. "At least he said he was sick." Everyone laughed.

"Con?" Madison said, realizing her long shot had not come in a winner. "I thought his name was Ben. My mistake."

"It is," one of the guys piped up. "Benjamin is his middle name. Some people know him as Ben instead of Conrad, especially outside the office where no one knows his dad, who's a big shot at the studio. At the office, he makes sure everyone knows who he is."

"Conrad Benjamin Winthrop Jr.," said the red-haired woman, drawing out the name with a nasal tone.

"Yeah, man," another of the men at the table said to Madison. "We're really sorry he gives you folks in here such a hard time. He's the same way at work."

"No problem," Madison told him with a smile. "People like him are definitely in the minority here." She started to walk away. "Have a nice day."

After putting the tea pitcher back, Madison rejoined the Dedhams. "Did you tune in to that?" she asked them.

"Sure did," answered Doug. "Sounds like he might be our guy after all. That long hair is probably a wig."

TWENTY-EIGHT

When they returned to the Dedham house, Doug and Dodie retired immediately. Madison was also very tired. She'd had only a couple of hours' sleep at Colin's and tonight would be out very late again. She wasn't sure what Samuel meant by "bring your toothbrush" but thought it a safe bet she wouldn't be returning to the Dedhams' until daybreak. She was burning the candle at both ends living both vampire hours and human hours.

Madison tried to take a nap, but the events of the night before and that morning were hard to ignore. She would have to spend several days cleaning out her apartment, trying to sort out what was salvageable and what wasn't, though much looked ready to be junked. Maybe it was time she looked for a nicer apartment. Seemed like now would be a good time, but that would depend on the job situation. She could hardly spend more on an apartment if she didn't have a job to go back to next week. She never talked to Kyle about it. With his own break-in on his mind, when he did emerge from the back office, he was irritable and not focused on anything but the vandalism. And the last thing Madison wanted was to alert him that his break-in might have been tied to her. Before leaving, she simply told him how sorry she was about what had happened at the diner and promised she would call him at the end of the week.

Realizing sleep was futile, Madison got up and went to her computer and turned it on. The Dedhams had WiFi, so Madison connected to the Internet right from her room. They were going to run a search on Conrad Benjamin Winthrop Jr. later, after everyone was rested, but since tossing and turning was getting her nowhere, Madison decided now would be a good time. Googling his name brought up some interesting items, especially about his father. Winthrop Sr. was one of the founders of the studio where Ben worked. No wonder he used his full name at the office; he was cashing in on Daddy's reputation and clout.

Madison sifted through the various articles that popped up. Most were about Ben's father. Ben had a Facebook page, but only his Facebook friends had access to it. The photo attached to the account was not a close-up, so she couldn't tell much from it. She moved on to the Google image search. There she found several photos of Ben with his father and tried to picture the younger man with long hair and sunglasses. There were none of Ben with his mother or any siblings, just with his father. She still didn't have any solid proof that he was the Ben from Dark Tidings, but there just seemed to be too many coincidences.

When she couldn't find an address for Ben online, Madison considered going back down for her nap. As she shut down her computer, she heard the doorbell ring. A moment later, there was a knock at her bedroom door. It was Pauline, bearing a large box.

"What's this?" she asked when Pauline brought the box in and set it on the bed.

"Won't know until you open it."

The box was white and tied with a blue ribbon. The logo of an expensive Beverly Hills clothing store was embossed into the cardboard. Madison opened it to find several articles of clothing separated by delicate tissue. She pulled out the top item. It was a cashmere turtleneck sweater the color of fine gold. Under it was a pair of copper-colored wool slacks. Another sweater and another pair of slacks were beneath them. At the bottom of the deep box was a fine-knit dress in deep green. Madison held the gold sweater up to her and looked in the mirror. It complemented her creamy complexion and brown hair and eyes perfectly.

"Did the Dedhams buy these?" she asked Pauline.

Pauline looked puzzled. "I don't think so. I think Mrs. D would have had more fun shopping with you than shopping for you." She fished around in the tissue until she found something. "Look, there's a card." She handed it to Madison.

Madison read the card over several times, not believing its contents.

"Well, what is it?" Pauline asked with impatience.

"It's from Samuel," Madison told her. "It's an apology for ruining my top last night."

"He ruined your top?" Pauline cocked an eyebrow at Madison.

"It was during the meeting here at the house. Just an accident." Madison had no intention of telling Pauline about the marks on her neck and Samuel's reaction to them.

Pauline fingered the fine weave of the slacks. "You tell that vampire if this is how he apologizes, he can ruin all my clothes if he wants."

"These are very expensive, Pauline. I can't accept them."

"Why not? To Samuel La Croix, the cost of these duds is like you and me going to Target. Enjoy them."

Madison flushed, thinking how Samuel had admitted that he wanted her, and not just for her blood. The flush turned to real heat remembering his fangs against her neck. The next mental image was of Colin ravaging Miriam. With short, quick movements, she shook the thoughts from her head and dropped down on the bed next to the elegant box.

"I'm so confused, Pauline. One minute Colin's turning me on, the next it's Samuel. I've never been like this before. I like it and hate it at the same time."

"It's the vampire charm," Pauline told her with sympathy. "There's something alluring about them, no doubt. Both of those men are handsome, rich, and mysterious—a perfect potion for turning a girl to jelly. I saw it plenty with Mr. D before he met and married Mrs. D. He had women following him around like he was the pied piper. It's the same with the female vampires. They're regular femme fatales when they want to be, especially that Isabella."

"But you fall for it, too."

Pauline laughed. "I'm just an old married woman soaking up the sweet talk like a kitten at a saucer. But you—you're different. Samuel La Croix isn't just apologizing here, he's wooing you."

"All I want is my life back," Madison said with a sagging sigh. "I want to go back to when I didn't know about vampires and blood sucking and bloodlines."

"From what Mr. D told me when you guys got back, you don't have much to go back to anymore."

Madison jutted her chin out. "Unless some crazy vampire worshiper gets to me, I still have my life. My apartment was just a box of things; I can replace those. And I can get another job if Kyle cans me. I have no intention of being the mistress of a vampire—not Samuel's or Colin's, no matter how rich or handsome they might be."

Pauline reached a hand out and touched the top of Madison's head. "Good girl." And Madison knew she meant it.

Later, when Samuel came by to pick Madison up, he eyed her old jeans, sweater, and sneakers with narrow eyes. "You didn't like the things I sent over?"

Madison walked over to the dining table where the big white box was waiting to be handed back to Samuel. "I can't accept these. You'll have to return them."

Samuel didn't ask why. He knew why. "They were an apology for the damaged blouse, nothing more."

"Then just replace the shirt you tore and we'll call it even."

Opening the box, Samuel looked inside. The clothing had been carefully folded and placed between the tissues like they'd just come from the store. "Instead of accepting them all, why don't you just pick one of these as a replacement? That's it. Just one."

"Just one?" Madison asked. "And only to replace my other top?"

He nodded. "Pick your favorite, and I'll return the others."

It sounded reasonable to Madison. She knew immediately which article she wanted—the gold sweater. Gently, she lifted it from the box and draped it across the back of one of the chairs. "There. You happy?"

Samuel grinned. "I'll be happier if you would put it on and wear it tonight."

After a slight hesitation, Madison went upstairs and slipped on the sweater. It fit her perfectly and felt as soft as an angel's touch against her skin. When she came downstairs, both Samuel and Pauline looked at her with approval.

Pauline left the house when they did. Samuel put the box containing the other clothing in the trunk of his car and climbed behind the steering wheel.

"No Gordon again tonight?" Madison noted.

"He's on a different assignment. Doug called and gave me Ben's real name. I'm having Gordon track him down. If he does, he'll stick to him like glue." He pulled out of the driveway. "With Colin and Doug at Bloodlust, Dodie at Dark Tidings, and Gordon tracking down Ben's home address, if that bastard shows up anywhere, we'll have him."

Madison was going to bring up the fact that Mike Notchey could get Ben's address in a heartbeat, but she knew they'd never go to him, especially now that he was out of the loop for his own good.

"And what about us? What's our assignment?" she asked Samuel as the car maneuvered the canyon streets toward the highway.

"We're off to meet Stacie Neroni. If she locates that homeless man, I want to question him myself."

When they reached Hollywood, Samuel found a rare parking spot on a side street just up from Hollywood Boulevard. The area was seedy and depressed in spite of the glitz of Hollywood attractions and the glow from souvenir shops. It was the height of the evening. Hookers, hustlers, and drug addicts mingled with thrill-seeking college kids and tourists snapping photos. Stacie was waiting for them by a twenty-four-hour newsstand.

"Find him?" Samuel asked as soon as they reached her.

"Yes." She pointed to a grizzled black man sitting on the sidewalk across the street. He had his back against a boarded-up shop and held a cup in his hand, holding it out to people who passed by. Most of the storefronts on that side of the street were boarded up, so few people walked on that side. Those that did either ignored the homeless man or gave him a wide berth. Next to him was a shopping cart stuffed with his belongings. Several yards away, a trio of hookers called to cars that slowed down.

"His name's Clarence, but everyone calls him Cubby. If he stays on that side of the street," Stacie explained to Madison and Samuel, "the police won't bother him. On this side, the cops or the shop owners will run him off. The other side of the street is where we usually run our legal clinic on Wednesday nights."

The three of them crossed the street and approached the homeless man.

"Hi, Cubby," Stacie greeted him cheerfully. "I brought some friends to meet you."

The man was old and dirty and smelled of garbage and filth. He wore several layers of ragged clothing against the night's chill. Looking up at Stacie, he flashed her a smile of jagged yellow teeth in recognition. When he turned toward Madison and Samuel, his face clouded with caution.

"This is Madison and Samuel," Stacie continued. "My friends. I told them what you said about vampires, and they want to help you."

"Vampires?" The old man asked, befuddled, then clarity made a brief appearance on his face. "Yes, vampires."

Samuel crouched down closer to the man. "Tell me about them, brother."

Cubby turned and fixed his runny eyes on Samuel. "Vampires are here." He held out a shaking hand and pointed an index finger toward the concrete beneath him. "Right here, I tell you. In the city of *angels*." He emphasized the word *angels*. "But no one listen to old Cubby. They say Cubby crazy."

Samuel stared into Cubby's eyes. "I'm listening. Tell me."

"I saw them," Cubby said, keeping his eyes latched onto Samuel's sunglasses. "They were doing unspeakable things."

"You have to tell us so we can stop them," Stacie told him.

"Unspeakable things," Cubby repeated, not taking his eyes off of Samuel. "They were drinking her blood," he said in a low, hoarse voice.

"Whose blood?" asked Samuel.

"Naked, she was. Skin pale as the moon. They cut her. Drank her blood." He barely choked out the words. "Poor girl."

Samuel crouched closer. "Where did this happen, Cubby? Can you show us?"

Cubby shook his head and withdrew into his rags. "Cubby not going back. No, sir. Evil things. Had to leave Porky. Have to find new home."

"That explains the shopping cart," Stacie said. "Usually he doesn't have it with him. He's on the move." She bent down.

"Please, Cubby, you have to tell us where you saw this. We'll make the bad men go away so you can go home."

Cubby looked up at Stacie. "Cubby never going back. Never. Place cursed." He retreated further into his dark mind, the light in his eyes fading into the fringe of madness.

Samuel glanced up at Stacie. "You know where he used to live?"

She shook her head. "Not really. Always thought it was a back alley around here somewhere. Bloodlust isn't far from here, though—maybe a half mile, maybe a mile, tops. It would have been convenient."

"Who's Porky?" Samuel asked her. "A pet? Another person?"

"Not sure about that either. I've never heard him speak of Porky before. Never heard of a street person out here called that either. Can't you see anything?"

Samuel shook his head. "Only bits and pieces. It's all jumbled inside his head."

Standing up, Samuel looked around. "Where's Madison?"

Both he and Stacie turned their eyes to the streets around them, searching for any sign of her.

"Damn it," swore Samuel under his breath. "How could she have vanished?"

It was then Stacie spotted Madison. She was across the street, coming out of an all-night coffee shop, heading back to them. In one hand was a bag; in the other, a large covered coffee cup. Samuel watched her carefully as she waited for the light, then crossed over to them.

"Couldn't you have eaten before you came out here?" Stacie snapped at Madison.

"It's not for her," Samuel said to Stacie.

Ignoring the vampires, Madison knelt down in front of Cubby, bracing her stomach against his stench. She transferred the paper cup of coffee to his dark hands with their dirt-encrusted nails, making sure he had a firm grip on it before letting go.

"Bless you," the old man said to her, clutching the warm cup.

She put the paper sack down next to him. "There are sandwiches in the bag, Cubby, and a couple of bananas."

Cubby gave her a nod of understanding and took a sip from the opening in the lid of the cup.

"Careful," Madison warned him. "It's very hot."

After a couple of sips of coffee, Cubby looked again at Madison as if seeing her for the first time. "You look like the girl," he said. "The naked girl."

"Where did you see her, Cubby?" Madison asked in a soft voice. "We're trying to find her."

Samuel bent down again and stared at Cubby, concentrating. Cubby, though, kept his eyes on Madison.

"They want you," the old man said to her, his eyes growing wide with fear. "They want your blood." His voice trembled.

"They want our blood?" asked Stacie.

"No," Cubby said, not looking at Stacie. He released one hand from the mug and pointed it at Madison. "Hers."

Madison stood up with a jerk and backed away. Samuel dug into his pocket and pulled out some cash. He tucked it into Cubby's donation cup.

"Thanks, brother," he told him. "If you remember anything else, you tell Stacie here. Okay?"

Cubby, forgetting about blood and vampires, gave Stacie a smile. Clutching his cup with both hands again, he went back to concentrating on drinking his coffee.

Samuel turned to Stacie. "Keep an eye on him. What he knows is in that head of his somewhere. Who knows when it will come out. But he does know something, I'm positive. I kept getting glimpses of what he saw, but not the place. Try to find where he used to live and who or what this Porky is. It might help."

"Will do," Stacie told him.

Samuel and Madison headed back across the street. Samuel kept a death grip on Madison's upper arm as they walked.

"Ow, that hurts," she protested.

Once at the car, Samuel spun her around to face him. "What were you thinking, going off like that without a word?"

"I was just getting him food," Madison said in her own defense. "He's probably only eaten garbage for who knows how long. Food isn't exactly anything you guys think about, but we beaters need it."

"You did a very good thing, Madison, but all you had to do was say something and we would have gone together to get it. Stacie could have gone with you while I talked to Cubby." When Madison turned away, Samuel put his hand on her chin and turned her face back, forcing her to look at him. "You're in danger, Madison. Get that through your thick skull."

"How did he know that?" she asked. "How did that homeless man, who I've never seen, know about them wanting my blood?"

Samuel took his hand away from her face. "I don't know, but sometimes madness opens other doors in the mind. He may have received some image or vision through his darkness."

Madison shivered and started to open the car door. Samuel reached down and opened it for her. As she stepped in, he bent close. "Millions of things in this world can't be explained, Madison. Vampires and visions are just two of them."

TWENTY-NINE

Samuel's house was a sprawling villa set high in the hills above Los Angeles. After entering a security gate, they had driven up a long private drive to reach the house. They'd entered through the garage, coming into a service room that fed into a huge kitchen with a tile floor and shiny appliances. Following Samuel, Madison was led into the great room. Colorful carpets covered the tile floor, and the walls were painted in varying earth tones. The furniture and overall décor had a Mediterranean feel, yet the furnishings were sparse, as at Colin's condominium, though here there were cut flowers throughout the room. And, as at Colin's, the view was spectacular, though Samuel's home looked out over the lights of Los Angeles instead of the ocean.

"You guys seem to like views," Madison observed.

Samuel came up beside her and looked out. "During the day it's just a boring cityscape, but at night it looks like a blanket of jewels against velvet. Since I'm up mostly at night, it made sense to buy a house with such a view."

"I also noticed none of you, not even the Dedhams, are big on a lot of furniture or knickknacks."

"We like to keep things simple, Madison. Vampires never know when they might have to disappear for a while. Sometimes we even have to move permanently."

"I like to keep things simple, too. Makes it easier."

Samuel chuckled. "Is that why you keep your money stashed in a feminine hygiene box?"

"How did you know that?" Madison turned, looking at him with surprise. "I'm not thinking about that at all."

"No, but you were when you got the call about your apartment," he explained. "Good thing you moved those boxes when you did."

"Can you read my mind now?" Madison zeroed her eyes in on his. He had removed his sunglasses and met her look head-on.

"Tsk, tsk, tsk." Samuel feigned offense. "For such a cute little thing, you certainly have a potty mind, and what you just said to me, I believe, is anatomically impossible, even for a vampire."

Now it was Madison's turn to chuckle. "That money is my inheritance from my great aunt Eleanor—or what's left of it. It wasn't much, about twenty thousand. I used some of it to buy a car and to get my ass out of Boise shortly after I turned twenty-one."

"Even we vampires trust banks, Madison. Maybe it's because they're blood suckers like us."

Madison smiled at the comment but shrugged. "As a kid, I got used to moving without notice. I was dragged from one foster home to another with little more than the clothes on my back and a small bag of backups. I guess once a gypsy, always a gypsy."

Samuel glanced back out at the view. "Most of my life," he paused, "both then and now, has been like that, too. I've been in Los Angeles quite a while. So have most of the vampires on the council. We like it here. It's easy for us to blend in with all the city's usual crazies and eccentrics, and most people here keep to their own business, unlike other parts of the country. We're trying to build a real community so we won't have to wander anymore."

"Dodie and Stacie told me it was very different before you got here. They said it was like the Wild West."

Samuel nodded. "There were bloodthirsty beater hunts and violent territorial fights between the vampires. It made it difficult for those who were simply in search of peace. They were afraid if it continued, they would be exposed." Samuel grunted. "Just as we're concerned about exposure now, only this time it's not other vampires causing the trouble."

The house was U-shaped, with its extensions reaching out like arms to embrace a large tiled courtyard. Beyond it was a large pool. Low-level lights lit the courtyard and set off the various pots of flowers and shrubs to their best advantage. Submerged lights in the pool made the water shimmer in a slow liquid dance like a mirage.

Madison watched the lights for a moment. "It's lovely, Samuel."

"Thank you. Maybe, in time, you'd like to come and stay for a visit." When Madison jerked her head to look at him, he added with a smile, "Just for a visit. A guest. Nothing else. I often have houseguests."

"Live ones?"

"Yes, and undead ones." He laughed. "The wing to the right houses two large guest suites. The wing to the left contains the master suite and my office. Most of the rooms have doors that open up onto the courtyard."

Samuel led her through the house into the right wing and showed her to a guest suite that consisted of a spacious bedroom with a roomy sitting area and private bath. The bed was large and covered with a quilt the color of terra-cotta pots. On the bed, pillows of different sizes and shapes were clustered like green- and peach-patterned mushrooms. The sight of the bed made Madison yawn.

"You must be tired," Samuel said. "I'll bet since last night you've hardly gotten any sleep."

"Just the couple of hours at Colin's." Madison yawned again. "I'm sorry, but I'm ready to drop."

"Understandable." Samuel placed the small bag of toiletries and clothing Madison had brought with her on the bed. "Through that door is the bathroom. Feel free to use the whirlpool tub; it might help you sleep. Also, there is some food in the kitchen—I'm not sure how much, but don't hesitate to check out the cupboards and refrigerator. I always keep things on hand for my living friends. There's no one else here tonight. Gordon lives in an apartment over the garage, and my housekeeper doesn't come until after eleven in the morning."

Samuel pointed to drapes pulled back close to the wall, away from the French doors. "You will find that all the bedrooms have room-darkening drapery panels to the side of the windows. My undead guests generally use those, but you might enjoy leaving the windows uncovered to enjoy the moonlight and the morning sun."

Before he left, Samuel bent and kissed Madison lightly on the cheek. "Good night, little one. Put the events of the day aside and sleep like the dead." He winked, closing the door behind him.

A few minutes later, Madison wandered into the kitchen in search of food. Finding a small bag of gourmet cookies in a cupboard and some apples in a bowl on the counter, she retreated to her room with her booty and ate while soaking in the deep tub.

The life of a vampire didn't seem that bad, Madison thought to herself as she relaxed in scented bubbles. They lived in luxury homes, drove expensive cars, and had money. Then she remembered Doug sniffing food he couldn't eat and Dodie baking cookies to keep her memories alive. Bowls of oranges and lemons instead of scrapbooks. And Kate Thornton with a mate who would grow old and die—Jerry being nothing but a heartbeat in Kate's eternal world. Under the wealth and power, it seemed a lonely and painful life, and one filled with worry of exposure and concern about who to trust and who could not be trusted. It was a secret life lived in darkness. And it was forever.

Madison started to cry and wasn't sure why.

Sometime in the night, Madison woke to find herself in total darkness. Someone had come in and closed her drapes. Maybe Samuel had, thinking it would help her sleep longer in the morning. Slipping out of bed, she went to the window and peeked through the heavy curtain. Everything looked the same in the large courtyard: the pool was still blue and inviting, the moon bright. In their outdoor dim light, the trees and potted shrubs stood like dancers in the wings, waiting for their cue to step into the spotlight.

Madison was about to return to bed when she spotted a shadow leaving the house from a back door on the other wing.

She scooted farther back behind the drapes and watched. It was a man. He seemed short and squat and moved like a nocturnal animal across the courtyard and past the pool. When he reached the far end of the property, which was bordered by an ivy-covered fence, he disappeared. A moment later, another figure left the opposite wing. This time it was a woman. She strolled with confidence, taking the same path as the man before her. For a brief moment moonlight crossed her face, and Madison recognized Stacie Neroni. Like the man before her, she approached the ivy fence and disappeared.

If Stacie was here, maybe she'd learned something more from Cubby, but why was she outside? Why couldn't she just meet with Samuel in the living room? And who was the man who'd arrived before her? Bursting with curiosity and hoping Stacie's presence meant they'd found the killers, Madison slipped into her jeans and her sneakers. Quietly opening the French doors from her room to the courtyard, she crept out into the night and followed the trail to the fence.

The night was cold and damp. Madison hugged her arms to herself as she scurried across the courtyard tiles and onto the grass on the far side of the pool. Besides her jeans and sneakers, she was only wearing the tee shirt she'd worn to bed. Once at the fence, she couldn't see where they'd gone.

Reaching through the ivy, Madison discovered it wasn't a fence at all, but a building on the other side. She quietly felt her way along until her hand hit something familiar. It was a door handle. She pulled on it just far enough so she could look inside.

On the other side of the door was a long, narrow storage room with its lights on, but no sign of Stacie or the man. Madison slipped inside. Once inside, she heard voices and followed them to the far side of the room, where she found another door. This one was slightly open.

From here, she could recognize Samuel's voice but couldn't see him. He sounded cold and menacing. She also recognized Colin's voice, and Stacie's. Madison wondered if they were arguing. She stepped through the door to get a better look and found herself in a small, dark area with a thick curtain separating it from the main area. She pulled back the drapery an inch and peered through the slit.

The room was the size of a large garage and bare except for chairs set up in a circle around a table. Seated in the chairs were Stacie Neroni, Colin Reddy, Isabella Claussen, and the man she'd seen crossing the lawn. Samuel La Croix stood at the head of the table, looking down.

Madison clenched her teeth to keep from screaming.

On the table was Lilith, leader of the Fang Me coven. She was naked and moaning. Blood dripped from her body onto the floor like wax from a melting red candle.

"Tell us where Ethan and Ben are," Samuel demanded.

"I don't know," Lilith answered in a weak voice. Her eyes were closed. Her head sagged to one side.

Stacie got up, sunk her fangs into one of Lilith's wrists, and sucked hard. Lilith screamed, but the sound was ragged and feeble.

"How does it feel to bleed to death?" Blood dripped from Stacie's mouth as she asked Lilith the question. "This is how your victims died. Talk or you'll die the same way."

"I don't ... I don't know where they are. I haven't seen them since last night."

Lilith raised her head slightly and turned it toward Isabella. "I was with you all last night and tonight—tell them."

Isabella got up and walked to the table. Stacie moved away, taking her place back on a chair. Isabella stroked Lilith's hair. "We were together, and it was lovely." Isabella smiled down at Lilith. "But you need to tell us everything you know." Isabella's voice was tender. "Who's behind this, Lilith? We know it's not you. Who is calling the shots on the kidnappings and killings?"

"I don't know," Lilith whimpered, her former arrogance drained from her as her blood dripped from her body. "Really. Ethan told me they knew how to become real vampires and asked if I wanted in. That's it. I'm telling you the truth." Lilith sobbed, then choked back the tears. "But you're real." She moved her head to look at the rest of them. "You're all real." She caught her eye on Colin. "Even you. All this time, you were a real vampire."

Colin stared at her, his dark, handsome face molded into a terrible mask.

Isabella nodded and continued to stroke Lilith's hair. "Yes, darling, we're the genuine article." She flashed her fangs.

Lilith shrank against the table. "But we worship you. We want to be like you … to be one of you."

"So much so," Colin finally said, his voice thick with disgust, "that you were willing to kill innocent people? Even we don't do that." He stood up and covered the distance to the table in a single stride. "Only people with bloodlines can become vampires, Lilith. You killed at least five potential vampires in your fruitless quest to become one yourself. We don't take that lightly. It's like killing our children." Colin unleashed his fangs. He reared back and thrust himself forward, latching himself onto one of Lilith's upper thighs. Lilith screamed while Isabella held her head.

Acidic bile rose in Madison's throat as she fought the urge to vomit.

When Colin finished sucking on Lilith's thigh, he returned to his chair. Samuel stepped up to the table. Isabella continued to hold Lilith's head, keeping it steady and turned toward Samuel.

"Tell us everything you know, Lilith," Samuel demanded, "or your life ends right here, right now."

Madison shrunk away, stumbling on rubbery legs to find her way out of the building and across the lawn and courtyard to her room. She knew no matter what Lilith said or confessed, the high priestess of Fang Me was going to die tonight on that table. The council had already sentenced her.

The weak light of dawn woke Madison as it crept into her room like a stealthy cat. She turned toward the French doors to find that someone had pulled back the drapes, just as they had been when she'd first gone to bed the night before. Again, she'd heard nothing.

The frightening memory of Lilith's screams filled Madison's morning thoughts. She got out of bed and looked out across the courtyard toward the ivy. Everything appeared peaceful, and there was no sign of a building beyond the ivy. Then her eye caught her sneakers where she'd kicked them off upon returning to her room. Wet grass clung to them. It hadn't been a dream. She had been out in the night. Madison looked again at the ivy and shivered. She wanted to crawl back in bed and stay there forever.

Turning, she looked out again into the courtyard and saw movement out of the corner of her eye. It was Samuel. He was standing in the doorway that opened to the living room, beckoning her to join him. Wrapping herself in a thick white terrycloth robe she'd found the night before in the bathroom, Madison padded down the hallway and through the house to the living room, where she found Colin and Samuel together, deep in discussion. Colin was slouched on the sofa, facing the French doors. Samuel was pacing. Neither were wearing the same clothes they'd had on the night before.

On the large coffee table in front of the sofa was a tray with a small pitcher of fresh orange juice, a glass, and a plate of croissants.

Samuel indicated the tray. "That's for you, Madison. Help yourself."

Madison poured herself a glass of juice and curled up on one end of the large sofa, tucking her legs beneath her. With their super hearing and Samuel's ability to read thoughts, they had to know she'd seen them last night. She took a drink of juice and waited for it to play out, knowing she was powerless to avoid it.

"Seems our surveillance turned up nothing," Samuel told her. "Neither Ethan nor Ben showed up anywhere last night."

Colin turned to her. "It's almost like they knew someone was looking for them and took off."

"Maybe they realized I overheard them and decided not to stick around in case I called the police." Madison took another drink, hoping the vampires didn't notice her shaking hands. "Maybe what happened to my apartment was just vandalism by kids."

Samuel shook his head. "Doug didn't think so. He said it looked like someone was angry at you. But we have to consider all the options."

"What about Gordon?" Madison asked. "Did he find out anything?"

"He checked in with me right after we got home last night. He said he had a lead and was checking it out. I haven't heard from him since." Samuel ran a hand over his bald head. "Not like him. It worries me. No answer on his cell phone either."

"And Lilith?" asked Madison, addressing the elephant in the room.

Samuel sat down in a chair across from the sofa and studied Madison before speaking. "She was bragging to Isabella about how she was going to be running all the covens shortly."

The information surprised Madison, and she pushed the thought of Lilith's death aside for the moment. "But of all the covens, hers was the one going downhill fast. In fact, Ethan told us he was trying to get Lilith to merge her coven into his."

Samuel sighed. "Well, something had her thinking that after she turned, she was going to be the queen bee of vampirism here in California."

"But," Colin added, "even if their cockeyed theory had been correct, she'd still have to deal with Ethan and Ben also being vampires. I find it difficult to believe they would let her take control."

Madison nodded. "I agree with Colin. There's no way those two would let a woman even share power with them, let alone be over them. I'm surprised she was even in on it."

Colin leaned forward, one dark brow lowered, the other arched in thought. "Isabella thinks they just let Lilith in for her money. Hiring thugs to kidnap people is costly, even if the thugs are on the cheap."

Samuel got up and stretched. "Stacie will continue looking into this Porky angle tonight. That old guy knows where those deaths occurred, I'm sure of it. We just have to unlock it from his mind. I think if we find that spot, we'll find Ethan and Ben, or at least someone else connected to them."

Colin looked angry. "We have to end this, and soon."

"I couldn't agree with you more, Colin." Samuel turned to look out the windows. With the morning had come a light rain. "Madison," he said, not turning around, "why don't you get dressed. I'll have Colin take you home." He turned to look at Colin. "If you don't mind, Colin."

"Not at all. I can fill the Dedhams in on last night."

Samuel shook his head. "No need. I've already spoken with them this morning."

"Home? Home as in back to my apartment?" Madison's voice was tinged with hope. "Or home as in back to the Dedhams'?" Trashed or not, after last night, Madison was thinking she'd rather be back in her tiny, ruined apartment in Culver City.

Instead of answering, Samuel gave her a soft, slow smile. He turned back to look out the window again. "And ease your mind about the rain, Madison. Colin brought a car today."

Madison gasped softly, always surprised by Samuel's ability. Her displeasure about riding on the back of Colin's motorcycle in the rain was one of the concerns occupying her mind, but it wasn't the foremost one. Without a word, she started to leave.

"And Madison," Samuel called to her just as she reached the arch leading to the guest wing. She turned around to find both Samuel and Colin watching her. "What happened last night," Samuel told her, "that was justice. Our justice. Remember that."

She gave the two vampires a short, quick nod of understanding and left.

THIRTY

I t was true, Colin didn't have his bike with him. Instead, he was driving a Porsche. He drove it fast and deliberate, as he did the motorcycle, making Madison almost ask for a helmet.

When they arrived at the Dedhams', Doug and Dodie were waiting for them, eager as two puppies hoping to go out for a walk.

"We're so glad you're home," Dodie said to Madison, taking her jacket and shaking the rain out from it before hanging it on a hook by the back door. "We have something we want to discuss with you before we go to bed."

"Just put her bag down on the floor, Colin," Doug directed, "and come join us. You hungry?" Before Colin could answer, Doug turned to Dodie. "Sweetheart, you have any of that special blend left?"

"That's okay, folks," Colin told them. "I'm not hungry at all."

Madison cast Colin a quick look. His eyes met hers but revealed nothing.

Madison turned back to the Dedhams, wondering if they were going to bring up Lilith. Her head bulged with questions, but she wasn't sure when to ask them or who to ask. Samuel was in charge, but the Dedhams were her hosts. "Everything okay?" Madison asked instead.

"Everything's wonderful, dear," Dodie told her. "What can I get you for breakfast? Want me to scramble you a couple of eggs?"

"Ah, nothing, thanks. I'm not very hungry either, and I had some juice at Samuel's." Madison looked at the Dedhams like they'd lost a wheel off their wagon. She was expecting a birds-and-bees talk about vampire justice, not eggs.

"Sit down," Doug told her, holding out a kitchen chair for Madison, "and we'll tell you our news." He looked at Colin. "You, too, Colin. You might as well hear this now. Samuel already knows."

Colin took a chair and again exchanged looks with Madison. He seemed as confused as she was about the Dedhams' behavior. Madison lifted her shoulders in an exaggerated shrug.

The Dedhams took seats at the table. Dodie looked at Doug, urging him to begin. "This morning," he said, "we're celebrating Madison's new home."

Madison sat up straight with surprise. "My new home? Have you found me a new apartment?"

"No, dear," Dodie said with a smile. "Something much better."

"What are you guys talking about?" Madison felt like she'd missed something.

"Here," Doug told her with excitement. "You're going to live here."

Madison stood up in disbelief. "Here? With you? In a house of vampires?"

Doug scowled. "You say that like it's a bad thing. I mean, after all, haven't we been good to you?"

With an audible thump, Madison sat back down and put her head in her hands. "Yes, of course. You and Dodie are the best. I'm grateful to you for everything, but … ." In her mind, the goodness of the Dedhams collided with the death of Lilith.

"No buts about it," Dodie said, with a jerk of her head to seal the deal.

Madison turned to Colin. "Help me out here, will you?"

Colin held a hand up. "Don't get me involved in family matters."

Getting no help from Colin, Madison looked back at the Dedhams. They seemed genuinely confused by her lack of joy.

"Listen," Madison started, "you've both been great. I mean, I'd be dead if not for you. But I have a job and school, and I need to find a new apartment—one that's close to both of those things."

"You can still work and go to school but live here," Doug told her. "Rent free."

"That's a longer commute than I'd like to make," Madison advised him. "Especially for the kind of money I make."

Dodie laughed. "What Doug means, silly, is you'll have a new job and you can go to school next semester. There are several good colleges not far from here."

Madison shook her head, still not understanding what they were saying. "What job?"

"With us. With the council," Dodie told her, excitement building in her voice. "You can assist Samuel—be the council's connection to the living, sort of like Mike is with police matters. You can start right after we clear up this nasty mess with the covens."

It was becoming clear to Madison what was going on. Knowing what she knew, Samuel meant to keep her close. "Samuel put you up to this, didn't he?"

"No, he did not," Doug said with knitted brows. "You living here was our idea. After seeing your apartment destroyed, we were going to invite you to stay here until you got back on your feet. But then Dodie thought why not have you stay permanently, like you're really our family."

"We called Samuel this morning after we got back from our duties," Dodie added. "We wanted to make sure it was all right with him since you're, well, alive and all, and we have to be so careful about that."

"But Samuel loved the idea," Doug joined in. "It was his idea that you go to work for the council. He said we could use a bright young woman like you." Doug beamed so bright, Madison wanted to shield her eyes.

"It's not that I don't care for you two," Madison began. "I do. You've been more like family to me these past few days than anyone I've known since my great aunt Eleanor died." She gave the Dedhams a sheepish smile. "And it was fun introducing you to people as my grandparents."

"So keep introducing us as your grandparents," Doug said in a matter-of-fact voice.

"But to live here," Madison continued, "is another story. I'm used to being out on my own. And I wouldn't want to be underfoot."

Dodie waved a hand, letting Madison know it was no big deal. "We sleep most of the day. You sleep most of the night. You could even decorate your room any way you'd like."

Doug reached out and patted Madison's arm. "Tell you what. Just give it a try for a little while—say, a few months. If it doesn't work out, you can move into an apartment. We'll even help you find a new one."

"But you should definitely take the job with the council," Dodie stressed. "They will pay you much better than that waitress job, and the hours will be more flexible when you need time for school."

Madison laughed in spite of the confusion and darkness dulling her brain. "Mostly night work, right?"

"Not necessarily," Doug said in all seriousness. "There are a lot of things Samuel and the council need help on during the day, when we're all sleeping. That's why we need someone like you."

Madison looked at the Dedhams, moving her eyes back and forth from one to the other. They really did look like picture-perfect grandparents. "Do I have to answer right now?" she asked them, thinking about the events of the night before. "I have a lot to think about."

Dodie clutched Doug's arm to stem her excitement. "No, dear, take a few days. We know it's an important decision."

When the Dedhams went upstairs to retire, Madison walked Colin out to his car. It had stopped raining, leaving the morning air fresh and filled with the damp, musty scent of the surrounding earth and trees.

"So what do you think?" she asked him. "About me living here and working with the council?"

Colin leaned against his car and considered his reply. "To be perfectly frank with you, having you here has given the Dedhams a spark I've not seen in them before. I'd like to see it continue. And maybe it's time for you to have a new start and a loving family. Nothing wrong with that."

"And the job?"

"I heartily agree with that. We've talked from time to time about needing a beater who can run interference for us. And everyone you've met on the council likes and admires you." Colin gave her a wide, genuine smile, the type of smile she had seen him give Isabella at Bloodlust. "Trust me, the admiration of a vampire is a difficult thing to come by."

Madison looked into Colin's eyes. "But what about last night? Isn't that the real reason Samuel wants me to stay? He wants to keep an eye on me because of what I know." She glanced at the house. "Do they know what I saw?"

"Undoubtedly. Doug is on the council, so Samuel would have told him this morning." Colin placed a hand on each of Madison's upper arms and held her directly in front of him. "Listen, I know you're terrified by what you saw. The entire council knows you're scared." He paused, then plowed on with blunt reality. "The truth of the matter is, if we thought for a moment you were going to talk, you'd be dead already."

She jerked away from him. "Is that supposed to comfort me?"

"What I'm trying to say, Madison, is that if an invitation to live and work among us was extended to you, then it was authentic and not a trick. Vampires don't do things like that lightly."

Madison was quiet for a moment, then asked, "Who was that other man there last night? Was he a vampire?"

"Yes. That was Eddie Gonzales, another council member. We have to have a certain number of members present to carry out an execution."

"And what about Lilith's body? Did you munch on it until it was gone? Pick your teeth with her bones?" Madison shuddered, then another issue that had been nagging her for days popped out of her mouth. "And Bobby Piper's body—what happened to that? If we dug up Samuel's back yard, would we find dozens of beater bodies?"

Colin was silent as he weighed his words. "No, you wouldn't find any bodies." He paused. "We have a special service that disposes of inconvenient corpses."

"Inconvenient corpses." Madison shook herself in disgust. "That's a civilized way of putting it."

Another few minutes of silence passed. A soft rain started up again, but neither Madison nor Colin made a move to take cover. Madison glanced over her shoulder at the house. "My grandparents, the vampires."

Colin stood up and placed a hand on either side of Madison's face. She looked into his black eyes but didn't pull back.

"We got off to a rocky start, Madison," Colin said, his voice taking on a genuine tone of tenderness. "But I really like you and hope we can become friends ... in spite of everything."

He bent forward and grazed her lips with his. Then he kissed her—a light but lingering kiss. Almost against her will, Madison leaned into it, surrendering to its soft, erotic pull until a vision of Lilith's white body and the memory of her screams broke through, destroying the moment.

Madison jerked back. She didn't look at Colin but just stared at his mouth—the mouth that, hours ago, had sucked the life out of another woman.

Again, silence fell between them until Colin walked around to the driver's side of his car. Before getting in, he gave her another long look.

"Give it a try, Madison, both the job and living here. We vampires aren't always such a rotten lot."

THIRTY-ONE

When were you going to tell me about this?"

The question came from Mike Notchey. When he'd arrived at the Dedham house to check up on Madison, she'd brought him up to speed on the break-in, both the one at her apartment and the one at Auntie Em's.

"I just did."

"A day late and a dollar short, aren't you?" He looked pissed.

"There was nothing you could do about it," she explained. "Culver City isn't your jurisdiction."

When Notchey had arrived, Pauline told him Madison was on the back patio. He'd discovered her tucked under a blanket on a chaise longue, getting some fresh air and reading a book. Or rather, the book was in her hands and open, but he'd found her staring off into space.

"It was just some vandalism, probably by kids," she said, pulling the blanket up farther to ward off the damp chill in the air. "At least that's what the police said. Someone probably noticed I hadn't been home in a few days and broke in."

"That doesn't explain the break-in at the diner on the same night."

She stuck her nose back into her book.

"Considering you were kidnapped and nearly murdered less than a week ago, you seem pretty cavalier about the whole thing." Notchey took a pack of cigarettes out of his pocket and lit one. He took a long first drag, savoring each second he held it.

"I thought you and the vamps thought I was snatched by mistake?"

Notchey took two more long drags, then snuffed the cigarette, saving the rest. "I'm still leaning that way, at least for the moment. But even if you were grabbed by mistake, it's pretty obvious someone is looking for you now."

Madison didn't like the idea of keeping Mike out of the loop on things, even if she did understand why the vampires wanted it that way. And after last night, she understood their reasons more.

Changing the subject, Madison announced, "The Dedhams asked me to stay and live here with them." She watched the detective, looking for some sign of approval or disapproval. His face was a blank.

Notchey drew up a patio chair and sat down. "Are you going to?"

"I'm not sure yet. It's a very generous offer, but there are a lot of things to consider."

Notchey blew out a gush of air. Madison could smell smoke on the breath he expelled.

"You're still very young. Sure you should be shut up here, in vampire world?"

"I'm not sure about anything right now." She let Mike think she was only talking about living with the Dedhams, but in truth she was also thinking about Samuel and Colin, and Lilith. And Colin's kiss.

"They said I could live here," she continued, "and go to one of the colleges in the area. Transferring wouldn't be a problem. I've only been taking general classes. I don't even have a major yet."

"And what about a job?"

"Samuel offered me a job working with the council—kind of a combination secretary and liaison is how I understand it."

Without a word, Notchey pulled out his cigarettes and removed the one he'd just saved. He lit it again.

"You don't seem happy about that news," Madison said, sensing that this time Mike would smoke the butt right down to his fingers.

"I'm neither happy nor unhappy. I'm concerned." He took a drag, held it, and exhaled before continuing. "Once you're in with the vampires, you'll never get out. Then again, you're already in pretty deep, but this will be the big and final plunge."

Madison scoffed at the idea. "I'll be able to move on anytime I want. They know I won't say anything."

"Ever see the Godfather movies?" He took another puff.

"Sure. Everyone has." Madison tilted her head and looked at him, not sure where he was going with the reference.

"Remember that famous line?" Notchey asked. "I think it was in the third one: 'Just when I thought I was out, they pull me back in.'" He shrugged. "Or something like that."

Madison laughed at Notchey's bad impression of Michael Corleone.

"Well, the vampires are like that," he told her, taking his last puff before snuffing and tossing his cigarette. "They're monsters, Madison. No matter how civil they seem."

Unbidden, the mental snapshot of Lilith's execution popped into her head.

"They're horror film legends come to life," Mike added. "Throw in seductive and mysterious, and that's an alluring combination."

"Is that what happened to you?"

"In some ways. I got close to Doug and Dodie. Like you, they saved my life. I owe them."

"The council didn't save your life," Madison pointed out. "So why do you help them?"

"Because I want to work with them to make sure the lid stays on between their community and ours. These current murders could blow all that to smithereens. Speaking of which, did you guys learn anything at Bloodlust?"

Madison was torn. She didn't want to lie to Mike Notchey, but neither did she want to go against Samuel's wishes. In the end, if it was between Mike or Samuel getting mad at her, she'd take Mike's wrath over the head vampire's any day.

"Not really. Both Colin and Doug went there last night and came back empty-handed."

Notchey started to leave. "Well, at least there haven't been any more murders—not that we know of, anyway."

Madison got up and went inside with the detective. "Mike, you know the Hollywood area well, don't you?"

"It's not my beat, but I'm familiar with a lot of it. Why?"

"Have you ever heard of a place called Porky's? Someone mentioned it to me, but I couldn't find anything about it on the Internet. I'm not even sure if it's a place—could be a person."

Notchey twisted his face in thought. "Doesn't ring any bells. Who told you that? Was it at Bloodlust?" He studied her face, waiting for an answer.

Madison wanted to tell him about Cubby and how Porky could be a lead to where the murders took place, but she wasn't sure how to do it without telling him everything. "No, it wasn't," was all she said.

About an hour later, Pauline left for the day. Madison had approached her almost as soon as she came in that morning about how she felt about Madison moving in permanently.

"You still going to keep your own room tidy?" was all the housekeeper had asked.

"Of course. Don't see why that would change."

"Then I say welcome. I think it would be good for both you and the Dedhams."

In the afternoon, Madison was restless. Her mind was buzzing with the pros and cons of living with the Dedhams and accepting the job with the council. Her lips were buzzing with the feel of Colin's kiss, and her ears were buzzing with the impact of Samuel's words. And everything was overshadowed by Lilith's death. She knew she would never forget what she'd seen, but she wondered if she'd ever be able to put it aside.

Mike Notchey was right. Once she made a commitment to work and live among the undead, they would always have a hold on her.

Shaking herself out of her thoughts, Madison went to the computer and tried again to find a reference to Porky or Porky's in the Hollywood area. Still nothing. She came to the conclusion that it had to be someone's name. She wondered if Stacie had found out anything more since last night, then remembered that it was likely she was sleeping, or whatever it was vampires did, just like the Dedhams, Colin, Samuel—all of them were out of commission for several more hours.

It occurred to Madison that, vampires aside, living with the Dedhams and having the house to herself most of the day could have both an upside and a downside. The big house seemed empty without Doug and Dodie's cheerful banter, and Madison wondered if she would get lonely rattling around the place. Pauline would be company, but she had work to do. But, Madison countered in her head, once she returned to school and started working with the council, she'd be occupied most of the day and would have several hours in the evening when she could interact with the Dedhams. During the day, it would be almost like living alone, and she'd done that for several years. It was all part of the process of weighing the pros and cons of the offer.

Still antsy, Madison grabbed her car keys and jacket. She was almost to her car when she had second thoughts about leaving. But, she reasoned with herself, no one told her she couldn't go anywhere today. And it was still daylight. She'd be safe in the daylight. Now would be a perfect time to find Cubby and see if she could pinpoint the Porky connection. Once it started getting dark, she'd come back.

Turning on her heels, Madison returned to the house. Just in case the Dedhams rose before she got back, she scribbled out a quick note saying she was running an errand and would be back before dark. If they needed her, they could call her cell. Earlier in the day, she'd made sure to save the Dedhams' number to her cell phone's address book. If she ran late, she would give them a call and let them know she was fine. Samuel had made her add both his and Colin's numbers before she left his home that morning.

Excited to get out of the house on her own for a change, Madison never noticed the dark sedan pulling away from the curb and following her through the canyon.

Without the cloak of darkness, the section of Hollywood Boulevard where they'd found Cubby looked seedier than it had the night before. It had drizzled on and off most of the day, making the broken concrete sidewalks look like soggy cardboard. In the gutters, sodden trash stuck together like lumps of dirty Velcro. She drove past the boarded-up storefronts where Cubby had sat the night before, but he wasn't there.

Remembering that Stacie had said she thought Cubby had been living in an alley not far from the spot, Madison turned down the first street and then turned into the alley that ran behind the storefronts. It was short and a dead-end. She turned the car around and slowly made her way back out to the street, keeping her eyes peeled for signs of Cubby.

Working her way methodically through the maze of alleys, side streets, and parking lots, Madison covered the area between Hollywood and Sunset Boulevards and found nothing. She crossed the major intersection and did the same to the large block to the east; again, nothing. Mostly she just spotted people trotting through the rain from buildings to their cars and vice versa. It was nearing the end of the business day, and people were mostly leaving.

Moving another block east, closer to the freeway, she spotted a ragged couple hovering in a back alley doorway. She got out of her car and approached them. "Do you know a man named Cubby?" she asked.

The man, white, with long, straggly gray hair, nodded but didn't look up. The woman, a female copy of the man right down to the smell of cheap booze, glared at her.

"Do you know where I can find him?" Madison asked.

The man remained silent, but this time he looked at Madison. His eyes were bloodshot. He shook his head.

Madison prodded with another question. "Do you know Porky?"

The man looked down and nodded. The woman said nothing but continued to stare, her eyes as runny as her nose.

"Know where I can find him?"

The man jerked his head up. "Porky ain't a him."

"Is it a place? Can you tell me where it is?"

"Porky ain't a place neither."

The puzzle and the man's cryptic answers were frustrating Madison. She fought to contain her composure. Whatever Porky was, at least the man had acknowledged knowing it. "Okay," she said, trying again. "How can I find Porky?"

The man started to say something, but his words were interrupted by a spasm of coughs. He lifted a trembling hand and pointed off in the distance. "Near the freeway."

"Anything more specific?"

"Fuck off, bitch," snapped the woman. "Can't you see he's sick?"

"Can I get you something?" Madison asked. "Some help?"

The woman glared at her. "Just leave us alone."

Madison dug into her purse, pulled out ten dollars, and held it out toward the couple. Between tipping the waitress at Bloodlust, feeding Cubby, and now this couple, Madison was going through her paycheck pretty damn fast. The woman eyed the money as if it were a snake, then snatched it before Madison could change her mind. Madison figured they were probably going to spend it on booze, but maybe the booze would at least keep the old guy warm.

As she walked away, Madison heard the man mutter between coughs, "Near Hollywood. Freeway near Hollywood."

It was a few blocks to where Hollywood Boulevard crossed over the Hollywood Freeway. Madison pulled into the parking lot of a corner burger joint almost next to the freeway. Ordering a burger and Coke, she sat in her car and ate while looking around at the area. It was going to be easier to continue on foot here. Several streets crisscrossed at odd angles, and building positions were less orderly. It would be almost impossible to cover the area in the car. The rain had stopped, but the sky didn't look like it was through dumping.

Swallowing the last of her burger and taking a big swig from her Coke, Madison scrounged around in the back seat of her car until she located a ball cap. It was navy blue, with *Auntie Em's* emblazoned in white across the front, a gift from Kyle to all his employees last Christmas, along with a small—a very small— bonus. Madison put the cap on her head and pulled her hair into a ponytail, threading it through the opening in the back of the cap. Then she stuck her ID and some cash into her jeans pocket and her cell into her jacket pocket. After stuffing her purse under the front seat, locking the car, and using the filthy ladies' room at the burger place, she was ready to go. She had a lot of area to cover before darkness sent her back to Topanga.

The man in the alley had said Porky was near the freeway and Hollywood Boulevard. Even though that narrowed it down considerably, it still left a lot of nooks and crannies to investigate in a short time. Before leaving the restaurant, she'd asked one of the counter guys if he knew anything about Porky. He'd screwed up his face, then shook his head in the negative.

"How about homeless people?" she prodded.

The guy behind the counter, a scrawny twenty-something Latino with a sparse moustache and tattoos dripping from under the short sleeves of his tee shirt with the burger joint logo, looked at her with suspicion.

"I'm a journalist," Madison lied, "doing a piece on the homeless in Hollywood. I'm told several homeless live here near the freeway."

He nodded, giving her more attention than she welcomed. He looked her up and down, the suspicion giving way to a lascivious grin. "They around. But the real story is here, *chica. I'm* the story you lookin' for."

"You ever hear of a guy named Cubby?" she asked, ignoring his come-on. "Old black guy."

"Yeah, I know him." The grin turned to a scowl of disgust. "Comes in now and then for a burger when he's got money. Drives off customers with his stink and crazy talk."

"Crazy talk?"

"Vampires, *chica*." The guy laughed as he wiped down the counter with a dirty cloth. "Last time the old guy was in here, he says he seen vampires." He squinted at her with a slow smile. "You lookin' for vamps, baby? I'll bite you if you want."

Madison gave him a smile, thinking how the guy would piss his pants if he ever saw a real vampire at work.

"Thanks, but maybe another time." She looked out the door, at the freeway. "So this Cubby guy," she said, continuing with her train of questions. "He might be interesting for my piece. He live around here?"

The guy shrugged, realizing he was getting nowhere. "I seen him a few times on the other side of the freeway, digging in trash—maybe there. Haven't seen him in a couple of days, though." He threw the dirty rag in a nearby sink. "Good riddance."

"Can I leave my car here while I take a look?"

"This ain't no park 'n ride." He gave her the up-and-down stare again. "Then again, maybe I could be persuaded."

Madison dug a ten-dollar bill out of her pocket. "I hear this is the going price these days for non-valet parking in Hollywood."

Just as customers came into the greasy shack, the guy snatched the money. "I'll watch it for ya."

"Thanks. It's the old silver Honda. I shouldn't be long."

Madison took off, hoping the guy didn't call his 'hood friends to boost her car while she was gone.

THIRTY-TWO

Since the guy in the burger joint said he'd seen Cubby on the other side of the freeway, that's where Madison headed first. She jogged down Hollywood Boulevard, crossed over the freeway, and came to a stop at the first cluster of buildings. The guy hadn't said which side of Hollywood Boulevard he'd seen Cubby on, north or south, just that it was on the other side of the freeway.

Standing in front of a squat building that housed a second-hand store, Madison took a minute to think about where she would go if she was homeless and needed shelter. Then again, she *was* nearly homeless—with questionable options.

If she needed shelter and chose this area to live in, Madison thought she might stick close to the buildings next to the fence that bordered the freeway. They might afford some protection against the elements and provide a little privacy. Even though there was a decent clearance between the fence and the buildings and it was paved, it wasn't wide enough for cars to drive down. And along the fence, weeds had been allowed to grow unchecked.

Anyone holed up along there would not be disturbed very often or easily seen.

Madison carefully entered the space, keeping her eyes peeled for signs of life, both human and animal. As much as it was a perfect spot for homeless squatting, it was also a great spot for rats. Scraps of paper, fast-food bags, and disposable cups littered the vegetation along the fence, stuck fast to the tall, thin weeds like large chunks of dandruff. When her sneaker landed on a slippery piece of decayed fruit, Madison started to lose her balance. Suppressing disgust, she put out a hand to the stucco side of the low building to steady herself and found it sticky and grimy from rain-drenched dirt. Before moving on, she wiped her hand on her jeans and scraped the bottom of her sneaker against the pavement, then reminded herself this was no time to be prissy. Her time was growing short.

Behind the low building was a set of dumpsters. Madison stood on her toes and peered in. Nothing. Nothing around them either. There were a couple of cars parked behind the second-hand store but no sign of people. The rain was keeping most visitors to this dismal area at a minimum.

Across the parking lot was another depressing building, followed by another. It seemed to be an old, run-down business complex. The buildings were all gray, their walls showing chunks of missing stucco, especially at the corners of the buildings, as if they'd been chewed on by large rats. They stood near each other, one after the other, with small parking alleys between them. Each had faded, unlit signs describing what type of business they held, and most looked closed, with iron bars on the windows and doors. Only the secondhand store had cars in its parking area.

Madison moved past each depressed building, checking each one's dumpster area for signs of life. So far, she'd met neither human nor animal. The rain had started up again, coming down soft but steady. She zipped up her jacket against the cold and wet and kept moving.

Just after the last building in the group, she spotted another set of similar-styled buildings. These looked in worse repair than the others, possibly even abandoned. They were set vertical to the first set, their fronts facing in the direction of a small, dingy side street instead of Hollywood Boulevard. She wove her way in and around these buildings and their dumpsters. Cubby had said he wasn't going back to his former place, but she might find someone who knew where he had gone or who knew more about this Porky.

Behind the last building, the one with its back close to the freeway fence, Madison found something promising. In a nook made by one building abutting another was a heap of cardboard. It wasn't stacked one piece on top of the other, ready for trash pickup, but was arranged in a crude shelter. Two sides of the small abode were made up by the rough sides of the buildings. The front and top were of thick, flattened cardboard.

With caution, Madison looked inside, expecting to find someone trying to keep out of the rain, but it was empty except for scraps of ragged cloth and pieces of crushed plastic pushed up against one wall and covering the ground. Like the group of buildings, it had an abandoned feel about it. It might have been Cubby's home, or it might have belonged to another unfortunate soul. She moved on.

Hunkering down more inside her jacket, Madison moved forward, slower now, her eyes scanning every detail of the area around the cardboard house. Her ponytail was soaked, and her feet were wet. A chill was building, working its way from the outside in toward her core. It only added to the creepiness of the place. Good sense told her to turn back. Madison beat back her fear, setting it off to the side, along with the cold, to be dealt with later. Whatever direction her life took, she knew she could not move forward until the killings were resolved.

A little farther past the building, she found evidence of another possible dwelling. This one was under a low corrugated piece of metal that had been wedged against the fence and a short shrub. Around it, cardboard had been used to establish crude walls affixed to the fence and metal roof with scraps of twine. Compared to the size of the last one, this seemed like a duplex. Again, it looked abandoned.

Now that her eyes knew what they were looking for, Madison started seeing them. Scattered throughout the area between the dilapidated buildings and the fence was a small village of crude shelters made of cardboard and other cast-off materials. There weren't many, maybe a half dozen or so. She approached each one with care. She didn't want to frighten anyone, nor did she want any unpleasant surprises, but each appeared abandoned. She wondered if the occupants had gone in search of drier shelter or if something had frightened them off, as it had frightened off Cubby. If Cubby had seen killings in the area, maybe other homeless had, too. Maybe this was why the drunk in the alley had been so reluctant to tell her about it. He'd said Porky was out this way. Having found the cluster of makeshift shelters, Madison felt certain she was close to identifying Porky. Once she had the information, she would go back to her car and contact Samuel; she'd leave the rest to them. Thinking about Geoff and the dead girls, and what was done to them, Madison was feeling less squeamish about the council's methods of meting out justice.

She'd gone a little farther when she let out a faint squeak of surprise. Scooting over to the side of a building just past the last shelter, she examined the wall near a rusty dumpster. She'd found Porky.

Porky wasn't a person and it wasn't a place: it was a drawing. Painted on the wall, partially concealed by the dumpster, was the faded likeness of Porky Pig, complete with his little blue jacket, red bow tie, and perky smile. The paint was faded and chipped, but it was clear to Madison's eye that at one time it had been a very good rendition of the popular Looney Tunes character.

Madison stepped back and surveyed the area around the drawing. The buildings had gotten more and more dilapidated as she'd moved farther away from Hollywood Boulevard. She looked back toward the busy street and was surprised by how far she'd walked in her single-minded quest for Porky. Cars and trucks on the freeway buzzed by below, hidden from view behind tall weeds and oleander that edged the fence. Overhead, the sun was a fading memory.

Excitement filled her. She was no longer bait set out by the vampires. She'd found the key to Cubby's mumblings. The killings had to have happened here or near here. Samuel and his crew could search the place tonight.

It would only take her a few minutes to jog back to her car, but she didn't want to wait. As she started walking away from Porky, Madison pulled her cell out of her pocket and started to find the speed dial for Samuel. She didn't know if he'd be up yet, but she could at least leave him a message to call her.

In her triumph, Madison didn't hear the steps coming up behind her or feel the blow that sent her sprawling to the ground.

THIRTY-THREE

My, my, my," said a voice coming out of the dark fog that engulfed Madison's brain. "Looks like we got an early Christmas present."

Madison opened one eye. Her head hurt like it'd been cracked open with an anvil. She shut the eye and squeezed them both tight against the pain. Then she opened it again, followed by the other.

Hanging overhead was a long fluorescent light fixture wrapped in a wire casing. Madison tried to cover her eyes with an arm but found both of her arms secured tightly by her side. She tried to move her legs and found the same thing with them. She was laid out on a cold, hard surface.

Madison still couldn't see who was speaking, but the voice sounded familiar. Not far away, another joined in. "What in the hell is she doing here?" another familiar male voice asked. "How the fuck did she find us?"

"Who cares how. She's here now, and we didn't have to lift a finger or pay some thug to grab her for us."

It was then one of the speakers came into view. It was Ethan Young. He was dressed totally in black, including a black watch cap on his head. He peered down at her through his glasses and smiled. "Miss me?"

It wasn't until Madison tried to speak that she realized her mouth had been taped shut.

"If you promise not to scream," Ethan said, "I'll take it off."

"Leave it," the other voice ordered.

"Aw, that's no fun. Besides, no one can hear her. These walls are concrete, and the area's abandoned."

"Maybe, but I'll still find the noise annoying."

Ethan looked over toward the direction of the voice. "You find everything annoying." He looked down at Madison. "You promise not to annoy Ben?"

After Madison gave Ethan a consenting nod, he lifted the tape from the corners of her mouth, then yanked it fast the rest of the way. She let out a yelp as the tape took some of her skin, leaving behind a sharp, painful burn. She licked her lips and tasted blood.

Ethan bent over Madison and lowered his face to hers. His tongue darted out and quickly caught a dribble of blood. "Mmmm," he murmured with a wink to her. He then turned Madison's left hand over and examined the bloodline. "I don't know if this line makes you lucky or unlucky," he told her. "Depends on your viewpoint, I'm sure."

"You can't become a vampire by drinking my blood," she said to him through her swelling lips.

"How do you know I want to drink your blood?" he asked, bending back over her. "Maybe I want to eat your heart instead."

He gave her a monstrous grimace and pretended to take a bite from her chest.

"I heard you and Ben talking that night at Bloodlust," she admitted in a low voice. "You think by drinking the blood of someone with one of these lines, you'll become a vampire." She wiggled the fingers of the hand Ethan held. "But only people with these lines can *become* vampires; that's how it works. And only a vampire can turn them."

Ben stepped into her line of vision. "She's only trying to save her skin."

Ben was also dressed in black, without the cap. But this time he wasn't wearing his sunglasses. Even though he was wearing his long-haired wig, Madison could see clearly that Ben was the Cobb salad guy from the diner. Fearing he might snap, she kept the truth of his identity to herself. Since she could only see the top half of the men, she guessed she was tied to a table. She also noticed that both Ethan and Ben were dirty. Turning her head one way as far as it could go, then the other, she saw that they were in a concrete building with no windows, like a garage. The ceiling overhead was low, with light fixtures like the one over her extending down in fairly even intervals. The interior appeared mostly bare as far as she could see, with just a few boxes stacked against one wall. To her other side, a van was parked. Its side door was open to reveal an assortment of items packed inside. The van had been backed in, its nose facing the large main door to make an easy exit. It looked to Madison like they were moving, but she didn't know if they were moving in or moving out. Her gut told her moving out.

"Who told you about those lines?" Ethan demanded. "You said you were new to vampirism."

"Colin. He told me what they meant when he met me. That's why I wanted to learn more." Madison's mind worked fast, making up a story and hoping to sell it. "We were trying to find a real vampire to turn me."

Ethan laughed. "So what Colin did with Miriam was really to help you?"

Madison turned her head away, trying to convey hurt. "I went looking for him that night." She turned her head back to Ethan. "I wanted to tell him that I thought you might know some real vampires who could help us. But when I found him with ... well, I just took off."

Ben glared at her. "Doesn't explain why you're here or how you found us."

The question worried Madison. She didn't want to give Cubby up, but she had to feed the killers something plausible. "Dumb luck, really," she said. "I was in Hollywood last night with friends. There was an old bum on the street yammering about vampires in Hollywood. Said he saw them drinking some poor girl's blood. I paid the bum to show me where." She shrugged as far as she could in her restraints. "I had no idea you'd be here. I thought I'd find real vampires."

"But we are real vampires, Madison," said Ethan. "You heard wrong that night. We know that only vampires can make other vampires. What that bum saw, it was us helping that girl become a vampire."

The two men studied her, but it was Ben who spoke first. "You really want to be a vampire?"

Madison wasn't sure how dumb they thought she was, but she was going to give them as much dumb as she could muster. "Doesn't everyone want to be one?"

Ben wouldn't give up the questions. "Who were you calling when I found you?"

"Colin. I wanted to tell him I'd found the vampires."

Ethan picked up her cell phone from somewhere and held it within her sight. He scrolled down through the numbers. "Colin Reddy. His name's right here." He showed it to Ben.

"But this Reddy guy doesn't have a bloodline, does he?" asked Ben.

"No," Madison answered. "But he's dying to see a vampire turn someone. What can I tell you, the idea of it makes him hot. And when he's hot, he's hot."

Again, Ethan laughed. "So claims the maid Miriam."

After a short consideration, Ethan held out her phone. "Tell you what, Madison. Why don't you give Colin a call and ask him to meet you here. Ben and I will turn you, and he can watch."

Ben started to protest. "We need to get going, Ethan. Who knows who else that bum told."

Ethan ignored him. "What do you say, Madison? We'll turn you, then you can suck Colin Reddy dry. He'll be your first official vampire kill. It'll serve him right for the two-timing he did back at Bloodlust."

Madison narrowed her eyes and gave Ethan a sly grin. "I like the sound of that."

Ethan looked up at Ben. "She's a natural."

"Ethan, no." Ben was getting angry.

Still ignoring his partner, Ethan pushed the speed dial for Colin. Madison didn't know if Colin would be up yet or not, and she sighed in silent relief when he answered. Ethan put the cell on speaker.

"Hey, Colin," Madison said into the mouthpiece. "It's me." Before he could answer, she gushed with forced excitement, "Guess what? I found Ethan and Ben. I was wrong that night—*they're* the vampires. They said they'd turn me and let you watch."

"Where are you?" Colin asked, his voice deadpan.

Ethan moved the phone closer to him. "Hear that, buddy? We've agreed to turn your little lady. But she told us you'd want to see it."

"Yes, of course!" Colin answered with enthusiasm.

Ethan laughed. "Bet it makes you hard just thinking about it."

"Hell, yeah," Colin said, sharing the male-bonding moment. "Just tell me where."

Ethan gave him the directions. "Come alone," he ordered. "We're pretty private about such things."

"Colin lives by the beach," Madison told Ben and Ethan when the call ended. "It might take him a bit to get here, especially this time of day."

"Get your stuff from the van," Ethan told Ben.

Ben's face contorted in anger. "Are you out of your mind? We need to get out of here."

"Think about it," Ethan said. "By the time that clown gets here, we'll be done. We'll have her blood and can set him up to take the fall. If we're lucky, they'll pin the other murders on him, too. We can make it look like he killed her, then killed himself out of remorse."

On the table, Madison struggled. "What are you talking about?"

Ben looked down at Madison, watching her wiggle on the table. Reaching under his shirt in the back, he pulled out a gun and held it up in front of Ethan. "We can use this to kill Reddy. It's untraceable—a throwaway from the street."

Madison struggled more as she understood their plans. She knew the gun couldn't kill Colin, but she didn't want to be cut and bled out before he got to Hollywood.

"Come on, guys. Let me loose so we can have some fun before he gets here."

Ben looked down at her. With the hand not holding the gun, he reached up and pulled off his wig, revealing his short hair underneath. "Remember me?"

Madison put on the best pretend shock she could muster. "You? The guy who loves Cobb salads? You're a vampire? How cool is that?" Then she paused and, as if changing shoes, changed her look to puzzlement. "Wait—if you're a vampire, how come you're eating salad?"

Ben laughed for the first time. "Vampires not eating is just a myth. But we prefer blood—especially the blood of young, stupid girls."

Before Madison could say anything more, Ethan slapped tape back over her mouth.

Ben put the gun back under his shirt and went to the van, returning with medical paraphernalia. It looked to Madison like the equipment used when she donated blood.

"We'll drain it here and drink it later," Ben said to Ethan. "With her, we should have enough for the three of us."

"The three of us?" inquired Ethan. "So Lilith's definitely out?"

"Those were my orders as of this afternoon." Ben smirked. "You didn't really think we were taking her all the way, did you?"

"Of course not. I just thought we wouldn't kill her until we were sure our plan worked."

"Even if it doesn't, we don't need Lilith anymore."

Ethan looked down at Madison. "Aren't you going to give her something to calm her down?"

Ben shook his head. "The more she struggles, the faster the heart should pump it out until near the end, when she gets too weak to fight."

From behind the tape, Madison grunted as a needle found its way into one of her veins.

Ethan stroked Madison's hair as her blood began to flow down the plastic tubing into a bag. "I'm really going to miss drinking it straight from the vessel this time," he told Ben with regret.

"When we're done," Ben told him with a sick grin, "I'll let you lick the spoon."

They both laughed.

Madison stopped moving and lay perfectly still, not wanting to rush the process.

After a few minutes, Ben said to Ethan, "It's probably dark out by now. Why don't you go outside and try to spot that guy." He brought the gun out again and handed it to Ethan. "Here, take this in case he gives you any trouble."

Ethan left the table and walked away, heading around the van to the side door of the building. "Man," he said from behind the van. "You have to be more careful. You left the side door open again."

Ben swore under his breath. "Well, it's not like you helped me lug her in here."

Without warning, a shot rang out, and Ben fell to the floor like a sack of manure.

Scared out of her wits, Madison jerked her head as far as she could to see what was going on. From the narrow space between the front of the van and the main garage door, Mike Notchey emerged. Madison's heart jumped in her chest with surprise and relief. He looked at Madison but didn't make a move toward her. Instead, he stayed pressed against the van as Ethan ran in, gun drawn.

When he spotted Ben on the floor, Ethan spun on one foot and fired the gun before seeing what he was firing at. The bullet hit the side of the van. He got off a second shot, which tore through Notchey. Notchey also fired three times, the second and third bullet hitting Ethan Young dead in the chest.

Notchey stumbled to Madison and removed the tape from her mouth, taking more skin with the adhesive. She let out a sharp yelp. "Let's get you out of here." He started working on her bindings but had to stop as pain ran through his body like an out-of-control freight train.

"Oh my god!" Madison yelled when she saw blood spreading across Notchey's shirt.

"Don't worry about me." He tore off the binding on her left arm and removed the needle, being careful with the tubing and blood bag. "Bend your arm to stop the bleeding," he ordered. She obeyed.

Removing the binding on Madison's other arm, Notchey stopped to take several deep breaths. It was then his eyes caught sight of the bundle against the wall, near the boxes. With her arms free, Madison sat up and focused on what had snagged Mike's attention. A scream started in her throat, but she cut it short. Propped against the wall, wrapped in clear plastic, was the body of Gordon, Samuel's bodyguard.

Madison forced her attention back to the living. "Forget him—we have to get *you* help."

He shook his head. "I'm waiting for Colin. I overheard he's on his way. As soon as he gets you out of here, I'll call for backup." He went to work on the bindings on Madison's legs.

Madison grabbed Notchey's arm. "I'm not leaving without you."

"Nothing I can't handle if Reddy doesn't dawdle. Now shut up and help me."

Madison was nearly free when Colin came through the side door. The vampire came around the van, took one look at the chaos, and ran to help Notchey, only pausing for a half second when his eyes snagged on Gordon's body.

"He's bleeding bad," Madison told Colin.

"Forget me," Notchey told Colin. "Get her the hell out of here. And take that blood shit with you." Notchey also wadded up Madison's bindings and handed them to Colin. "Take anything that could link her or her DNA to this place," he ordered as he leaned against the table for support.

Colin, understanding instantly, helped the wobbly Madison to her feet. She hung on to the table for support. Grabbing Madison's jacket from the floor, he threw it over her shoulders. Then he policed the area again, looking for other traces of her being there.

"That your phone?" he asked her, pointing to one on the floor, by the table. When she nodded, he picked it up and handed it to her. Then he took his own jacket off and wrapped the blood bag and tubing in it. "Come on, Madison," he said in a firm voice. "Mike's right, we have to get you out of here."

"What about Gordon?"

"It's too late to help him."

A cell phone rang, but it wasn't Madison's. The sound was coming from Ben's body. Carefully, Colin retrieved the phone from Ben's pocket and looked at the display, surprise registering at the name. He slipped the phone into his own pocket and continued to help Madison.

Holding his bloody side, Mike grimaced and turned to Colin. "You have two minutes, then I'm calling for backup."

"But ...," Madison stammered, still not wanting to leave Mike behind.

"Go with Colin," Notchey demanded. "I'll call as soon as I can."

Reluctantly, Madison let Colin lead her around the van and out the door. Once outside, they walked as fast as Madison could. Colin held his bundle in one arm and wrapped his other arm around Madison's waist to support her. They kept close to the buildings and in the shadows until they reached his motorcycle, which he'd parked out of sight, next to a dumpster behind one of the first buildings. Once safely on, Madison directed him over the freeway to the burger joint where she'd parked her car.

"You okay to drive?" Colin asked, unsure no matter what she answered.

"Yes. I'm feeling much better now." She sucked on a Coke Colin had bought her and leaned against her car. Her eyes wandered across the freeway. Seconds earlier, sirens had screamed down Hollywood Boulevard and turned in the direction they had just come from.

"Mike's going to be fine, Madison," Colin assured her.

"And Gordon? He won't be."

"No, he won't, but Samuel will handle that."

THIRTY-FOUR

As Colin had promised, Mike Notchey was fine. When the police reached him, he was sitting propped against the van holding his gun on the men on the floor. Ben had been killed instantly; Ethan died on the way to the hospital. Traces of blood linking them to the deaths of the women and Geoff Baxter had been found in the van, including a cooler holding bags of blood, some of it from Geoff. The police were trying to trace the sources of the other blood.

Ben's gun had also been the weapon that had killed Gordon. Gordon's connection to Ethan and Ben was never made clear, and the police assumed he'd been part of the killing spree, though they couldn't prove it. Since Gordon had no family, Samuel didn't set the record straight, which would have required a detailed explanation. He also managed to keep his name as Gordon's employer out of it, though privately he mourned the man who'd served him faithfully for so many years.

Several days later, Mike and Madison were enjoying some fall sunlight on the Dedham patio. After leaving the hospital,

Mike had come to stay with them for a few days until he got his strength back, giving Dodie a full house and a patient to look after, much to her delight.

"I would never have forgiven myself had you died," Madison told Mike, being alone with him for the first time since the shooting. "You should have let me stay and help, even if Colin couldn't."

Notchey shook his head. "No way," he insisted. "They would have interrogated you until you dropped—not that you would have folded willingly under the pressure, but we couldn't take that chance. As far as the police know, I went to that garage on a tip from an old bum and found them packing their shit to disappear. Young fired on me. I fired back, hitting both of them. Four bullets for two scumbags." He shrugged. "Perfect ending to a shit story."

"But I'm the one who got the tip from Cubby." Madison looked over at Mike, who was settled on a chaise. She could tell he was itching for a cigarette, but he'd made the decision to use his convalescence to stop cold turkey.

"Yes," Notchey admitted. "And I followed the tip by following you. I knew when we talked that day you were hiding something." He shook his head. "I may not be Samuel, but I am a trained detective, Madison. I know when people are avoiding the truth. And you were so caught up with playing Nancy Drew, you never noticed anyone shadowing you. I'm sorry I wasn't close enough to stop him from clubbing you."

"So why did you wait so long before breaking into the garage?"

"I didn't break in. That jughead really did leave the door open. And I needed to hear as much as I could. I also wanted to give Colin enough time to get there." Notchey looked straight into her eyes. "Believe me, I would have stepped in sooner had I thought they were going to kill you outright. If Colin hadn't arrived when he did, I wouldn't have been able to get you out, and it would have been a lot messier for all of us."

"And what about Ethan and Ben?"

Mike shifted uneasily on the chaise, grimacing as pain rippled through his middle. He knew where Madison was going with her question, and he knew he would have to tell her or she'd pester him to death—or worse, go hunting for the answers on her own.

"What about them?" he asked, stalling for time to collect his thoughts.

"From what I heard, it sounded like their orders were coming from someone else."

With a nod, Mike confirmed her guess. "As we originally thought, Bobby Piper and the creep in custody were foot soldiers. Ethan and Ben were the middlemen answering to someone else."

"You know who?"

This time when he moved, the pain showed on Mike's face.

"You okay?" asked an anxious Madison.

"Yeah, I'm fine." He gingerly adjusted himself into a more comfortable position, then took a deep breath before dumping the info he had in her lap. "Ben Winthrop was traced to Lady Harriet. Ben's her son."

Madison felt her jaw fall to her chest. "Her *son*?"

"Seems she and Winthrop Senior divorced ages ago. There's no doubt she was the one behind the kidnappings and killings—the big brains of the outfit."

"But she seemed so sweet and laid-back."

Mike scoffed at her words. "Yeah, so sweet she had a sound-proof, completely furnished torture room in her home."

Madison nearly stopped breathing at the news. She had been in that home.

"One of the bedrooms had been tricked out with a false wall with a hidden door. Behind the wall was quite the dungeon. It's no wonder the guy in the can was scared shitless. As soon as he found out Ben and Ethan were dead, he broke down and told the cops everything. Guys like him were hired to kidnap specific targets. They were paid when the victims were handed over. He claims they never did any of the killing."

"Do you believe him?'

Mike gave it some thought before answering. "Yeah, I do. He doesn't seem the killing type. His priors were mostly assault and robbery. Kidnapping alone was a big step up for him."

Madison leaned forward in her chair, both fascinated and repelled by the turn of events. "And what's happening with Lady Harriet? Did they arrest her?"

"She's disappeared. Probably sensed everything went sour and took off. No one in her coven has any idea where she's gone."

"How do you know all this?"

"My partner told me at the hospital just before I was released."

"You have a partner?" Madison paused, then blurted, "Partner as in another cop, or partner as in gay couple?"

"As in cop." Mike laughed, then grabbed his side as a stab of pain radiated through him. "You seem more surprised at that than the dungeon." When she didn't respond, he added, "You know, I am a real detective with a real caseload when I'm not on vampire duty."

Madison shrugged. "Just that you never mentioned him … or her."

"It's a him."

They remained silent for a while, each lost in their own thoughts, before Notchey asked, "So, you going to take the job with the council and live here?"

Madison drew in a long drag of air and blew it out. "Yes, I am. I'm in up to my neck now, so why not?" She glanced at Notchey. "Besides, I'm quite fond of the Dedhams. It might be nice to see what having a family is like, even if they are vampires."

"You could do worse."

"Yep, and I have."

She'd broken the news about her decision to both Samuel and the Dedhams the night before. The Dedhams had been elated. Samuel had taken Madison to dinner at Scarlet to celebrate. While at dinner, he'd handed her a jewelry box. She started to protest, but he'd stopped her and told her to open it.

Inside wasn't a fancy, jewel-encrusted trinket but a sturdy handmade bracelet of woven material. Madison took it out of the box and held it up, puzzled. "Thanks?"

The question in her tone made Samuel smile. "Put it on and leave it on," he told her. "It will protect you."

Madison studied the homespun bracelet. "What is it, some voodoo trinket?"

"In a matter of speaking." Samuel took the bracelet from her and slipped it onto her slim wrist. "It has my hair woven through the fabric."

"But you're bald," she pointed out.

Samuel laughed. "Who said the hair came from my head?"

Madison grimaced and stared at it. "Does this mean we're pinned in some creepy vampire way?"

"Sort of." He touched the bracelet. "As long as you wear this and I'm alive, no other vampire will hurt you."

"Oh, so it's really like a pet ID tag." Madison frowned. "'If found, return to owner'—that sort of thing?"

She started to take it off, but Samuel stopped her. "It is to protect you," he insisted. "We don't know why this works, but thousands of years have proven that if a living person wears the hair of a vampire, no other vampire can hurt them. But this is just temporary. The council is having a special one made for you—several, actually, in case of loss or damage. Your new one will be more feminine and will contain hair from each council member. As long as one of us is alive, you will be protected. In the meantime, wear this. It was one of Gordon's spares."

"What about you?" Madison asked, looking for clarification. "Can you hurt me?"

"Yes. Only the vampire whose hair is worn can hurt the person wearing it."

Madison gave that some thought. "But what if I wanted …," she whispered, looking around the restaurant until she spied a handsome vampire with blond hair. "Say I wanted him to bite me. He couldn't?"

When the blond vampire turned her way and flashed a wide grin, Madison blushed, realizing he had super hearing like Colin and the Dedhams.

Samuel turned to look at the vampire in question. "Keep your fangs to yourself, Eric," he told him. "The lady was just making a point."

Ignoring Samuel, the other vampire raised his blood glass to Madison. "Just say the word, beautiful."

Turning back to Madison, Samuel explained, "If you give another vampire permission, he or she can bite you or hurt you. Otherwise, you're off-limits. Once you're wearing the council's bracelet, you will be protected by all of us, and none of us will be able to harm you or bite you without permission from the others or from you yourself."

"In other words, when it comes to the council, I'll get my day in court before execution."

"That's one way of looking at it."

Madison studied the bracelet again. "I've seen something like this on Pauline, but I always thought it was some Jamaican thing."

"Her bracelet contains hair from the Dedhams."

"And Mike Notchey? Does he have one?"

"We've offered him one, but he refused."

"I didn't know refusing was an option."

Samuel shook his head. "For you, it's not—not if you're going to work for us. We need you to be protected, not just for your sake, but for ours."

Sadness crossed Madison's face as she looked at the bracelet again. "I'm so sorry about Gordon. Too bad his bracelet couldn't protect him against living freaks."

They were quiet while their food was served, then Madison spoke again. "I have a question. And please don't read my mind," she added quickly. "Let me ask it like a normal person."

Samuel raised his glass of imported blood. "Normal is boring."

"Are you through?"

He smiled, indicating for her to continue.

"What happened to the blood those creeps took out of me? Last I knew, Colin had it."

"Then why don't you ask him, not me?"

"I haven't seen him since that night." Madison took a bite of her grilled salmon, chewed, and swallowed. "And something tells me you know. You seem to know everything." She paused to sip some iced tea. "Don't you ever get bored with knowing everything?"

"I don't know everything," he admitted. "Just most of the things important to me."

"So make this important enough for you to know."

Samuel gave her a coy shrug but said nothing.

Madison leaned forward and hissed, "He drank it, didn't he, the little bloodsucker?" She cut another piece of fish and stuck it in her mouth, chewing with annoyance.

"Don't be angry with Colin, Madison. He just did what comes naturally." Samuel lowered his sunglasses and winked at her from across the table. "And he shared, like the good sport he is."

Madison dropped her fork.

THIRTY-FIVE

An hour after dropping Madison off at the Dedhams' house, Samuel had changed his clothes and was heading across his back lawn toward the ivy. When he arrived at the council room, he was pleased to see everything in order.

The prisoner was seated, her hands tied in front of her. Her feet were also bound and her mouth gagged. Standing guard next to her was Isabella. The prisoner's chair faced the large council table. Behind the table sat various council members.

A quick head count told Samuel the required number of council members was in attendance. Not wanting to alert Madison that something special was up with the council, Samuel had instructed Doug Dedham to remain at home. It was enough that Madison had witnessed Lilith's execution. She would have to be handled like Mike Notchey, with care and sensitivity. Like Notchey, Madison wasn't stupid, but it would serve no purpose to make her a direct accessory to the council's harsh but necessary governing methods.

Samuel took his place at the head of the table. With a slight nod of his bald dome, he indicated for Isabella to remove the prisoner's gag. The woman coughed and cleared her throat before staring at her captors with a mixture of defiance and fear.

"How dare you?" she began, looking straight at Colin. "You know who I am, yet you and this ragtag coven treat me like this?" The woman sputtered, using her indignation to mask her fright. "This is an abomination! Totally against all coven rules of conduct."

"This is no coven, Lady Harriet," Colin informed her, his voice even and solemn.

Lady Harriet looked at the face of each person on the other side of the table. "Then what is this? An abduction? A kidnapping to extort money from my ex-husband?" She cackled. "Good luck," she said with scorn. "Conrad stopped caring about me long before he divorced me, and now that Ben is dead, he cares even less." At the mention of her son, Harriet's voice cracked, and her defiance faltered as she lowered her head.

"I can assure you, Lady Harriet," began Samuel, looking directly at her, "this is no kidnapping." With a short sweep of his hand, Samuel indicated the council members. "We are the California Vampire Council. You are here because you are on trial for murder and conspiracy."

Harriet's head snapped up. "Trial? Murder? You can't be serious." She looked to Colin again. "You said this wasn't a coven."

"It's not, Lady Harriet," Colin told her again. "We're the governing board for vampires living in California. Real vampires." Colin flashed his fangs. Kate Thornton, Stacie Neroni, and Eddie Gonzales followed suit. Samuel and Isabella kept their fangs covered.

Lady Harriet's eyes widened, but she didn't look shocked. "I always knew you existed," she told the council with a tight-lipped smile. "I had to convince Ben and Ethan, especially Ethan, but I always knew it was just a matter of time before I found you."

"And what about Lilith?" asked Stacie, getting to her feet to stand in front of the prisoner.

"Her? She was insignificant. Ethan convinced her to join us. She'd have done anything to save that sorry-ass coven of hers."

Stacie continued with her questions. "And who told you about the bloodlines?" Stacie turned her bare left hand out and tapped her palm to get her point across.

Lady Harriet looked down at her own left hand but couldn't see her bloodline because of the way her hands were tied. She looked back up at Stacie, her fear gone, replaced with budding confidence and hope. "During some recent research and studies, I found a very old text on vampires. It was in a foreign language I didn't recognize so I couldn't read it or have it translated, but the drawings showed someone sucking the blood out of a young woman with one of these hand marks. Then the person sucking the blood became a vampire."

"So you thought if you drank the blood of those marked as such, you'd also become a vampire? Is that correct?" Stacie waited for a response.

"Yes. At first I thought it was just the blood of young women, but when Ethan met Geoff, and he had a bloodline, too, we decided to try his blood."

Stacie came in close to the prisoner, her fangs still out and menacing. "And what about your own bloodline? Weren't you worried that Ben or Ethan would try to kill *you* for your blood?"

Lady Harriet scoffed. "Ben was my son; he'd never kill me. But he never had a real backbone or leadership qualities. Ethan was smarter, but not by much. They needed me and what I knew if they wanted to become vampires."

Stacie turned to the table and picked up a cell phone. She showed it to Lady Harriet. "According to the messages and voice mails on this, it seems you controlled the whole operation."

"That's Ben's phone." The older woman's eyes narrowed. "How did you get that?"

Colin answered, "I took it off his dead body."

"You? *You* killed my son?"

Shaking his head, Colin clarified, "No, the police killed him. I just happened to be there after, when you were trying to call him." He paused and looked at Samuel, who gave Colin leave to continue. Stacie sat back down. "You see, Lady Harriet," Colin explained, standing, "you got it wrong. Only people with those bloodlines can *become* vampires. Had he lived, your son could have told you that. I understand he learned of it just before he was shot."

"No!"

Colin ignored her cry and continued. "To turn a human into a vampire, a vampire must suck the blood of a human with a bloodline. At the exact moment the human is about to die, the vampire forces the human to drink his—the vampire's—blood. It's like a transfusion. It's very dangerous, and if it's not done correctly, the human can die. If the human survives, he will come back from the brink of death a new vampire." Colin reached out and touched Lady Harriet's left hand. "All along you had the power to become a vampire, but only a real vampire could have turned you. Humans have no ability to do it without one of us."

Looking down again at her bound left hand, Lady Harriet stared at it as if seeing it for the first time. "All this time." She looked back up at Colin, her eyes red and wet, yet bright with new eagerness. "Colin, please—I beg you—turn me. It's all I've wanted my entire life."

"It's too late for that, Lady Harriet." Colin turned away and took his seat with the other council members.

"It's not too late!" the high priestess of Dark Tidings shouted. "Turn me," she begged. "My son is dead because of wanting to be a vampire. Turn me so that his death was not in vain."

"And what about the innocent blood you shed in your ignorance?" Samuel demanded, standing at his place at the head of the table.

Now Lady Harriet really did look surprised. "What do you care if people were killed? You're vampires. Surely you understand my desire to become one of you—to live for eternity." Passion filled her voice as she pled her case. She stopped to sniff as her nose started to run from her tears. "What's a few deaths when you're seeking the higher calling of immortality?"

When she received no answer, Lady Harriet snarled at the vampires before her. "It's not like a single one of you have clean hands. How dare you judge me for killing so that I can have what you have."

Samuel addressed the council. "Lady Harriet, high priestess of Dark Tidings, is charged with murder and conspiracy to commit murder against bloodline holders. You've heard the accused. What is your verdict?"

Samuel went around the table, asking each council member to verbally cast his or her vote. It was a unanimous vote of guilty.

Samuel nodded to Isabella, who lifted Lady Harriet to her feet to stand before the council. The legs of the high priestess shook in terror, but her face was set in anger and disbelief.

"Lady Harriet," Samuel pronounced, his rich voice steady and stern, "you are found guilty as charged and are hereby sentenced to death."

Isabella and Colin lifted a struggling Lady Harriet to the table and secured her to it, then proceeded to tear her clothing away from her body.

"You can't do this," the condemned woman shouted at the council. "If I'm guilty, then turn me over to the police."

Samuel leaned in close. "When it comes to vampires, we're the only law that matters." He unleashed his fangs. "And besides, if we handed you over to the police, it would spoil our fun."

With a nod from Samuel, the remaining council members rose, unfurled their fangs, and approached the table.

The Lady Harriet's screams went unheard by a single living soul.

Lord Wilhelm parked behind Bat Beauty. Being Monday, the club was closed and the parking lot deserted. He'd just come from a date with a promising young acolyte and had a spring in his step.

Wilhelm was about to unlock the back door to the club, the door that led to his private quarters, when he heard a soft weeping coming from the alley. Curious, he followed the sound until he found a woman crouched against the wall of his building. She appeared to be in her late sixties and didn't look homeless.

"May I help you?" he asked.

"Bless you," the woman sobbed.

Wilhelm held out a hand and helped the woman up. Her outfit was smart but dirty.

"I was coming home from playing bridge and took a wrong turn," she explained. "When I stopped a young man to ask for directions, he pulled me from my vehicle, stole my purse and the car." Her crying increased. "I'm so confused. I've been walking in circles for hours."

"Come, dearie," Wilhelm told her, taking her arm. "Come in, I'll make you some tea, and we'll call the police."

"I don't know how to thank you."

As soon as Wilhelm turned his back to unlock his door, the old woman jumped him, pushing him down to the ground with surprising strength.

Stunned, Wilhelm tried to get up but couldn't. Then the woman turned him over and flashed her fangs at him.

"You're … you're…," Wilhelm stammered in horror. "You're real?"

"You bet your hiney, she's real," said a tall, good-looking older man stepping out from the shadows. He looked down at Wilhelm and flashed his own fangs. "And so am I."

"Oh, dear," said Dodie, still holding Wilhelm down. "I do believe he's wet himself."

Doug Dedham shook his head in disgust. "Don't you just hate it when they do that?" He moved in toward their prey, but Dodie stopped him.

"Samuel said he's mine. He gave permission to me, not you."

"Then by all means, my love." Doug gallantly bowed to his wife. "I don't mind taking sloppy seconds."

Dodie studied Wilhelm. "You really should be ashamed of yourself, Lord Wilhelm, for taking advantage of impressionable young people. But your fatal mistake was sinking your fake fangs into our granddaughter."

Wilhelm, speechless with terror, looked into the burning eyes of the vampires, something he'd wanted to do all his life. As the first bite ripped through the flesh of his thin neck, his eyes rolled back in a mixture of excruciating pain and ecstasy. Then the irony of the moment hit him, dulling both his pleasure and pain: he knew he'd never live to tell anyone.

THE END

Read on for a sneak peek
at the second book in the
Fang-in-Cheek Mystery series
by Sue Ann Jaffarian

EXCERPT

The dead body floated facedown in the pool like an inflatable joke, something meant to scare people at parties and on Halloween. But to Madison Rose's eye, it didn't look like some plastic gag. It looked real. Dead real.

"Mike," she said into her cell phone. "We have a problem at the Dedhams."

"What kind of problem?" he asked.

"Um, it's not something I want to discuss on the phone. Can you get here sooner rather than later?"

"Hmmm." He paused, thinking about his schedule. "I could be there in a little over an hour. That soon enough?"

"Not really." She looked at the body, wishing it would swim away or vaporize into the December daylight. "But I guess it'll have to do."

"Sorry."

"I'll have fresh coffee waiting for you," she coaxed.

"Then I'll see you in an hour."

"And there's leftover pot roast."

"Make that closer to forty-five minutes."

Madison went back out onto the patio and stared at the body. Lifting her gaze to the surrounding trees and foliage that covered the surrounding hillside, she scanned them for signs of peeping eyes but noticed none.

It was just after two in the afternoon. Madison had spent the night at Samuel's after working with him until almost four in the morning on council matters. Samuel La Croix was the head of the California Vampire Council. Madison was employed by the council to assist it and Samuel in its day-to-day business affairs —things that were often best handled by a live person during the day. She also helped Samuel with some of his personal business matters. It was a good job—a lot better than her last job as a waitress at Auntie Em's, a diner in Culver City. The council job paid better and was more interesting, although at times it was lonely, and she missed being around the people at the diner. Madison usually did her work for the vampires during the day, depending on e-mails and voice messages for direction, but once in a while she'd have to work through the night with Samuel or attend middle-of-the-night council meetings.

When she'd returned home from Samuel's, Madison had grabbed the Sunday paper and her iPod and headed out to the patio to read and relax. Doug and Dodie Dedham lived in a charming and spacious home tucked into a hillside of Topanga Canyon. She'd come to live with them last October when her own apartment had been destroyed by killers. The Dedhams had adopted her as their granddaughter, and that was how she was introduced to outsiders. Like the job with the council, living with the Dedhams was much nicer, but at times it was lonely because of the opposite hours the Dedhams kept to hers. Doug and

Dodie were upstairs now, suspended in what passed for vampire sleep. Their bodies wouldn't revive until the sun started to set. It was the same with Samuel. She'd gone to sleep in one of his guest rooms while he was still awake, then left his sprawling villa in the hills above Los Angeles long after he'd gone to bed. Except for the couple of hours between sundown and her own natural bedtime, Madison and the vampires were often like ships passing in the night.

Leaning against a post that held the roof over the patio, Madison wrapped a large pool towel around her wet clothes and studied the body. The body was of a naked black man, slim but very fit, with wide, muscled shoulders and strong legs. From his build, she guessed him to be on the young side. His black hair was cropped close to his skull, but she never looked at his face.

As soon as she'd seen the body, she'd kicked off her shoes and jumped into the pool to check for life. Once close, she'd noticed the body had been impaled through its chest with a large stick, the end of which was protruding from the man's back. Still, she'd checked his pulse and found no sign of life. She crawled out of the pool at that point, not wanting to destroy any evidence. No matter who the man had been, it was crystal clear to Madison that he was now a murder victim.

After getting out of the pool, she'd spent a few minutes trying to think of what she should do. Because the Dedhams were vampires, it wasn't like Madison could call the local police. They would arrive and wonder why the Dedhams couldn't be wakened. When sleeping, the Dedhams looked and passed for dead; they *were* dead. How would Madison ever explain that to the authorities? So she'd called Mike Notchey.

Mike Notchey was a detective with the Los Angeles Police Department. He knew about the vampires and was friends with many of them, especially the Dedhams. When he arrived, they would figure out something together.

Madison and Notchey had become close friends in the past couple of months. Like her, he was human. Besides the Dedhams' housekeeper, Pauline Speakes, he was her only regular human contact that she could talk to about the vampires. Since today was Sunday, Pauline was off work, otherwise she might have been the one to find the body. She'd been employed by Doug Dedham for many years, even before he had met and married Dodie. Pauline would have known what to do, although Madison was sure Pauline's first call also would have been to Mike Notchey.

When it was no longer possible to ignore her chattering teeth, Madison decided to run upstairs to pull on some dry clothes. The dead man wasn't going anywhere. Again, she looked around the Dedham back property, wondering if whoever dumped the body in the pool might be watching, but she saw nothing.

Hurrying, it only took Madison a couple of minutes to slip out of her wet clothing, scrub herself dry with a towel, and slip on a sweatshirt and yoga pants. She'd also pulled on wool socks and slippers. Drying her long brown hair would have to wait. Grabbing another towel and her brush, she started back downstairs to wait for Notchey. She was on the upstairs landing when she stopped in her tracks. Quickly, she reversed direction and covered the hallway to the master suite. She knocked. Receiving no answer, she opened the door a crack and peeked in.

The Dedhams were on the bed, cuddled together in the spoon position, with Doug's arm wrapped lovingly around Dodie's middle. The Dedhams appeared to be in their late sixties, early seventies. Doug had been a vampire for a few hundred years, but Dodie had been turned less than twenty.

"Guys?" Madison called to them, hoping that maybe they were nearing the end of their daily death sleep. Since it was winter and daylight hours were shorter, the vampires slept less than they would during the spring and summer. But even in December, the sun wouldn't be going down for a few hours yet. Madison closed the door and ran back downstairs to wait for Notchey.

Walking through the house, Madison yanked out the band holding her hair and started towel-drying it. When she got out to the patio, she plopped herself down on a patio chair and bent at the waist, letting her hair fall forward while she ran it through the folds of the towel. When she came back up into a sitting position and tossed her damp hair back, she screamed.

It was a short shriek, as if someone had come from behind her and slapped a hand over her mouth, cutting it off—a scream of surprise that turned into silent horror.

The body in the pool was still in the pool, and it was still the only body in the pool, but it was no longer floating with its arms extended in a perfect textbook display of a dead man's float.

Dropping the damp towel, Madison jumped to her feet and stared at the pool in disbelief. Her feet were frozen to the concrete pad of the patio as if the cement had become quicksand and swallowed her up to her ankles.

The body was at the far end of the pool, near the wide steps that led down into the water. It was still facedown, but its arms were over the edge, its head resting on the apron, as if someone had tried to haul it out of the water and then abandoned the project.

Madison looked around the back yard and wooded property and again saw no sign of anyone else. When she'd left the body to go inside and change, it had been near the steps but definitely still in the water.

Finally loosening her feet, Madison took a few careful steps toward the body. Doing some quick calculations in her confused head, she added up the time that had passed since she'd first seen the body, called Notchey, and then left to go upstairs. The man couldn't be alive. No one could float facedown that long and not drown. And there had been no pulse. She hadn't been hasty in her determination. She'd checked thoroughly. She was sure of it.

Then his right arm moved ...

WWW.MIDNIGHTINKBOOKS.COM

From the gritty streets of New York City to sacred tombs in the Middle East, it's always midnight somewhere. Join us online at any hour for fresh new voices in mystery fiction.

At midnightinkbooks.com you'll also find our author blog, new and upcoming books, events, book club questions, excerpts, mystery resources, and more.

MIDNIGHT INK ORDERING INFORMATION

Order Online:
• Visit our website, www.midnightinkbooks.com, select your books, and order them on our secure server.

Order by Phone:
• Call toll-free within the U.S. and Canada at
  1-888-NITE-INK (1-888-648-3465)
• We accept VISA, MasterCard, and American Express

Order by Mail:
Send the full price of your order (MN residents add 6.875% sales tax) in U.S. funds, plus postage & handling to:

> Midnight Ink
> 2143 Wooddale Drive
> Woodbury, MN 55125-2989

Postage & Handling:

Standard (U.S., Mexico & Canada). If your order is:
  $24.99 and under, add $4.00
  $25.00 and over, FREE STANDARD SHIPPING

AK, HI, PR: $16.00 for one book plus $2.00 for each additional book.

International Orders (airmail only):
  $16.00 for one book plus $3.00 for each additional book.

Orders are processed within 2 business days.
Please allow for normal shipping time.
Postage and handling rates subject to change.

A spirited new series from award-winning, critically acclaimed Odelia Grey mystery author Sue Ann Jaffarian

A GHOST OF GRANNY APPLES MYSTERY

Along with a sprinkling of history, this ghostly new mystery series features the amateur sleuth team of Emma Whitecastle and the spirit of her pie-baking great-great-great-grandmother, Granny Apples. Together, they solve mysteries of the past—starting with Granny's own unjust murder rap from more than a century ago.

Coming in February 2011: GHOST IN THE POLKA DOT BIKINI, book two in the Granny Apples series!

Ghost
à la
Mode

Granny was famous for her award-winning apple pies—and notorious for murdering her husband, Jacob, at their homestead in Julian, California. The only trouble is, Granny was framed, then murdered. For more than one hundred years, Granny's spirit has been searching for someone to help her see that justice is served—and she hits pay dirt when she pops into a séance attended by her great-great-great-granddaughter, modern-day divorced mom Emma Whitecastle. Together, Emma and Granny Apples solve mysteries of the past—starting with Granny's own unjust murder rap in the final days of the California Gold Rush.

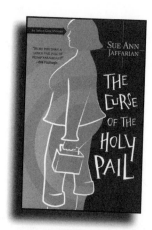

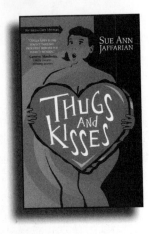

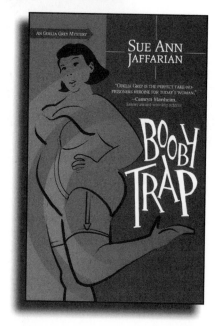

The hugely popular mystery series that features unforgettable amateur sleuth Odelia Grey

You'll love Odelia Grey, a middle-aged, plus-sized paralegal with a crazy boss, insatiable nosiness, and a knack for being in close proximity to dead people. This snappy, humorous series is the first from award-winning, critically acclaimed mystery author Sue Ann Jaffarian.

An Odelia Grey Mystery

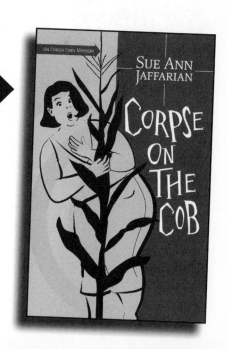

Too Big to Miss

BOOK ONE

Too big to miss—that's Odelia Grey. A never-married, middle-aged, plus-sized woman who makes no excuses for her weight, she's not Superwoman—she's just a mere mortal standing on the precipice of menopause, trying to cruise in an ill-fitting bra. She struggles with her relationships, her crazy family, and her crazier boss. And then there's her knack for being in close proximity to dead people...

When her close friend Sophie London commits suicide in front of an online web-cam by putting a gun in her mouth and pulling the trigger, Odelia's life is changed forever. Sophie, a plus-sized activist and inspiration to imperfect women, is the last person anyone would ever have expected to end her own life. Suspecting foul play, Odelia is determined to get to the bottom of her friend's death. Odelia's search for the truth takes her from Southern California strip malls to the world of live web-cam porn to the ritzy enclave of Corona del Mar.

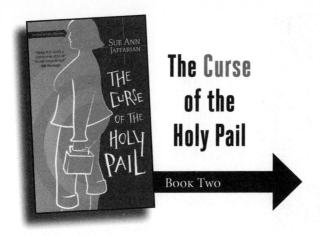

The Curse of the Holy Pail

Book Two

I s the "Holy Pail" cursed? Every owner of the vintage Chappy Wheeler lunchbox—a prototype based on a 1940s TV Western—has died. And now Sterling Price, a business tycoon and client of Odelia Grey's law firm, has been fatally poisoned. Is it a coincidence that Price's one-of-a-kind lunch pail—worth over thirty grand—has disappeared at the same time?

Treading cautiously since her recent run-in with a bullet, Odelia takes small bites of this juicy, calorie-free mystery—and is soon ravenous for more! Her research reveals a sixty-year-old unsolved murder and Price's gold-digging ex-fiancée with two married men wrapped around her breasts—uh, finger. Mix in a surprise marriage proposal that sends an uncertain Odelia into chocolate sedation and you've got an unruly recipe for delicious disaster.

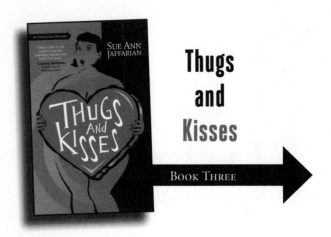

Thugs
and
Kisses

BOOK THREE

With the class bully murdered at her thirtieth high-school reunion and her boss, the annoying Michael Steele, missing, Odelia doesn't know which hole to poke her big nose into first. This decision is made for her as she's again swept into the action involving contract killers, tangled relationships, and fatal buyer's remorse. Throughout this adventure, Odelia deals with her on-again, off-again relationship with Greg and her attraction to detective Devin Frye.

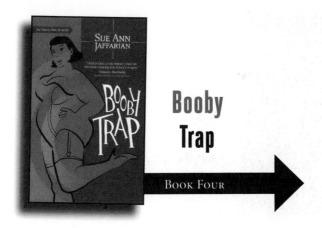

Booby Trap

BOOK FOUR

C ould the Blond Bomber serial killer possibly be Dr. Brian Eddy, plastic surgeon to the rich and famous? Odelia never would have suspected the prominent doctor of killing the bevy of buxom blonds if she hadn't heard it directly from her friend Lillian—Dr. Eddy's own mother!—over lunch one day. This mystery gets even messier than Odelia's chicken parmigiana sandwich as Odelia discovers just how difficult—and dangerous—it will be to bust this killer.

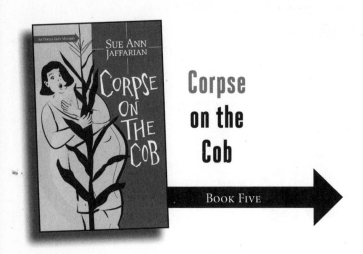

Corpse on the Cob

BOOK FIVE

What do you have to lose when you go searching for the mother who walked out of your life thirty-four years ago—besides your pride, your nerves, and your sanity?

Odelia finds herself up to her ears in trouble when she reunites with her mom in a corn maze at the Autumn Fair in Holmsbury, Massachusetts. For starters, there's finding the dead body in the cornfield—and seeing her long-lost mom crouched beside the corpse, with blood on her hands…